Death of a Nationalist

Death of a Nationalist

Rebecca Pawel

Published by

Soho Press, Inc.
853 Broadway
New York, N.Y. 10003

Library of Congress Cataloging-in-Publication Data

Pawel, Rebecca, 1977–
Death of a nationalist / Rebecca Pawel.
p. cm.
ISBN 978-1-56947-344-3 (alk. paper)
1. Spain—History—Civil War, 1936–1939—Fiction.
2. Nationalists—Fiction. I. Title.
PS3616.A957 D43 2003
813'.6—dc21   2002026921

10 9 8 7 6 5

For Persephone Braham,
who gave me the idea in the first place,
and then urged me to write the whole thing.

*"From ancient grudge break to new mutiny,
Where civil blood makes civil hands unclean."*

—William Shakespeare, *Romeo and Juliet*

*"Oh, city of gypsies, with all your flags flying,
extinguish your green lights, the Guardia's coming."*

—Federico García Lorca,
"Romance de la Guardia Civil Española"

Maria Alejandra was on her way home from school when she saw a man dressed as a guardia civil creep out of the bomb-blackened building that had been Señor Merello's bakery before the shell hit it. The man glanced in both directions and then crossed the street quickly, looking over his shoulder, as if he were frightened of something. Then he headed down the Calle Amor de Dios. Maria Alejandra looked after him, surprised. The man had been dressed like an officer, and the officers of the guardia weren't frightened anymore.

For a moment, Alejandra thought about going home from school a different way. But her books were heavy, and one man acting oddly didn't seem like a reason to walk farther. She started down the Calle Amor de Dios after him. She was just passing another roofless building when she heard gunshots. To her practiced ear, the shots sounded like pistol, not machine-gun, fire and her mother had told her that there would be no more shelling now. But nearly half of Alejandra's seven years had been spent in wartime, and she knew better than to take foolish chances. A little annoyed at the possible damage to her school clothes, she dropped her book bag and flung herself to the ground, covering her head automatically as she did so.

For a moment there was no sound. Cautiously, Alejandra raised her head. Ingrained habit made her glance upward.

Everyone knew that the German planes didn't pass over this part of town after four o'clock, and there had been no bombing at all in the last few days, but Alejandra was unable to stop herself from nervously checking the sky. She had always been scared of airplanes. Even the grownups were scared of airplanes. She rose and gathered her books, some of which had fallen onto the ground. Someone was coming down the street, from the opposite direction. Alejandra shrank into the doorway of the ruined apartment house, stepping over the threshold and behind the one standing wall. She heard footsteps and saw the legs of a guardia uniform pass by again. This time, they were not hurrying. The man was humming under his breath.

Alejandra waited until the sound of his footsteps had died away. She did not like the guardias civiles. Her uncle said they were traitors. Her mother said that there were some good guardias, who fought for the people, but that most of them supported the rebels who were fighting against the Republic. But the good guardias had probably been arrested now, like her friend Candela's father. Or maybe even taken for a stroll. Alejandra was not quite sure what happened when you were taken for a stroll, but she knew that the grownups had sometimes laughed when they said that one day the Fascist generals who had started the rebellion would "go strolling." And she knew that Maricarmen in the fourth grade had been absent for a week after her grandfather, who lived outside Madrid in country that had fallen to the rebels six months ago, had been "taken for a stroll." Maricarmen's school clothes had been dyed black when she came back to school.

Alejandra crouched behind the wall and tried to stuff her books back into her bag. But her teacher had helped to pack them tightly and she couldn't fit them all in. She tucked her composition book under her arm, glad that the man had gone. At the intersection of Amor de Dios and Fray Luis de

León she stopped again. The man she had seen before, the guardia civil who had looked afraid, was lying facedown on the pavement, in a puddle of blood. Maria Alejandra looked at him for a long moment. Then she dropped her composition book and began to run.

Chapter 1

"Sir! There's been a murder, sir!" Guardia Adolfo Jiménez stamped up to the flat surface that his commanding officer was pleased to call a desk and gave a stiff-armed salute.

Unfortunately, Jiménez's last stamp shook loose the battered copy of *La España del Cid* that was holding up the fourth leg of the table, and several papers cascaded over the edge. Lieutenant Ramos steadied the remaining papers, and looked up at the young guardia with a glare. "Well, have you arrested someone for it?" he demanded impatiently.

"No, Lieutenant!" Jiménez saluted again, but was careful not to stamp.

The third man in the room unobtrusively stooped, and began to gather the fallen papers from the floor. He glanced at them as he rose, trying to figure out which pile each belonged in: a requisition for two hundred rounds of ammunition, a handwritten denunciation of someone named Méndez, a schedule of assignments to night patrol, and two typed memos from the division commander. After a moment, he carefully shuffled them into a stack, and placed them randomly on the table.

"Well, damn it, why are you coming to me then?" the lieutenant asked. "You're supposed to be restoring public order. Go and restore it. Thanks, Tejada," he added, as the papers were replaced.

"We think the murderer's a Red, Lieutenant," Jiménez explained.

Sergeant Tejada reflected that saying a Red was a murderer was rather like saying that the sun rose in the east. "Why do you think that, Guardia?" he asked.

Jiménez forgot himself and stamped again, causing both of his superiors to dive for papers. Then he looked chagrined. All of the recruits looked up to Sergeant Tejada Alonso y León. Not many men who started out as guardias were made officers, even with the rank of sergeant, before their thirtieth birthday. And Tejada had entered the Guardia late on top of that, coming from a university instead of from one of the military academies.

"The victim was a guardia civil, sir. Rank of corporal, sir."

"Hell!" Lieutenant Ramos's attention was caught. "One of our battalion?"

"Don't think so, sir. He had no identification on him. Just the uniform."

"Poor bastard." The lieutenant was shuffling papers furiously. "I'll send around a memo to the other posts, and ask them who's gone missing. Goddamn it, where's the carbon paper? Oh, thanks, Tejada." He unearthed an ancient portable typewriter and began to insert the sheet that the sergeant had offered. "Go take a look, will you? And arrest anyone in the neighborhood who seems suspicious. If they're Reds, put them up against a wall. Take Jiménez with you."

Tejada saluted, somehow managed to stamp without shaking any papers, and left without speaking. Jiménez followed him, excited to have been assigned to accompany the sergeant. Outside the temporary barracks, really a dormitory abandoned by the university and commandeered a few months earlier, Tejada turned. "Where are we going?"

"It's over near Atocha Station, sir. A little street called Amor de Dios."

Tejada's mouth curled briefly. "Not a very appropriate name. Lead the way, Jiménez."

It was not a long walk, and they passed very few people. It was nearly eight o'clock, and those who had food were cooking dinner. Those who did not were preparing for bed. An evening stroll had become a dangerous custom, and in a city without fuel, darkness meant bedtime. The few people on the streets slid away from the two red-collared guardias, as the north pole of one magnet turns from the north pole of another.

Tejada liked the silence. It was almost like being in the country, with the shadows falling so naturally, and no glare of streetlights to block out the moon rising ahead of them over the city. A breeze was blowing at their backs . It's peaceful, he thought, and then was surprised. It had been a long time since he had thought of peace in the present tense. The streetlights would come back, of course. But he hoped that the streets would stay like this at night: cool, silent, empty except for those on legitimate business. No demonstrations, he thought, as they passed through a deserted plaza with the gutted and flame-blackened ruins of a townhouse sitting silently on their left hand. No rabble-rousers. No rock throwing. No general strikes. No petty crime. Maybe now an honest man will be able to walk the streets without fear. His mouth tightened as he remembered their errand. The streets were not quite peaceful yet. But they would be. Tejada was under no illusions as to what Lieutenant Ramos had meant by "put them up against a wall." Rough and efficient justice was still necessary in Madrid. Maybe in a few years it would be possible to prettify it with legal niceties again.

Jiménez broke in on his reverie. "It's just at the end of this street, Sergeant."

Tejada nodded, but did not reply. Jiménez was too much in awe of the sergeant to offer further comments. So there was no sound except the echo of their boots as they approached

the intersection of Amor de Dios and Fray Luis de León.
Tejada sometimes wondered afterward what would have happened if they had made more noise.

Maria Alejandra was already breathing in great gasps when she
reached her home, and the climb to the third-floor apartment
took away any breath she might have had left for crying. She
fumbled with the key and tore through the darkened living
room to the kitchen at the back.

The kitchen was empty except for Tía Viviana. Tía Viviana
wasn't really a relative, but as far as Alejandra was concerned,
she was almost as good as her mama. She told jokes and knew
good songs, and best of all, she was never afraid of anything.
Alejandra loved the way Tía Viviana greeted her every afternoon with, "*Hola,* Aleja," slurring the words together so that
it sounded like the name of a princess in *The Arabian Nights*:
"*La'leja.*" Tía Viviana looked up from her mending now.

"La'leja," she said. Then, dropping the patched clothing on
the kitchen table and kneeling quickly, "Aleja! What's the
matter?"

Maria Alejandra leaned against her shoulder and sobbed.
She had seen dead people before. The year after the war
started, her grandfather Palomino had died of pneumonia
and she had gone to the wake. She and her mother had been
on their way to the Merellos' bakery when the bomb had hit
it, and they had seen Señor Merello and Danilo, who had been
three grades ahead of her, carried out of the rubble. But something about the dead man lying alone in the street terrified
her. Perhaps she could only bear seeing a certain number of
dead, and the guardia in the Calle Amor de Dios had been the
corpse that had broken the camel's back.

Viviana rocked the little girl back and forth, and crooned
to her. "It's all right, sweetheart. It's all right." As pieces of
Aleja's story emerged, the young woman's voice gained

strength. "It's all right, precious. If he was a guardia then it's all right. Let them fight among themselves. Don't cry, sweetheart. He wasn't a Republican, I'm sure. Don't cry." She kept up the flow of soothing words until Aleja was calm again, and then Viviana distracted her with chores and songs and fantastic stories about princesses and ghosts and imaginary kingdoms where all the children ate roast pork every night. After a few hours, when she could think of nothing else to amuse the girl, Viviana asked if she had homework.

Alejandra required only a little coaxing to begin her work but as she retrieved her book bag she gave a stricken cry. "My notebook! I dropped it. By the man I saw."

Viviana frowned, once again concerned. "Are you sure, Aleja? You didn't put it in your bag?"

A quick search and more tears confirmed that Aleja had indeed lost the notebook. Her aunt frowned in thought for a moment. Aleja's homework for the night was a trivial thing, but Aleja's mother placed great value on the child's education. And Aleja's notebook had been only half-filled. Paper was rationed, and God alone knew when they'd be allowed more now. At the beginning of the term—in another life—the teachers had emphasized that all students must take special care of their materials. Viviana bit back the impulse to snap at her almost-niece for carelessness. It wasn't fair for a child to see so much of war. It wasn't fair to ask her to go and retrieve a notebook from the place where she had practically seen a man die. It was neither fair nor safe. There was a curfew, and Aleja would not be able to return before it went into effect. But to lose the notebook. . . . Another loss, Viviana thought, and choked back tears. How much more can we lose now? Can we keep losing when there's nothing left? She was brought back to herself by a warming flash of anger. There was no reason to lose it. She knelt by Aleja and gave her a quick hug. "Don't cry. Tell me exactly where you left your notebook, and I'll go and get it. It's probably still there. When she comes in, tell your mother where I've gone."

She left hurriedly, without bothering to change her clothes. The wind whipped her hair away from her face, and she wished that she had thought to tie it back. It was nearly long enough to braid now. I should cut it again, she thought automatically, smoothing flyaway strands behind her ears. She shivered slightly. It was too cold for spring. Too cold and too silent and too deserted. She tried to remember summer afternoons, when the streets were choked with people and it was impossible to find a table at cafés that had already turned on their colored lanterns. Before the cafés had closed. Before the shelling. Before the war.

She reached the spot Aleja had described. Yes, there was the man, his life's blood clotted around him on the cobblestones. He had undoubtedly been a guardia civil. Viviana glanced at his uniform, saw the red collar of the Nationalists, and sighed with relief. Funny, with those collars, that they were called the Blues. So she had not lied to Aleja. He had been a Fascist. One of the victors, Viviana thought, though it still hurt to admit it. She was not ashamed of having lost: the army, the rich landowners, the church with all its wealth, the old aristocrats with all their power, had been behind the Nationalists. And their German and Italian friends had provided them with all the arms and soldiers that they could well have afforded to purchase anyway. It was amazing the Republicans had held out for so long, even with the help offered by the Soviets for the sake of the Communists who had supported the Republic. Viviana knew she had no reason to be ashamed of the fight she had put up. But it was grief and not pride that made her want to deny that the Republic was dead. She had fought for a new way of life: for a world where people shared things in common and no one starved so that rich men could become richer; a world where women were equal to men; where every new acquaintance was greeted with the familiar *"tú,"* like a friend, instead of the servile *"usted,"* like a servant to a master. Viviana had not fought purely to win. That was what made losing so hard. I'm damned if Aleja loses her notebook though, she thought. Whatever happens to us all now, she's *not* going to be a chambermaid or a factory girl all her life, at the mercy of some señorito's busy hands! We can't let them spit on *her* even if they do bring back the old ways! She scanned the ground. Yes, there, barely a foot from the dead man's out-flung hands, was Aleja's notebook. It had fallen open, facedown on the stones and one corner was slightly stained with blood. She knelt to pick it up, with a rush of relief, and quickly leafed through its pages. No harm done.

It was not the sound of footsteps that alerted her. It was the way they suddenly speeded up, as if someone had broken into a run. She looked up and saw two men approaching from the street opposite. They were silhouetted against the setting sun, but Viviana had seen this particular silhouette before, and the shape of their three-cornered hats and of the rifles sticking over their shoulders was all too clear. Viviana straightened rapidly and whirled, prepared to run.

She was too late. Behind her came a shout: "Guardia Civil! Hands above your head!"

Chapter 2

Tejada had expected to find the street deserted. He could hardly believe his luck when he caught sight of a figure kneeling in the street beside the corpse, apparently taking something from the dead man's hands. He gestured Jiménez to silence with one hand and drew his pistol with the other. Then he advanced as quickly and quietly as possible before challenging the crouching figure. Their quarry froze for a moment when he shouted and then turned slowly, hands in the air. Beside him, the sergeant heard Jiménez murmur, "Christ, it's a woman!"

Tejada inspected their prisoner. The sun was shining full in her face, as brightly as an interrogator's lamp, and he had a good view. She was thin-faced, and the blue overalls that she wore looked too large for her. They looked like the uniforms of the Red militias, and they were much stained and mended. The wind lifted her hair off her neck and outlined her skull. Hunger and grief had bitten lines into her face but Tejada had considerable experience with both besiegers and besieged, and he guessed her to be in her early twenties. A few years older than Jiménez, and a few years younger than himself. She squinted into the sunset at him, with a familiar look of sullen resignation. "Decent women are at home at this hour," he said mildly.

"I had an errand to run." She spoke calmly.

"She's a miliciana, sir," Jiménez broke in with some excitement. "I've heard about them. The Reds have their women fight for them. I've heard they're worse even than the men. And whores too, terrible. They. . . ."

"Thank you, Guardia," Tejada interrupted, without taking his eyes from the woman. "I'm interested in this errand, Señorita." And then, as she attempted to push her bangs back from her eyes. "If you move again, I'll shoot."

She bit her lip, and said nothing.

"Guardia," Tejada said, still in the same conversational tone. "Will you please keep her covered?" He waited until Jiménez's pistol was trained on the woman and then returned his own to its holster. "I'm inclined to agree with my colleague," he continued, carefully giving the prisoner a wide berth, and then approaching her from behind. "You are a miliciana. Drop that, please," he added, clamping one of his hands over the hand that held a battered notebook and grabbing the prisoner's forearm with the other. "Or I'll break your wrist. Thank you. Now, as I was saying, I don't think we're in any doubt as to what you are. But I'd like to know why you were fool enough to come back here after killing a guardia."

"I didn't kill him." The woman's voice was firm but she gasped slightly as Tejada pulled her arms behind her back.

"It's in your best interest to tell the truth, Señorita." The sergeant began to twist one arm.

The woman's breath hissed between her teeth. "The truth?" she repeated, her voice suddenly contemptuous. "The truth is that I wouldn't have offered him a glass of water in hell but I didn't kill him. I wish I had."

She would probably break down and tell the truth when they got her back to the post, Tejada thought dispassionately. Of course, it would be too late then. It would not bring the man she had killed back to life. Tejada felt the beginnings of distaste. He had no problem with interrogation for information, but there was no question as to her guilt.

The woman was carefully obeying his command to stand still. The wind was whipping her ragged hair into a dark halo, and her bangs must be blinding her, but she remained inanimate. Loose strands brushed the sergeant's face, triggering an unpleasant recollection: in the beginning of the war, a little village had defied the command to surrender and held out for another two days under shelling before its defenders finally ran out of ammunition. Most of the Red troops had been killed in the fighting, and only a handful were left as prisoners, including two women. Tejada had guarded the men until the firing squads were ready for them, and seen to it that they had access to an army chaplain. Once the executions were over, he cleaned up the office in the Guardia Civil post that the Reds had tried to destroy. When he emerged into the autumn sunset, a knot of laughing men had drawn his attention. "Join us, sir?" one of his comrades greeted him.

He remembered drawing closer and realizing that the men were grouped around one of the women who had been captured. He remembered the way a tangle of bloodstained chestnut hair had fallen across the woman's face in the evening breeze, obscuring eyes that seemed to stare at nothing, just as the Madrid miliciana's eyes were probably staring at nothing now. He remembered thinking that she must be in pain, and wondering why she was making no sound. He remembered thinking that she must be unconscious and remembered the moment when he had realized that she was dead, and that the others were raping a corpse. He remembered excusing himself abruptly, and then retching in a deserted alley. Thankfully, he remembered very little else, because he had taken the unprecedented step of getting thoroughly drunk that night.

Jiménez was still regarding their prisoner with a mixture of disgust and fascination. Tejada knew that the boy was only waiting for orders. "Who did kill him, then?" he asked her. "One of your friends?"

Viviana felt the beginnings of real terror. They don't know about Gonzalo, she reminded herself, and then cut off the thought, afraid that they would somehow read her mind. "One of *your* friends, more likely!" she spat. Anger was good. Anger kept fear at bay. "I'm not friends with murderers!"

"Not the most convincing of statements," Tejada said, torn between incredulity and disgust. Disgust—with her youth, her mendacity, and the knowledge of what would happen to her if she was arrested—won out, and he made a quick decision. "We don't have time to play around." He released her arms as he spoke, thrusting them upward again with such force that she stumbled forward a step.

Viviana, preoccupied with keeping her balance and puzzled by his last nonsequitur, hardly noticed as he stepped to one side. She was still working out his meaning when, in her peripheral vision, she caught him raising his arm.

The echoes of the pistol shot bounced off the darkened buildings, making it sound as if a firing squad had been at work, instead of a lone man. Tejada looked at Jiménez, who was still crouched, pointing his pistol expectantly. "Put that gun away, Guardia. There's no need for it now."

"Yes, sir." Jiménez shook himself out of a stupor. "It's just I didn't think . . . I mean . . . She didn't even . . . You're very fast, sir."

"Practice," Tejada said briefly, turning past Viviana's body to crouch by the murdered man. He looked consideringly at his colleague, wondering if the young man had ever seen a woman tortured, and if he was one of those who would enjoy the sight. "How long have you been in the Guardia, Jiménez?"

"Almost four months officially, Sergeant. My birthday's the middle of December. But I was in the youth movement before that, sir. And it's in the blood. My father was a guardia too, and both my grandfathers."

The sergeant looked up at Jiménez and marveled for a moment at the gulf ten years created. Or perhaps it had only been the last three. There was some amusement in his voice when he said, "Suppose you help me turn him over, Jiménez," but it was kindly amusement.

The young recruit scrambled to obey, afraid Sergeant Tejada had thought that he was cowardly or slow-witted. This, Jiménez thought, as he heaved the body onto its back, is something to tell Durán and Vásquez. I've never seen a man so fast with a pistol. Wait until I tell them. "We don't have time to play around," and boom. There you are. He didn't need me at all. Maybe I can ask him about Toledo on the way back. Wait until they hear I went out on patrol with Tejada Alonso y León.

"Oh, shit," said the sergeant. "Oh, shit. Paco!"

Jiménez's jaw dropped. He was not surprised that Sergeant Tejada seemed to know the dead man. Jiménez would not have been surprised if the sergeant had suddenly demonstrated a knowledge of Chinese. What surprised him was the sergeant's tone, and the way Tejada was kneeling, with one hand cupping the dead man's forehead, like a mother feeling for fever in a small child. "You know him, sir?"

"Yes." Tejada stared down at the stiff body. Someone was frying something in oil in one of the nearby houses, and he was tempted to arrest whoever was creating such a stench. "He is Francisco López Pérez." Then, because Jiménez had obviously meant *how* do you know him, Tejada elaborated. "I knew him in Toledo."

Jiménez thought of a number of things to ask. Since most of them sounded, even to his ears, like the questions of a starstruck adolescent, he resisted the urge to say something like, In '36, sir? Was he also a hero of the siege, sir? Was he decorated too, sir? Instead, he said simply, "You're sure?"

It was Tejada's turn to hold words back. There would have been no point in saying, As sure as if he were my brother. You don't forget a man you shared a bunk with during a tour of hell. You goddamn idiot, I would know Paco if he shaved his eyebrows and dyed his hair purple. "Yes," he said.

"Do you know his battalion, sir?" Jiménez asked practically.

"No." The sergeant sounded slightly dazed. "No, he was transferred to the north, and we lost touch. I didn't know he was in Madrid." He looked down at the body, trying to ignore the bullet hole in its back, and the sprawling limbs. *I'm off to the Basque country, buddy.* Arriba España, *and all that good stuff. See you when the war's over.*

Jiménez was trying to think of a way to ask the sergeant, tactfully, what they should do about the two corpses in the street when Tejada rose, walked over to the body of the miliciana, and kicked it several times, without speaking. Jiménez coughed.

"Idiot," Tejada said, his back still turned. "She didn't deserve to die like that."

"But, sir," the guardia protested. "If she killed Corporal López—"

"She deserved something much worse for sneaking up on Paco and shooting him in the back," Tejada said. He gave the woman's body a final kick, which dislodged the notebook lying under her.

"What's that, sir?" Jiménez asked, more to distract his superior than from any real curiosity. Jiménez was not exactly frightened by the sergeant's reaction, but he was not at ease either.

"It's what she took from his body." Tejada looked down at the notebook, consciously seeing it for the first time. "It was important enough for her to come back and take it, after he was dead," he added thoughtfully, and bent to pick it up.

The sergeant said nothing more, and Jiménez, who felt silly kneeling and waiting for further orders, stood up after a moment. He stepped away from the body of Corporal López, and went to peer over Tejada's shoulder, at the carefully lettered words on the inside cover of the notebook: PROPERTY OF

MARIA ALEJANDRA PALOMINO. "That must have been her name," said Jiménez, pleased. "Maybe it's a list of Reds and she killed him to get it back."

"I don't think so." Amusement was back in Tejada's voice, but it was a good deal less kindly now. "Unless you think our miliciana was in Señorita Fernández's second-grade class. Look." He gestured to the facing page, where someone had worked out a series of arithmetic problems, underneath a somewhat smudged heading.

"It's dated in January, sir. It could be a code. For troop movements or something."

Tejada reflected that the phrase $324-62=262$ might conceivably be a code, but if so it was one of the most subtle in existence. It was hard to believe that a mind capable of that kind of encryption would also have the shaky hand of someone just learning to print. He flipped through the pages of the little book. There were several more pages of arithmetic. Then some writing caught his eye:

Señorita Fernández   February 3, 1939
Leopoldo Alas School Grade 2   History

GERONA—Gerona was besieged twenty-one times. The French besieged it in 1809. It risisted the siege for seven months. That is why Gerona is called the Imortel. Gerona is besieged now. Dr. Negrín is in Gerona now. We hope Gerona the Immortel will keep risisting.

Spelling Words: besiege
                  ~~immortel~~ immortal
                  ~~risist~~ resist

In a different hand, someone had written, "Recopy misspelled words 3x." Jiménez peered at it. "Do you suppose it could have been a school for adults, sir? I mean for illiterates?"

Tejada shook his head. "I don't think so. Look at this one."

Señorita Fernández   February 21, 1939
Leopoldo Alas School Grade 2   Writing

WHEN I WAS LITTLE—When I was little my father took me
to the front. There was no Front then~~than~~ and my father was
alive. The front was a big park. We played in the park, and
ate ice ~~ereem~~ cream.

"But," Jiménez hesitated. "I don't understand. Why would
she have a child's book? And why would she kill your frie—I
mean, the corporal—to get it back?"

Tejada shook his head, in puzzlement rather than negation.
"I'm guessing that she was the mother of—" he glanced at the
cover again—"Maria Alejandra. But for the rest, I don't know,
Guardia."

Jiménez also had become aware of the smell of frying oil.
It reminded him that there was less than an hour of daylight
left, and that his lunch was a distant memory. "What are we
going to do with Corporal López, sir? And the miliciana?"

Tejada forced himself to turn and look down at the body of
his colleague. The murdered man's limbs were already beginning to stiffen. "Go back to the barracks," he ordered. "Get two
men, and bring a stretcher. We can't carry him back like this."

"Yes, sir. And the Red, sir?"

Tejada was briefly surprised, and then remembered the
decade, or aeon, that separated them. "It's none of our business. Her people will find her in the morning, I suppose."

"Sir." Jiménez saluted, and vanished into the sunset.

The sergeant squatted on his heels, next to his fallen comrade, and thought about the past. "See you when the war's
over." "In six weeks, you mean?" "If *you're* going to Madrid,
make it three." Tejada wished he had a cigarette. Something
to keep his hands occupied. To keep his mind occupied. He

turned over the little notebook again. Why had Paco taken it? And had he been killed for that? Or merely because he wore the uniform of a guardia, and the Reds were so blind in their hatred that they shot men for that alone? Jiménez was foolish to think the notebook was in code, of course, but . . . He turned to the last entry. The date was nearly illegible, partly blotted out by a light brown stain that ran along the top of the page and had splattered slightly onto the bottom. It might have been the 30th or the 31st of March. The subject was once again arithmetic. Nicely neutral, in these last few days, Tejada thought wryly. A set of simple division problems had been copied into the notebook, but only the first problem had been completed. Next to the second were the words, "Do at home." Tejada squinted at the date again, in the fading light. Today's date, or yesterday's. Paco could not have had the book in his possession long then. He stared again at the heading. Señorita Fernández, Leopoldo Alas School, Grade 2. It was ridiculous to imagine a man giving up his life for this notebook. He glanced over at the corpse of the woman and wished that he had questioned her more closely. Now he had nothing except the name of a little girl. And the name of her teacher, of course. And, his mind sharpened suddenly, the address of her school.

When Guardias Jiménez, Vásquez, and Moscoso returned, bearing a stretcher, they found Tejada alert and waiting for them. He gave them their orders with his usual calm, and the stretcher-bearers were convinced that Jiménez had been dramatizing the sergeant's shock and grief.

Tejada was silent until they returned to the barracks. When they had set the remains of Corporal López down in the back hallway designated the infirmary, he and Jiménez went to Lieutenant Ramos to make their report.

Ramos nodded when they had finished. "Excellent. That's one less thing to worry about. Stroke of luck that you knew him, Sergeant. Dismissed."

The two guardias saluted and turned on their heels. Ramos, who made it a practice to seem very busy with paperwork, did not watch them go. He heard the door slam. Then he heard Tejada cough respectfully. "There is one thing, Lieutenant."

Ramos hoped that he had not jumped. The sergeant was a good officer. He'd been promoted quickly on his merits, not because of who his parents were, though of course that might not have hurt. But he sometimes had a nasty habit of sneaking up on people. Ramos looked up, trying to pretend that he had only dismissed Guardia Jiménez, so that he could talk privately with a fellow officer. "Yes, of course, Sergeant," he agreed. "We still don't know his unit. But thanks to you, that will be easy to find out."

"Yes, but that wasn't what I meant." Though Tejada was standing at attention, there was an inquiring quality in his stance. "We still don't know why he was killed, Lieutenant."

"I thought you said the killer was a Red?" The lieutenant's tone was impatient.

"Yes, but she'd taken a notebook from him that doesn't make much sense."

"So?"

There was a pause. Then Tejada said. "I'd like to apply for some leave, Lieutenant. Three days. Personal reasons."

Ramos's jaw dropped. "Are you out of your mind, Tejada? I can't spare you now."

"I'm sure that Corporals Torres and Loredo can take my place, sir."

Ramos stood, and leaned across the desk. "Listen, Sergeant," he said quietly. "General Franco is going to announce to the world tomorrow morning that Spain is once more at peace, and Madrid had goddamn well better *be* at peace tomorrow. *No one* is going on leave now."

For an insane moment, Ramos thought that the sergeant was going to argue. Then Tejada saluted and said quietly, "Yes, sir."

"Dismissed." Ramos sat down again. "Oh, and Tejada?"

"Lieutenant?"

"I'll see about leave in a few days, if I can."

Tejada made a sound that might have been a snort. Perhaps of gratitude, perhaps not. "Thank you, Lieutenant. I wanted to go to Toledo, and tell Corporal López's mother in person."

The tone was casual, but the words were so unexpected that Ramos found himself without a reply. Tejada was generally about as sentimental as a mule. But he withdrew before Ramos could collect his wits, or the papers floating gently off his desk.

That evening Tejada sought out Guardia Moscoso. He found him playing cards with a number of other recruits. They eagerly moved aside to make room for Tejada, and offered to deal him in. He declined, but watched the game for a few rounds, intently inspecting Moscoso's cards and his play. The young man was flattered by this scrutiny, but unnerved. After ten minutes he mumbled an excuse and threw in his cards. Tejada watched him stand and take a few paces away from the game, then rose and followed him. "I wanted to ask you a personal question, if I may, Guardia."

"Sergeant?" Moscoso flushed slightly. Jiménez had bragged insufferably at dinner, about being chosen to go on patrol with Tejada Alonso y León. This might be a good chance to pay Jiménez back.

"Where are you from, Moscoso?"

"Here, sir," Moscoso smiled, relieved, and wondered why he had been so tense before. Feeling that this response might be inadequate, he added. "I'm a Madrileño. But we were in Mallorca when the war broke out, so my parents are all right, God be thanked."

"Ahh. Summer vacation?"

"Yes, sir. I had just finished my first year at the institute, sir."

Tejada said, "I'm sure you were devastated to leave school."

Moscoso grinned. "You want an honest answer, sir?"

"This isn't an interrogation. But if you're local, I would like to ask you a few questions about the lie of the land. I think the lieutenant might, as well."

"Anything I can do to help, sir." Moscoso had forgotten his nervousness.

Tejada hesitated. "Well . . . I don't suppose you've ever heard of a primary school called Leopoldo Alas?"

The recruit blinked in surprise. "Why, yes, sir. I think I have. It's a public school, isn't it?"

"Do you know where it is?"

"It's up near the Plaza de Colón," Moscoso answered readily. "Well, it was. It may have been moved because of the bombing."

"Thank you." Tejada's voice was warmer than Moscoso had ever heard it before. "I'll mention to Lieutenant Ramos that you have special knowledge that may be useful."

"Thank *you*, sir."

"It's nothing." Tejada retired, secure in the knowledge that the post patrol routes were scheduled by him. He was fairly sure that his own route was going to take him to the Plaza de Colón within the next few days.

Chapter 3

Gonzalo Llorente opened his eyes and wished that he were dead. It was hard to believe that less than two weeks ago he'd been happy to wake up.

A nurse with a white wimple was bending over him. He thought that she was the same one who had brought him a glass of water that first Monday, when he had awakened drenched with sweat and conscious only of being thirsty. She had not worn a wimple then.

"Are you awake, sir?" she asked, her voice polite and professional. "Your sister is here."

That first Monday she had smiled at him and said, "Congratulations, soldier. Looks like you've turned the corner."

"Yes, thank you." He spoke the polite words because Carmen was there, and Carmen wanted him to be polite. Not to use the familiar *tú*. To survive. It had been Carmen who had hastily spoken of a congenital heart defect, and of weakness as a child, to the strange doctor who had appeared three days ago. It had been Carmen, he was sure, who had pleaded with the staff: "Don't trouble him while he's still weak." So he had convalesced slowly until the afternoon the strange doctor appeared, and his siesta was ended by the sound of shooting in the plaza.

"What's happening?" he had asked. "What's happening?"

And his sister had said, "Shh-shh, it's nothing." And then, with a glance at the doctor, "Don't worry. There's nothing to fear now."

"But the shooting," he had protested. "If they're fighting house to house. . . ."

It was Viviana who had taken his hand and said quietly. "It's over, Gonzalo. The carbineros are disbanded."

He stared dumbly, wondering for a moment if they were humoring him, pretending that a miracle had happened, and that the war was over. The war could not be over. Winning was impossible, and losing was unthinkable. It must still be going on. "The shooting . . . ," he had repeated.

"Executions." The doctor had spoken then. "It's necessary to set an example, you know. You're a lucky man," he had continued, apparently changing the subject to Gonzalo's health. "That was a bad fever."

Gonzalo had let the words wash over him, hearing only the bursts of gunfire. Lying here, staring up at the whitewashed ceiling, it almost sounded like the front. But the noise was too regular. A round of firing; many men, shooting together. Then a short silence. Then firing again. On the front, the firing was ragged. Men reloaded as quickly as they could, and the rhythm was as erratic as waves on a shore. Viviana had sat by him, holding his hand, and he had noticed vaguely that she was wearing a dress, and that the doctor addressed her as "Señora" and referred to "your husband's illness." And that every time the sounds of firing filtered through the windows she squeezed his hand a little harder and shivered. Carmen had said something about his being well enough to come home soon. The doctor had asked him how he felt, and he had answered that he felt fine, just a little tired. Was that normal?

The doctor had assured him that it was normal. Carmen had spoken of how glad Aleja would be to see him. "She asks about Tío Gonzalo every day." The doctor had said that it was a fine recovery; Gonzalo and his country could make a new beginning together. They had agreed that he would go home that Saturday. Doctors and nurses had hovered during each visit. There had been no chance to talk to Viviana alone, to ask her what was really going on, and if she knew what had happened to Manuel and Jorge and Pilar.

He tried to be glad that he was going home today. He would be able to talk to Viviana. He could find out what had been happening. But why did a dead man need to talk, or to know what was happening? It was kind, or perhaps selfish, of Carmen to try to keep him alive, but he was a dead man now, for all that she might try to protect him. Better to have died in the plaza, with the compañeros. This pretending to be alive while he waited for the Guardia to catch up with him took effort. Carmen was there now, offering him his clothes, civilian clothes, that had belonged to him before the war.

Gonzalo allowed Carmen to take care of the formalities of signing him out of the hospital and thanking the staff. Walking upright after so much time required concentration. He would gladly have collapsed in a heap on the threshold but Carmen guided him firmly with one hand, dragging a bag with the other, until they were out of the door, and walking down the Gran Vía. With mild, academic interest he watched the guardias civiles lining the street. The majority of them were standing along the sidewalks, regulating—or obstructing—pedestrian traffic. Some appeared to be fiddling with wires. One was leaning out a third-story window in a most undignified manner, apparently fixing a loudspeaker attached to the side of the building. None of them took any interest in him. But he knew it was only a matter of time. The sky seemed to match his mood. It was gray, and overcast, but it did not seem to think that raining was worth the trouble.

He realized that Carmen was talking. She had talked almost nonstop since they had left the hospital, in the high, shrill, voice of a record played too fast. He wondered, with a flicker, if something was troubling her. It did not occur to him that he might be the problem. After all, he was dead. "How's Aleja?" he asked, for the sake of interrupting her.

"Aleja." Her voice died. "Aleja's . . . well, thank God."

"Did you leave her with Viviana?" Gonzalo spoke with only nominal interest.

"Viviana. . . ." For a moment his sister sounded dead as well. Then she rallied. "Aleja loved Viviana from the first, you know. Really. I was the one who had doubts about her. But she was such a blessing to me when you were ill. And so good with Aleja. I never realized what a treasure she was. Do you know, after we left the hospital on Wednesday, Viviana said to me that she supposed now you'd have to get married. She said she wasn't sure how you'd feel about it, but that she was willing to be married in a church if that was the only way to stay with you. She loved you, you know. She was crazy about you."

Gonzalo's numbed brain registered something odd about his sister's speech, but it took him a while to figure out what it was. Then it dawned on him. The verb tenses were wrong. He wondered if perhaps this was a narrative defect. If so, a simple correction was in order. He tried one. "I haven't thought about marriage," he said. "But yes, I suppose we'll have to discuss it, if that's what she wants."

This gentle reminder of the existence of the present tense did not have the desired effect. "I'm so sorry, Gonzalo," Carmen whispered. "I . . . you mustn't blame Aleja."

A clanging of bells distracted Gonzalo for a moment. It was noon. Church bells were ringing, all over the city. Gonzalo realized that some of the ringing sounds were coming from the loudspeakers along the street as well. The guardias must have rigged them to broadcast the church bells. "What mustn't I blame her for?" Gonzalo asked, when it was possible to talk without shouting.

"She lost her notebook." Carmen was crying now. "Viviana went out to look for it, and . . . she must have run into the Guardia Civil. I only knew this morning. I'm sorry, Gonzalo."

"She's been arrested?" It wasn't surprising. The only thing left now was for the soldiers to come and take him away. He wondered wearily if it would be worth the effort of raising his fist as they shot him.

"Manuela found her this morning." Carmen was looking at the sidewalk, perhaps because it was uneven and she was guiding their steps, or perhaps because she did not want to meet his eyes. "She was in front of the Arcé house. Manuela said she heard a shot yesterday evening. That must have been it. She looked out and saw some guardias so she didn't come out."

"Don't tell me she's dead?" Gonzalo had once suffered from frostbitten feet. He remembered the way they had hurt when feeling returned. He felt now as if his entire body were recovering from frostbite, and he understood suddenly why people died in blizzards. It was not because they were cold and fell asleep. It was because it hurt too much to come back to life.

If Viviana had been arrested, tried, condemned, past saving, he would have comprehended. But she could not be *dead already*. Not without some kind of warning. His sister's hand was on his arm, and he dimly realized that without her support he would have stumbled and fallen. Carmen was still talking. "Manuela says it was probably very quick. It doesn't look as if they hurt her or . . . or anything. Just an execution, Gonzalo."

The words were like cold water for frostbitten feet. They mingled with an interior voice that said: A soldier's death. No worse than dying in the plaza. You can't believe all the stories you've heard about what they do to captured women. Well, there was Mercedes, but that was an exception. This isn't the front. A girl can't be raped in broad daylight in the streets of

Madrid. The loudspeakers squawked and Gonzalo realized that they had gone dead for a few moments. A tinny voice was saying, "Ladies and gentlemen, His Excellency, Generalíssimo Francisco Franco," and then there was a burst of static that might have been wild applause.

"Why?" he asked in an undertone, as the loudspeakers hissed and squeaked an announcement about the coming of peace and prosperity, and the great destiny of the nation.

"There was a guardia civil, dead in the street," Carmen replied softly. "They must have thought she had something to do with that."

Gonzalo would have liked to cry, or vomit, or best of all hit something. He concentrated on walking, with each footstep echoing softly to the beat. Viviana's dead. Viviana's dead.

They turned to leave the Gran Vía, and found their way barred. "You want to hear the end of the Generalíssimo's speech," a guardia civil said, holding a rifle across his chest. It was a statement, not a question.

So they stood there, listening to a speech so distorted by amplifiers that it was nearly impossible to understand. When another burst of static marked applause, the guardias civiles shouted together: *"Viva* Franco! *Arriba España!"* A few prods with rifle butts gave the civilians on the Gran Vía the correct idea. *"Viva,"* the echo rose from the street like a sigh. *"Viva, viva."*

"Vivi," Gonzalo whispered the pet name hoarsely, unable to believe that she would never answer it again. "Oh, Vivi." The rest of the afternoon passed in a blur for him. Somehow, Carmen got him home and warned him away from the folding bed behind the curtain in the living room before he collapsed onto it. The undertakers were closed today, in honor of the first day of peace, so there had been no coffin available. Viviana had been laid out on their bed and covered with a sheet. Gonzalo pulled it back for a moment and felt the obscenity of his sister's words of comfort: "They didn't hurt her."

That night, curled up on the couch, his brain began to work clearly for the first time in days. His reasons for living were about as great as his chances. Sooner or later a neighbor would whisper a denunciation. Or the Guardia Civil would review the lists of the carbineros and realize that he had originally been hospitalized with a wound, and that only infection had caused the fever. He could stay here, with Carmen and Aleja, and without Viviana, waiting for the Guardia to come and rectify their mistake. He could go up to the nearest guardia in the street, shout, *"Viva la República!"* and die with his fist in the air. Or he could spend the free time he had left looking for the man who had killed Viviana. Killing one guardia wouldn't make a difference now. On the other hand, it couldn't hurt. Carmen said there was a guardia found dead near her. Just one guardia, though, and they always go in pairs.

So, start with the man who was murdered. Find his partner, and he's the man you're looking for.

Chapter 4

Lieutenant Ramos had told the truth when he had said
there would be no time off over the next few days. In addition to the patrols, there were prisoners by the hundreds who
had to be either executed or registered and housed and so-
called civilians looking for family members who had to be
taken down to the cells to look at prisoners or directed to the
morgue to identify bodies. Ramos had received a memo from
Burgos stating that all houses were to be checked for firearms
("Maybe they'd like an inventory of rat holes, too!" the lieutenant had exclaimed. "What the hell do they think this is—
some mountain village? Where are we going to get the
manpower for that?"). Then there were denunciations, written and oral, to be received and acted upon. The corps
worked through Palm Sunday, stopping to hear the mass that
inaugurated Holy Week with relief or impatience, depending
on individual temperament. Jiménez and some of the other
new recruits dutifully prayed for the health of General
Franco, so that he might continue to do God's work in Spain.
Ramos, who was preoccupied with God's work on a more
immediate basis, prayed for a consignment of trucks or a train
designated to remove the prisoners, or else for speedy trials
and sentencings, so that the prison would not be so danger-
ously overcrowded. After some consideration, he decided that
praying for an honest and efficient quartermaster was also an

unselfish prayer, and he requested that as well. Tejada prayed for the soul of Paco López. And for understanding, he thought. I don't question the need. Not my will, Lord, but thy will. But please, if there was an earthly reason, for my comfort, I'd like to find it.

Tejada did not have time to search for an earthly reason until two days later. A memo had been sent around to all posts, asking if one was missing a Corporal Francisco López Pérez. But other commanders were overworked as well, and a dead man whose murderer had already been executed was a low priority. No reply had arrived when Sergeant Tejada and First Corporal Loredo set out on a routine patrol, one whose route had been carefully planned by Tejada the night before.

He would have preferred patrolling with Jiménez, who knew of the strange piece of evidence he had found by Paco's body, or even with one of the other enlisted men. They were all younger than he was, and none of them would have thought to question his judgment. Loredo was in his midthirties, a career guardia, who would never rise beyond his present rank. He would obey orders, but was apt to resent them, especially if given by someone several years his junior. However, there was no help for it. Jiménez was on his way to Toledo, along with ten other guardias, with a trainload of prisoners. Moscoso had been commandeered by Lieutenant Ramos to update maps. Loredo would do.

As Tejada had arranged, they were making a circuit of the Plaza de Colón. As they walked down one of the side streets south of the plaza, they passed a high whitewashed wall. The shrill cries of children at play could be heard from the other side. The wall was pierced by a wrought-iron gate adorned with a plaque proclaiming, LEOPOLDO ALAS ELEMENTARY SCHOOL. Tejada read the sign with satisfaction. "Shall we take a look, Corporal?" he asked.

Loredo shrugged. "What for?"

Tejada had his answer planned. "We're supposed to get to know the neighborhood. Besides, we should get a register of the older boys. They'll be forming groups of Falangist Youth here. We want to know who to sign up for the movement."

Loredo grunted. This was typical of Tejada. This was the sort of idea that men with university educations had. This was the sort of idea that had gotten Tejada promoted. Loredo looked on such ideas with profound suspicion. Tejada was the sergeant, though. "Yes, sir."

Tejada rang the bell beside the gate. It took a few minutes for someone to come out of the main building and down the path to open the gate. Long before their guide arrived, the gym class in the courtyard had become aware of the silent scrutiny of the two guardias civiles. The shouts died to whispers, and the children bunched together, clustering around an elderly man who seemed a most unlikely instructor in physical education. The ball they had been playing with rolled away toward the gate. Someone in the class whimpered.

There was some low-voiced conversation and then the teacher shuffled after the ball. He was not so old, Tejada realized, looking at him more closely. Perhaps in his early fifties. It was his slight limp and frail appearance that gave the impression of age. He stooped awkwardly to pick up the ball, muttered, "Gentlemen," and turned away, without meeting their eyes.

By this time, a boy of perhaps thirteen had appeared at the gate. He turned white at the sight of the guardia civil, but said only, "Did you ring the bell, gentlemen?"

"Yes," said Tejada. "We'd like to speak to the director."

"Y-yes, sir." The bolts of the gates clattered as the boy drew them back, perhaps because his hands were shaking.

One of the little girls in the gym class began to cry as they marched across the courtyard. Someone hastily shushed her. The sergeant glanced at the little knot of children. "Coeducational," he remarked dryly. "Very modern."

Loredo grunted again, but this time it was a friendly grunt. "Can't hardly tell the boys from the girls," he agreed. "Unchristian."

Their guide whirled around, face burning. "We have separate classes after third grade! And you *can* tell!"

Loredo and Tejada glanced at each other, and then stared at the boy, until his face went from red to white. "You salute when you're speaking to an officer, son," Loredo said quietly.

Very slowly, as if it did not belong to him, the boy raised his right arm. His hand twitched a few times, and then seemed to clutch at the handle of an invisible teapot. Tejada reached out, gently pulled the boy's elbow straight, and uncurled the twitching fingers. The boy's eyes glittered, with rage or unshed tears. "You're young," the sergeant said. "You'll learn. That's why we're here."

"And a good thing, too," Loredo muttered. Tejada smiled, satisfied. If Corporal Loredo were convinced of the necessity of their visit, Tejada's task would be that much easier.

The boy said nothing more as he led them through an arched entrance and down a corridor, into the office of the director. The room contained a desk, a filing cabinet, and a chair. That was all. The director of the Leopoldo Alas School apparently did not favor unnecessary ornamentation.

The director, Señor Herrera, was, if not exactly pleased to see the guardia, at least anxious to appear helpful. He provided the two men with the rolls of the senior classes, and was quite willing to allow Loredo to copy them. Leaving Loredo thus occupied, Tejada turned to Herrera. "One other thing, sir. Does a Señorita Fernández teach second grade here?"

The day was cool but the director started to sweat. "Yes, Elena Fernández works here. Why do you ask, Officer?"

"I wonder if I could speak to her for a moment," Tejada said. "It's nothing serious. I'd just like to ask her a few questions."

Señor Herrera had been pale before. At the last phrase he turned slightly yellowish. "Her room is just up the stairs and to your right," he croaked. "Number 102. The children go home for lunch at one o'clock. But if you'd like to see her now. . . ."

"Thank you." Tejada turned to his colleague. "This is fortuitous, Loredo. I ran across Señorita Fernández's name last week, in connection with an incident. I'd like to clear up a misunderstanding now, if you don't mind. I'll be upstairs when you finish."

"Very good, sir." Loredo saluted, and returned to patiently copying the names and addresses of students onto the pages of a tablet that Señor Herrera had provided. Tejada turned to leave the office.

"Er . . ." The director cleared his throat desperately. "Do you anticipate . . . I mean . . . should I call a substitute teacher for this afternoon?"

In spite of the man's pasty face, and in spite of the fact that he was almost certainly a Red, Tejada was suddenly reminded of Lieutenant Ramos. He laughed, which unnerved Señor Herrera still more. "I don't think that will be necessary. Oh, and a piece of friendly advice, Señor, if I may. You don't seem to have a Spanish flag in your office. I'd recommend you find one. Very important to instill patriotism in the young by example."

"Of course, of course," the director gabbled. "I *had* a flag, only, er . . . it was . . ."

"Burned by the Reds?" Tejada suggested, the memory of his harassed commander still putting him in a compassionate mood. "I suspected as much." His eyes scanned the bare walls of the office and noted several rectangular patches where the paint was noticeably brighter. "You seem to have lost several wall ornaments also. A photograph of General Franco, perhaps? And the lyrics to the national anthem?"

Señor Herrera swallowed, uncertain how wide an escape route the guardia civil was leaving him. "Of course . . . I'll replace them with that. . . . I mean, with the photo and . . . I mean, with *another* photo and . . . just as you suggest, Señor Guardia."

Tejada made his way up to room 102, fairly certain that Señor Herrera would present no further problems. As he turned out of the stairwell, he saw an open door on his right, and heard a female voice spilling out of it, saying, ". . . The Count Lucanor heartily approved of Patronio's advice . . ." He stopped, just before the doorway, and allowed the voice to come to the end of the story. Then he stepped forward.

The square classroom that met his eyes contained perhaps fifteen children seated in the rows of battle-scarred school desks, in a promiscuous confusion of boys and girls. The walls had once been tan, but paint was peeling from them to reveal the white plaster beneath. Unlike Señor Herrera, however, Señorita Fernández obviously believed in decorating them. Childish drawings were stuck up all around the room, most with carefully lettered captions: "This is my house." "My older sister has brown eyes and looks like me." "The Germans bomb Madrid." One wall was devoted to a chalkboard, which was completely blank.

Señorita Fernández stood at the front of the room holding the book she had just finished reading. Tejada, whose impression of the school had led him to expect another militant like the woman by Paco's body, was favorably surprised. The teacher was unobjectionably dressed, in a long garment of so dark a blue it was almost black. Her hair was pinned to the back of her head in a dark, glossy coil, and looked as if it would be unfashionably long. As she turned toward Tejada he saw that she was about his own age. Her eyes widened as she took in his uniform, and the rifle over his shoulder, but her voice was steadier than Señor Herrera's had been as she said, "Good morning. Can I help you?"

The class, Tejada noted, had gone dead silent. He scanned their faces, trying to guess which one might be Maria Alejandra. It was hard to tell. Too many of them looked like they had been recently orphaned. "Elena Fernández?" he asked.

"Yes?"

"I have some questions for you."

"Of course." She turned toward the class. "Please read the next fable in the *Conde Lucanor* silently," she said. "It begins on page 53. I'll be right back."

Tejada gestured toward the hallway with one hand. "Should I get my coat?" she asked in a low voice designed to pass over the heads of the children.

The sergeant felt a moment of unwilling admiration for Señorita Fernández. She was cooler than many of the men he had arrested. She was either very courageous, or else she had a very clear conscience—and if she had stuck it out in Madrid as a Nationalist then she should probably get an award for courage in any case. "There's no need," he answered in the same undertone.

She let out an almost imperceptible sigh and stepped into the hallway.

He followed her, and then shut the classroom door. "I wanted to know if you recognized this?" He reached into one of the pouches on his belt, and pulled out the stained and crumpled notebook.

Her gasp was audible this time and he wondered if he had underestimated her fear. On the other hand, it was an unexpected question for him to ask.

"I don't know," she said after a moment.

He raised his eyebrows. "You don't know if you recognize it?"

She looked up at him, and her mouth twisted. "Guardia, as you probably are aware, all of the students at this school have notebooks like that one. I won't say that I recognize this specific one, because I don't, but I won't be entrapped into saying that I have no idea whose it is when I might very well know the owner."

Tejada smiled. "Very wise." He held out the book. "Open it. See if the inside looks familiar."

She opened the book to the inside cover right away, he noted, and looked for the owner's name there. "Alejandra," she said in a flat voice. "Yes, she's one of my students. Where did you find this?"

"Are you surprised?" The sergeant avoided her question.

"That you'd be interested in a child's notebook, yes." She flipped to the final entry on its pages and smiled, a little sadly. "She hasn't done Friday's homework, I see. Will I be arrested for asking if she's still able to?"

"I imagine it would be difficult to do without the problems," Tejada answered. "Other than that, I don't know. I've never laid eyes on her." He hesitated for a moment and then said, "Who are these notebooks valuable to?"

"Valuable?" The teacher stared at him. "Aside from the students and their families, no one."

"Their families?" Tejada repeated.

Señorita Fernández made an impatient gesture. "Paper's rationed, you know. Each child gets one notebook per semester. They have to make it last as long as possible."

The sergeant took the book back, and looked at the last entry. There were still nearly fifty clean pages left. A suspicion presented itself, but it did not wholly make sense. "So if a book was lost?" he suggested. "Or stolen?"

Señorita Fernández lifted her chin. "*We* don't steal from each other," she said.

Tejada ignored the implicit challenge. "Lost, then."

The teacher's moment of defiance passed. "It would be a disaster. Especially for a student from a poor family."

"And Maria Alejandra's family?" Tejada asked. "Are they poor?"

"All of the students are from poor families now." She looked down.

Tejada's eyes narrowed. "That's not an answer."

"It's the best one I can give."

"Would you suspect the Palomino family of political activity?" He changed course abruptly. "Any reason why her parents might wish to lie low now?"

There was a certain bitter triumph in Señorita Fernández's voice as she answered. "I don't think you need to worry about her parents. Alejandra's father died two years ago."

"Was he a soldier?" Tejada asked.

The teacher shrugged. Tejada considered pressing the question, but decided that there was probably an easier way to answer it. "Could you call Alejandra out here, please," he said. "I'd like to speak to her."

"No," Señorita Fernández spoke with satisfaction. "Alejandra has been absent for the past two days."

"You don't find that suspicious?"

Señorita Fernández had lost either her fear or her patience. "A third of my class is out today. On any given day I have three or four students absent. Runny noses, fevers, a death in the family. Anything could keep them at home. So no, I don't find it suspicious."

Tejada reflected that Maria Alejandra's mother had almost certainly died four days ago, but he saw no need to offer Señorita Fernández a possible explanation for her pupil's absence. "Would Señor Herrera's office downstairs have Maria Alejandra's address?"

"Very probably."

"Thank you for your time." Tejada bowed slightly and put his hand on the handle of the classroom door.

The teacher gasped again. "That's all?"

"Yes." It was Tejada's turn to look surprised. "Your students should have finished their assigned reading by now."

"Well . . . yes." Señorita Fernández was smiling broadly. "Yes, you're right. I . . . thank you, Guardia."

Her relief was palpable and so strong that the sergeant wondered how frightened she had been. He returned her smile.

Whatever else she was, she wasn't a coward. "Sergeant, actually," he corrected. "My name is Carlos Tejada. And I would have let you get your coat, you know." He opened the door for her.

"That's very gallant of you." The words were sarcastic but her voice was almost friendly. "Good-bye, Sergeant Tejada."

As he headed down the stairs he heard her say in a loud, clear voice, quite unlike the one she had used during their interview, "All right, those who have finished, raise your hands, please."

He found Corporal Loredo halfway through the final class list with Señor Herrera hovering anxiously nearby. The director was only too happy to let him look at the second-grade class rolls as well. They were admirably organized, and Tejada easily found the information he was looking for:

PALOMINO LLORENTE, M. ALEJANDRA
Contact: Señora M. Carmen Llorente
25 Calle Tres Peces

"Do you know where Calle Tres Peces is, Señor Herrera?" Tejada asked as he copied the address.

"Only in a general way, sir." The director gulped as he realized that this could be construed as being obstructive. "It's down near Calle Atocha, sir. South of it, I think. A bit of a walk for the smaller children but they were sent here because we remained open through the war."

Something clicked in Tejada's mind, with the unpleasant snap of a safety catch being released. Near Atocha. Near the Calle Amor de Dios, which ran south into Atocha, perhaps? A child with "a bit of a walk" would probably take the quickest way home from school. And if something—or someone—startled her, she might well drop her notebook. Something like a murder? Tejada thought. But why go to the trouble to retrieve it? The simplest thing would have been to let the notebook lie where it was. I wouldn't even have noticed it if I'd just found Paco's body. No one would connect the two. So what if Paco found the notebook? He'd have found Maria Alejandra as easily as I did. What if he thought he knew something about what she'd seen and wanted to ask her more about it? Something that was worth killing him to make sure that he wouldn't report it? The sergeant felt the beginnings of satisfaction. If Corporal López had been killed because he was on the verge of discovering a subversive conspiracy, there was an excellent reason to pursue the investigation into his death.

"Finished, Sergeant." Loredo broke in on his musings.

Señor Herrera, who had been unnerved by the sergeant's pensive silence, cleared his throat. "If there's any other way I can be of assistance, gentlemen? Would you like a list of the staff as well? And their addresses? To the best of my knowledge none of them have any political affiliations, of course, but it's been difficult to screen staff during the war."

Tejada had a sudden unpleasant vision of himself knocking on Elena Fernández's door and asking her to get her coat. She would, he was sure, be calmer than her employer under the same circumstances. He looked at Señor Herrera with dislike. "That won't be necessary, thank you," he said. "We trust your judgment."

Chapter 5

"Gonzalo! What are you doing here? Are you out of your mind? Don't you know they've been shooting people in the streets!" Manuela Arcé tried to slam the door. It was no use. Gonzalo's foot was firmly wedged in the crack.

"I know. That's why I'm here." The former soldier had braced both hands on the doorjamb. He glanced down the dusty apartment stairwell. "The street is deserted at the moment, Manuela. And I wasn't followed."

"Jesus, Gonzalo, if Carmen's been arrested I'm sorry. Really sorry. But you can't stay here. Forgive me, Gonzalo, but I have children. I can't risk it." Manuela tried to look over Gonzalo's shoulder to see if anyone was coming up the stairs, a difficult endeavor since she was several inches shorter than he.

"Carmen's fine." Gonzalo's voice was grim. "But I need to ask some questions. And the sooner you let me in, the sooner I'll leave."

"Gonzalo, I can't . . ."

"I'll ask them on the doorstep if I have to." He glanced down the stairs again. "Of course, someone might come up at any time. But if you won't let me in . . ."

"Oh, all right!" Manuela fumbled with the chain, and the door swung open. "Come inside, quickly. And stay away from the window."

Gonzalo slid inside. His sister's friend slammed the door behind him. He found his way out of the foyer and into a living room whose only furnishing was a table still dotted with coffee mugs, and a much-stained sofa. Above the sofa was a bare wall. Manuela had not offered him a seat, but he sank onto the sofa anyway.

"You've gotten rid of the flag?" he asked sardonically.

"Gonzalo!" she begged. "Don't be foolish."

She remained standing, obviously hoping that he would go quickly. A devilish impulse to be as leisurely as possible made him say, "So, how're the kids? And Javier?"

She put one hand to her cheek as if she had been struck. "You bastard!" It was almost a sob.

He leaned back and crossed his legs. "Hope he isn't out of a job now."

"He was arrested on Saturday." Manuela started to cry in earnest.

Gonzalo blinked, and then stood up rapidly. "Jesus, I'm sorry, Manuela. I didn't know. I thought . . . I mean it's not as if garbage collection's political. Hell, I'm sorry, Manuela. I'll ask my questions quickly and get out of here."

"If it isn't too much trouble." Her voice was bitter.

"Carmen told me you found Viviana." Gonzalo had to fight to say the name. Manuela nodded. She had turned away from him and was starting to clear the cups from the table. "She said you heard . . . whatever there was to hear Friday night," he persisted.

"I heard shooting." Manuela no longer sounded angry or grieved. Just exhausted. "But Javier was here, and the kids, and it wasn't any of my business."

Gonzalo sighed. She wasn't trying to be unhelpful. "At around what time?" he asked, without much hope.

"The first time? Right after Juana and César got home from school. Maybe five-thirty or six o'clock."

Gonzalo blinked in surprise. "The first time?" he repeated. "Was there a volley of shots then? Returned fire?"

"No." She shook her head. "Just the one shot. César went to the balcony, and he said there was a guardia civil dead in the street. So I told him to let him lie. The guardia don't travel alone."

"But Viviana?" Gonzalo persisted.

"That must have been a few hours later. I was making dinner when I heard the second shot." Manuela had finished clearing the table, and was scrubbing at it with a rag.

"Did you look out?" Gonzalo asked.

She turned to him and shook her head. "No. If there was a dead guardia, that meant there was a sniper somewhere along the street. I didn't think looking out would be healthy." She winced. "I didn't know it was Viviana until the next morning. I would have gone out if I'd known, Gonzalo. I swear to you. I would have tried to do something."

Gonzalo closed his eyes, remembering the wound to Viviana's head. "I don't think it would have helped."

Manuela put down her dishrag and laid one hand on his arm. "I'm sorry, Gonzalo. She was a wonderful girl."

He was silent, unable to trust his voice. Manuela's hostility was almost easier to bear than her sympathy. "Such a quixotic little thing," Manuela said gently. He nodded. "Ready to take on all of Franco's army with an old rifle." Manuela smiled a little. "I wonder how long she was holed up there, waiting for her shot. And how they caught her."

Gonzalo was about to explain the mistake to Manuela when he reflected that there was no real reason to do so. But that must have been what the guardia civil had thought as well. Why search for a phantom sniper when there was a flesh-and-blood Republican available for execution? Now that he thought about it, though, there was something odd about the timing. "You said more than an hour?" he said.

Manuela looked surprised at this change in sentiment. "Yes," she agreed. "It must have been well after eight o'clock when I heard the second shot."

"Why do you suppose they didn't search for a sniper right away?" Gonzalo spoke more to himself than to Manuela, but she offered a suggestion anyway.

"Maybe the one left alone was frightened," she snickered. "They're great ones for strength in numbers, you know."

"And ran for it?" Gonzalo smiled slightly.

"Could be. Or maybe the dead one was on his own."

"They always patrol in pairs," Gonzalo objected.

"They've got to go off duty sometime," Manuela pointed out sensibly. "And Javier says. . .," she faltered. "Javier says," she continued more strongly, "that some of what they do is best done alone."

Gonzalo, despite himself, was interested. "Oh, yes?" he asked.

"Javier collected . . . collects, around the barracks," Manuela explained. "He says some of their garbage is stuff that could only come off the black market. Foreign cigarette packages and such things."

"Couldn't they get those from the Italians?" Gonzalo asked, wondering with one part of his mind if the office of garbage collector was more political than he had previously thought.

"Steak bones?" Manuela asked bitterly. "English chocolates?"

Gonzalo whistled. "They threw this stuff out?"

"Just the leavings." Manuela spoke sadly. "Javier told us about it at dinner. He told the kids maybe there'd be chocolate in the city in a few weeks."

The human mind, or rather the human stomach, is resolutely egotistical. For a moment, Gonzalo grieved for steak and chocolate almost as much as for Viviana. "Fat bastards." He would have liked to end the topic with that. But a certain voyeuristic curiosity made him add, "Do you suppose their officers turn a blind eye?"

"I think most of their officers are in cahoots with the black marketeers." Manuela too seemed fascinated by the subject. "They shoot them, if they catch them, and then they take their goods and hoard them. Or else barter them, if they can."

"How do you know this?" Gonzalo asked, surprised.

Manuela flushed. "Just guesses. From what Javier's seen."

He nodded, but his mind was elsewhere already. "You don't know anything about who might have fired the second shot—the one around eight-thirty—do you?"

"Look, I told you. I was making dinner. We were all safe at home. I didn't look out." Manuela sounded exasperated.

"Carmen said you did look out and saw guardias civiles," he persisted.

"Not then," Manuela sighed. "Later. Javier wanted to go out for a stroll. He looked out from the balcony and saw a bunch of guardias."

"A bunch?"

"Four." Manuela was shifting from foot to foot with impatience. "I went and looked too, because I was surprised. There were two of them, lifting a body onto a stretcher. And a couple of others, standing around."

"I thought they'd left Viviana . . . where you found her?" Gonzalo forced himself to ask.

"Not Viviana, idiot. The dead guardia," Manuela explained. "He was gone in the morning."

"How much later was this?"

"Jesus, Gonzalo, I don't know! Why do you care?"

"Before or after dinner?" Gonzalo was not sure how useful this was going to be. But he had no other ideas for establishing the identity of Viviana's killers, and he was desperate to keep Manuela talking.

"Before," Manuela said positively. The squall of an infant interrupted her. "Listen, Pepe's up. I've got to see to him."

"Javier wanted to go for a stroll before dinner?" Gonzalo said, puzzled.

"Yes! He took . . . he *takes* strange notions sometimes," Manuela was shepherding him toward the door, and turning her head to listen to the sound of the baby.

"Around eight-thirty? It was still light out?" Gonzalo stood his ground.

"Sunset, yes. Look, I *can't* talk now."

"Would anyone else have seen anything, do you think?"

"Interview the whole building if you like!" Manuela abandoned her attempt to get rid of her unwelcome visitor, and headed for the bedroom, where the sounds of a baby's crying had become more intense. To her dismay, Gonzalo followed her. "Go around and knock on doors! Wear your uniform if you like, so you're nice and easy to identify! But if you're going to commit suicide, don't involve me!"

"I'm going to find out who killed Viviana."

"What for?" Manuela demanded harshly. After a glance at Gonzalo's face she added quickly, "Never mind. You're insane. I don't want to know." She picked up her youngest son with a gentle efficiency that contrasted oddly with her voice as she added, "Please, Gonzalo. I'm sorry, but I've told you all I know."

"You were Viviana's friend." Anyone else would have given up. But Gonzalo was accustomed to hopeless causes. "You don't have any ideas?"

The baby was still crying. Manuela turned away without speaking, and began to unbutton her blouse. After a moment, the cries subsided, and peaceful sucking sounds replaced them. Gonzalo was about to give up when she said quietly, "The nearest post is in the Ciudad Universitaria. The guardias who took away the body probably were from there."

Gonzalo opened his mouth to thank her, remembering the words of a drill sergeant who had trained the militias several lifetimes ago: If your gun jams, put your head down and count to five. Sometimes it's just nervousness. He held his breath, and counted to five. "There were two pairs of guardias civiles," Manuela said, just as he reached "four." "So probably the dead man was from another post. They'd have called his partner otherwise."

"Thank you," Gonzalo said to her back. She did not reply. "I'll let myself out," he added. "And I will try to make sure no one sees me."

She bent her head slightly but still said nothing.

"I hope Javier gets out soon," he said.

There was a more definite nod this time. "Thank you."

He glanced through the peephole of the front door before opening it. There was no one on the landing. Hastily, he opened the door and then shut it again and hurried to the next landing. With any luck, no one would see him leave. Once he was on the main stairway he breathed more easily. At least there was no longer a concierge to avoid. Before the war, there had been one, but the rich tenants on the first and second floors had left in '36, and the concierge was killed in '38, and no one had taken over the position. The tenants locked their doors at night from habit, but the front door of the building stood open. There was nothing left to steal.

At the entrance to the street, he paused in the doorway. He had a good view of the intersection of Amor de Dios and Fray Luis de León. A few men hurried by, perhaps late for work, or early for the siesta. There were no soldiers or guardias civiles in sight. Gonzalo stepped out of the shadow of the building and into the street, doing his best to avoid the overflowing gutters. Not much of a surprise, if they've arrested all the garbage men as Communists, he thought with some disgust. Damn, poor Javier. *City employee? Whoops, you must be a Red.* His heel skidded on a piece of paper, and he stopped a moment to steady himself. When he took another step forward, something squished under his sole. With an exclamation of disgust, he lifted his left foot and inspected it.

A square of crumpled silver foil, perhaps an inch across, was stuck to the sole of his left shoe. Surprised, he picked at it with his fingernail. It came away almost in one piece, leaving a dark brown stain on the shoe. It was, he saw, only silver-coated on one side. The other side was white, but with dark brown stuff sticking to it, and stained with something rust-colored, which had formed a darkish red sediment around the outside of the stain. Gingerly, aware that he was doing something foolish in the extreme, he sniffed at the brown gunk, prepared to recoil from the stench of excrement. But it smelled of chocolate. Manuela's voice echoed in his mind. "Their officers are in cahoots with the black marketeers." Gonzalo would have liked very much to stay and inspect the rest of the gutter. But a man of military age loitering for too long was bound to attract unwanted attention. He straightened, crumpled the wrapper, and slipped it into his pocket. Then he headed toward home, trying to look purposeful and inconspicuous.

A guardia civil on his own was an unusual thing. A possibly bloodstained piece of silver foil with chocolate clinging to it was also an unusual thing. Two unconnected unusual things in the same vicinity seemed highly unlikely. For the first time, Gonzalo wondered about the motivations of a guardia civil. It cost him some effort to place himself in the position of Viviana's killers, but he had to admit, however reluctantly, that they would have been fools not to search for a sniper if they suspected that their fellow had been killed simply because of his uniform. They *might* be fools, of course. But they might also have been aware that the dead man had been killed for a different reason. If he were a black marketeer, for instance, or if he had stolen goods from one. "They shoot them . . . and then they take their goods and hoard them. Or else barter them . . ." How convenient to say, "What a tragedy. Poor so-and-so, fallen for his country, a martyr to the dirty Reds. At least we got his killer" while enjoying the milk chocolate that so-and-so had been killed for.

When Carmen Llorente came home for lunch she discovered her brother seated at the kitchen table, staring intently at a piece of silver foil. "Did you have a good morning?" she asked, a little anxiously.

He nodded. "I went to see Manuela."

"You—? Gonzalo! Please, you have to stay indoors. It's not likely anyone will look for you, and when things die down. . . ."

"Where would I find someone with contacts on the black market?" he interrupted.

"You want to commit suicide," his sister said flatly.

Gonzalo smiled, a little grimly. "Not just yet."

Chapter 6

Tejada would have liked to have gone immediately to the Calle Tres Peces to search for Maria Alejandra. Unfortunately, he and Loredo were committed to heading north and east, directly away from the child's home. It was a long walk, and the constant low-grade hostility began to grate on Tejada's nerves. It seemed as if for every person who saluted or shouted, *"Viva la Guardia Civil!"* there were ten who dropped their eyes, turned their backs, or slid into doorways. The orders were to stop and search anyone acting suspiciously, but after four hours, nearly everyone looked suspicious, and the two guardias civiles were exhausted. Both Tejada and Loredo stopped looking for suspicious behavior and began covertly scanning the streets for bakeries or cafés. Awnings were not uncommon, but the windows beneath them were shuttered and lightless. Few shops even bothered with signs saying that they were closed.

By the time they returned to the barracks, a little after six, Tejada was too tired to consider going out again to Tres Peces. It would not have been possible anyway. "The lieutenant wants to see you, sergeant," a guardia said as soon as he entered the building.

Tejada sighed, and made his way to Lieutenant Ramos's office. The lieutenant was on the telephone when he entered. "Yes, Colonel . . . yes, Colonel, understood." Ramos thrust a piece of paper at the sergeant, and indicated that he should read it. "Yes, Colonel, very good." Tejada looked down at the paper. It was typewritten and addressed to Ramos, from someone named Captain Morales. "Yes, but that may be difficult, Colonel." Ramos's voice, a combination of deference and exasperation, hummed in the background, as Tejada read:

> Regarding your memo of March 31, 1939, Corporal Francisco López Pérez was a member of this post. He went off duty at 10:00 on March 31, leaving the post shortly afterward. His partner, Sergeant Diego de Rota, reported him missing on Saturday, April 1 at 09:30. Thank you for your information concerning Corporal López, and for your men's prompt action concerning his murderer. I have informed the López family. If it is your opinion that Corporal López should be a candidate for military honors I will initiate the process.

"At your command, Colonel. *Arriba España!*" Ramos hung up. "I thought you'd like to know that we've traced López."

"Thank you, sir." Tejada held out the memo to his commander.

"There's another shipment of prisoners going out to Toledo tomorrow," the lieutenant said, pleased. "I've assigned you to the convoy."

"Lieutenant." Tejada nodded, but did not seem overly pleased by the news.

Ramos made an exasperated noise. "I thought you'd be glad to go. You said that López's family was in Toledo. Drop off the prisoners, and take a couple of hours to see his family. It's better than just getting a telegram."

Tejada blinked. "Thank you, sir." There was nothing else to say. Three years had taught the sergeant that war was more apt to bring out men's worst qualities than their finest, but it did occasionally strike little sparks of decency from unlikely flints. Lieutenant Ramos was doing his best.

"You're welcome. You leave at nine A.M. tomorrow. Dismissed."

As a matter of fact, the convoy did not leave until after eleven, partly because the recruits under Tejada's command were late and partly because Ramos had willfully underestimated the number of trips it would take to get all of the prisoners to the train station. When the trucks arrived from their final trip, perilously overloaded, it was discovered that two of the prisoners had fainted on the journey. The truck driver, who had protested at the lack of space, was careful not to say "I told you so" but it was written on his face. Tejada bit back his annoyance. It would have been simplest to shoot the unconscious men, and thus make more room on the train, but he was unaware of what they were charged with, and it was possible that interrogators at the other end of the journey wanted to speak to them. "You have five minutes to get them vertical," he said shortly, and turned to another guardia. "Start the roll call, as they get onto the train." Naturally, the roll took rather longer than five minutes, partly because there was a crowd of civilians yelling to the prisoners, and since they were yelling back, they frequently missed their names. Tejada fired into the air, threatened to fire into the crowd, and mentally cursed his subordinates as incompetents. By the time the train crawled out of Madrid, he was more than half sorry he had ever expressed a desire to go to Toledo.

When the train arrived, the initial headaches of unloading prisoners prevented any time for reflection. One man made an ill-advised attempt to escape, and three of the newest and most enthusiastic guardias sprayed the street with several rounds of bullets before managing to hit him. Tejada, whose memories of Toledo involved rationing nearly everything, including bullets, winced at the waste of ammunition. The attempted escape meant another roll call, this time with angry and demoralized prisoners, and then a lengthy report to the prison authorities.

It was not until the midafternoon that Tejada had the leisure to stop and think. He stood in the courtyard of the alcázar, looking down over the town. Too many buildings still stood roofless, but at least there were no explosions, and no gunfire now. Behind him, the ruined towers of the fortress loomed, impressive even in the midst of rubble. He remembered staring down at the town at an earlier time, with the pleasant sense of an impossible task achieved. There were footsteps behind him. He turned, half expecting to see Paco coming toward him, grinning. "Hey, Carlos! Colonel Moscardó wants to see you. Looks like you're getting stripes."

"Excuse me, Sergeant. Lieutenant Adriano says there's a car here for us." It was Guardia Vásquez, looking and sounding a little nervous.

Tejada glanced at his watch automatically. It was almost four. "With a driver?" he asked.

"Yes, sir."

"Ask him if he can wait," Tejada said. "We're due for a break."

Vásquez gaped. Sergeant Tejada had not been in a forgiving mood today. And it was unlike him to suggest breaks. "Yes, sir," he managed.

After some discussion, it was settled that the guardias civiles from Madrid would return at six o'clock. Sergeant Tejada, after threatening dire punishments for anyone who was not present and prepared at the appointed hour, disappeared into the town. The other men stayed near the fort. "You'd think he'd want to hang around here," Vásquez commented. "I mean, get reacquainted with the alcázar."

"Idiot," Jiménez said scornfully. "He *knows* the alcázar. He doesn't need to get reacquainted. I bet he could find his way around it in the dark with his eyes closed."

"Is it true that General Franco gave him a medal for heroism in a special ceremony in '37?" Durán asked, wide-eyed.

"Of course. You know Corporal Torres? He's seen Tejada in dress uniform and he says there's a decoration."

Vásquez looked around him and shook his head. "Three months in here, with the Reds bombarding it," he said. "I heard they were eating rats when Varela lifted the siege."

"I can't picture the sergeant eating rats," said Durán thoughtfully.

"Sergeant Tejada could eat anything." Jiménez was stoutly loyal.

In fact, Sergeant Tejada was just tasting an excellent cup of coffee while this conversation was taking place. He had headed across the square from the alcázar and down one of the broader streets, stopping in front of a large building with a nineteenth-century facade. There had been elaborate stone carvings over the door, but some vandal had smashed them, and now there was only a suggestion of human forms carved into the yellow stone. The smashed statues, and a few panes of broken glass, were the only hints that war had come anywhere near this building. Its owners had thus far been fortunate. Tejada took off his hat, straightened his crumpled uniform as best he could, and rang the bell.

A man dressed in black opened it. "Can I help you, Señor Guardia?"

"Is Señora Pérez in?" Tejada asked.

"The señora is not receiving anyone today." The man's voice was uncompromising in the extreme.

Tejada had by this time taken in the man's black coat and gloves. The telegram had been delivered already then. "I know this is a house of mourning," he said. "I'm here as a friend of Corporal López's, to present my condolences."

The doorkeeper scanned Tejada, and the sergeant wished that he had been able to wear a dress uniform. "Whom shall I announce to the señora?" he asked.

"Sergeant Carlos Tejada Alonso y León." The sergeant matched the doorkeeper's stare.

He was led into an arched hallway dominated by a staircase, undoubtedly once carpeted and now bare wood. A large portrait hung on the opposite wall. It showed a gray-haired gentleman wearing the dress uniform of a colonel from the War of 1898. One hand rested lightly on his sword. With the other, he beckoned to someone just outside the canvas. Tejada looked at the portrait for a long moment, trying to trace a resemblance to his friend Paco. The servant reappeared. "The señora will see you," he announced and turned toward the stairs.

The parlor at the top of the stairs was a handsome room. Sunlight slanted through windows that looked out on a flower garden. In one corner, a piano was open, with a few sheets of music lying on it. The mantelpiece held a cluster of porcelain figures, shoved awkwardly but not carelessly to one side, to make room for two photographs. The first was a photographer's vision of the portrait in the hallway, set in a heavy silver frame. The second photograph, also silver-framed, was set in the exact center of the mantelpiece. It was a portrait of Paco in a cadet's uniform, looking very young, and very pleased with himself. Someone had placed vases of lilies around it.

Paco's mother had risen from the sofa to greet her guest. She was dressed in black and a black lace veil covered steel gray hair. "Sergeant Carlos Tejada Alonso y León, Señora," the doorkeeper announced, standing to one side.

As Tejada crossed the sunlit room, he felt a strange sense of familiarity. The room, the lady, his own actions—all of them were governed by a set of rules that he had learned a long time ago and that he had imagined he had forgotten. So it was not knowledge of the rules of etiquette but a sort of muscular memory, similar to that necessary for riding a bicycle, that made him bow over his hostess's hand and kiss it. "Your servant, Doña Clara." He kissed one cheek and then the other, still acting from some half-remembered script. "My deepest sympathies."

"Thank you." She gestured him to a seat, and then resumed her own. "It was good of you to come, Carlos. Forgive me—I should say Sergeant Tejada."

"No." He shook his head. "You have the right, Doña Clara."

She turned to the black-clad servant. "Bring us coffee please, José."

There was a pause. The script was deserting him at the crucial moment, leaving only ugly truths to be spoken. "I hoped to arrive earlier, to tell you in person."

"I am surprised you came so soon," she replied reassuringly. "How did you know? Did Paco contact you in Madrid before . . . the end?"

"No." Tejada found himself wishing that he was already on his way back to Madrid. "No. Actually, I identified him."

"What happened?" she asked.

Tejada hesitated. Doña Clara twisted a handkerchief in her lap. "Please, Carlos. The official notice gave no details. And I want to know. I can bear it better if I know."

She had been a soldier's wife, Tejada reminded himself, and she was a soldier's widow. She had borne the siege along with her husband and son. Slowly, he began to sketch the scene for Paco's mother. It seemed to take a long time although there was actually very little to tell. There was too much that he did not know, and too much of what he did know was too sordid to discuss. There was no need to mention the way Paco's limbs had stiffened before the stretcher arrived. No need to mention that his eyes had not been closed. Tejada found himself suppressing the episode of María Alejandra's notebook as well. Too many unanswered questions surrounded it. He mentioned the miliciana who had presumably killed Paco, but only briefly. Doña Clara closed her eyes. "A woman! Their women, too! May God have mercy, Carlos. They aren't human!"

"No," he said quietly.

The door opened and José reappeared, bearing a tray. He poured the coffee, and Tejada, judging that more discussion of the details of Paco's murder would be tasteless, cast around for a change of subject. "I wish I had known Paco was in Madrid," he said. "When was he transferred, do you know?"

"He was in the north until after we won Gerona." Doña Clara tacitly agreed to the conversation's new direction. "I believe he was a border guard for a while."

"In Cataluña?"

"Yes, he was sent there just before my husband passed away. Francisco"—Doña Clara crossed herself, in memory of the departed—"was very relieved that he was leaving Basque country. He used to say that the Catalans would go to hell, but that the Basques would go *home* to hell."

Tejada smiled. "I had a few letters from Paco now and then, and I think he agreed about the Basques. But he would have hated anywhere that wasn't Toledo, I think. I've never met anyone who loved Castile so much."

Doña Clara smiled, too. "Yes, he was like his father. *'La mía Castilla,'* they always said. As if the land were their sweetheart. It was a shame he had to leave. Even his father sometimes thought it hadn't been a good idea, but you know after that business . . . ;" she trailed off.

"A lot of people were transferred after the siege," Tejada agreed. He was starting to remember why he had chosen the Guardia Civil, and not the civilian life his parents had urged on him. It was difficult referring to sieges and battles as "that business."

"What? Oh, the siege, yes, of course. After that." Doña Clara looked vaguely discomfited.

The sergeant felt a flicker of surprise. He had assumed that Paco's transfer had been random: the fortunes of war. But Paco's mother seemed to think otherwise. "Was there some other reason?" he asked, and then kicked himself for cross-examining a grieving woman on what was supposed to be a condolence visit.

"Oh." Doña Clara was blushing faintly. "I assumed you knew . . . it was nothing serious really. Just . . . well, it's not a woman's place to judge these things."

"I'm sure Paco was always the soul of honor," Tejada said, fighting against a disloyal and discourteous desire to pursue the subject. He tried to recall some clue to Doña Clara's embarrassment.

"Of course." Doña Clara smiled at him warmly. "That was what *I* said. Francisco—may he rest in peace—was . . . well, a good husband, of course, but perhaps more . . . susceptible himself. But *I* knew that my son would never get entangled with that painted hussy."

Tejada choked on his coffee. *Hussy? Jesus, Paco, you could have told me!* He struggled with an unreasonable sense of betrayal. He was just hurt enough to commit a further breach of good manners. "I assume he . . . er . . . didn't give his father any more cause for concern?"

"Not the slightest," Doña Clara agreed complacently. She bit her lip, perhaps aware that she had expressed herself rather strongly. "Would you like more coffee?"

"Yes, please." Tejada, awash in surprising disclosures, felt his feet strike solid ground. "It's delicious," he added truthfully.

Doña Clara smiled, but her eyes were tear-filled. "It was my last gift from Paco. He knew how hard rationing was for civilians, so he always tried to send me supplies. The coffee came last month, with a pound of sugar as well. He must have starved himself to be so generous."

Tejada nodded. "That's like him. I remember, during the siege, it must have been the middle of August, I thought I'd go insane. He handed me half his morning's rations and said, 'Here, eat, Carlito. You need it.' And God help me, I ate it. I don't think I even thanked him."

Doña Clara wiped her eyes. "You didn't have to, Carlos. You know, before each of the girls were born, he kept saying to me, 'Remember, Mama, I want a little *brother* this time.' And afterward, oh, he was so angry he wouldn't speak to me. He found a brother in you."

"I'm honored," Tejada said softly.

He would have liked to linger over the coffee, talking more of the siege, of Paco, and Paco's father, and the early days of the war, when he had believed that victory would be quick and painless. But the chiming of the little clock over the piano was insistent. "I must go," he said, at five-thirty. "I'm supposed to be on duty. And my men and I have to return to Madrid tonight."

Doña Clara rose, and gave him her hand. "Thank you for coming," she said.

He kissed her on both cheeks again, before leaving. Another phrase from a past life came unbidden to his lips. "I am always at home to you."

José showed him out.

A few minutes after six, Tejada and his men rolled out of Toledo. Jiménez and a few of the others would have dearly liked to question the sergeant about the deployment of troops during the siege and about several prominent pockmarks in the walls of the alcázar. But Tejada was in an abstracted mood, and none of them dared to raise the subject. Finally, Durán said hesitantly, "Did you have a good afternoon, Sergeant?"

"Hmm?" Tejada had been staring out at the dry yellow fields. "Yes, thanks. I visited . . . an old acquaintance."

The guardias civiles were forced to be content with that.

Chapter 7

Carmen Llorente had not been among the crowd at the railroad station who had seen the Guardia Civil transporting prisoners to Toledo. She heard an account of it from her employer that afternoon though, and came home white-faced. Her brother was pacing the floor when she arrived.

"I have an idea," he announced, as soon as she came in. "Those people you work for . . . they're rich enough to buy things on the black market. Where do they go, can you find out?"

Carmen had taken off her coat. It took some effort for her to hang it up as she said shakily, "No."

"Damn it, Carmen. Are you sure?" Gonzalo had spent all day indoors. The little piece of silver foil that had seemed like such a good lead yesterday now seemed to mock his hopes. He had started at every creak in the boards, and gone so far as to hide himself in the closet a few times. This contact with the black market had been his only idea all day. It had seemed sure-fire.

Carmen stepped forward and slapped him as hard as she could. "You self-centered bastard." Her voice was shaking with the effort of keeping it low, when she wanted to scream. "Don't ask what happened today. Don't ask how the hell I'm supposed to feed us now that I'm out of a job. Don't ask what happens to women like me who are *stupid* enough to try to hide carbineros. Just look at that damn chocolate wrapper, and try to find out about the black market!"

"You lost your job?" Gonzalo rubbed his jaw, irritated. There was, he thought, no way he could have known that Carmen would be in a bad mood. It wasn't his fault. "I didn't know. Why?"

"Why should you care?" Carmen turned her back to him and leaned on the table. "It doesn't concern you. You don't care about anything except getting some stupid vengeance for Viviana."

"I care if we eat," Gonzalo retorted.

"We! You mean Aleja and me, too? Big of you!"

"Look, I'm sorry," Gonzalo whispered, uncomfortably aware that his sister's voice had gotten steadily louder. "I'm sorry, I just . . . why don't you tell me what happened?"

Carmen sank into a chair and rubbed her forehead. "Señor del Valle was arrested yesterday evening. They found some articles he'd written before the war. The señora thinks that it would be better for me not to come anymore. Safer."

"So we're safe and starving?" Gonzalo transferred his irritation to the absent Señora del Valle. "Brilliant!"

Carmen shook her head and made a conscious effort to hold on to her temper. "It would have happened sooner or later. I overheard them a couple of days ago. They were talking about going to France."

"Sounds a bit late for that," Gonzalo remarked.

"Much too late," his sister agreed. "The señora told me that Señor del Valle was taken out of Madrid today. There was a whole convoy leaving by train. She said she called to him but there were so many people he didn't hear. And guardias civiles were holding off the crowd."

"Did the train come back?" Gonzalo asked.

"She stayed until this evening, hoping to see." Carmen shuddered. "There's a rumor it went to Toledo. They say it's a bad sign if it comes back empty too quickly."

"Shit," said Gonzalo.

"I know. Señor del Valle was a good man."

"Shit." It was the atheist's equivalent of "May he rest in peace."

Carmen stood up, and went back to her bag. "Señora del Valle paid me through the end of the week."

Gonzalo rubbed his eyes. "With what?"

"Bread. Almost a whole loaf. And there's an orange for Aleja."

"She's been saying she's hungry."

"At least she's saying something," Carmen sighed. "Where is she?"

Gonzalo pointed without speaking.

"Oh. Damn."

There was still a blanket draped over a string in the living room screening off the bed he had shared with Viviana. Gonzalo had made the bed again after her burial, turning back the sheets and placing the two pillows in an awkward L shape, because it was too narrow for them to fit properly. ("You'd think we'd be very uncomfortable," Viviana had said, laughing, the first time she made the bed.) Then he had continued sleeping on the couch. Carmen walked over to the blanket and then pushed it to one side. Aleja was curled up on the bed, hugging her knees.

"How are you, sweetheart?" Carmen sat down and put one arm around her daughter. There was no reply. "You're so quiet, I didn't even know you were there. Are you angry because I snapped at Tío Gonzalo? I didn't mean it." Carmen was stroking the little girl's hair now, her voice coaxing. "Would you like a piece of bread?"

"All right." Aleja's voice could not be called enthusiastic but it was a voice.

Relief flooded through Carmen. "You'll feel better after you eat, precious. And then maybe tomorrow you'll go to school."

Aleja tensed and shook her head. "I can't go to school."

"But, sweetheart, you've missed three days."

"Tío Gonzalo doesn't have to go out," the little girl pointed out.

"Shh-shh," Carmen said automatically. "Remember, I explained. Tío Gonzalo isn't going out because he's hiding. We have to be very careful to say that it's just us two here. But you have to go back to school, Aleja."

Aleja burrowed her head against her mother's stomach. "I don't have my notebook." Her voice was the whine of a much younger child.

Carmen looked toward her brother for support. But he was standing with his back to them, and the set of his shoulders told her that he did not feel like intervening. "But you can't miss school forever," she wheedled. "Think how Señorita Fernández would feel if you went away and never said good-bye to her. Maybe she'll be able to help you get a new notebook."

"Tía Viviana promised me *my* notebook." The end of Aleja's sentence was drowned in tears.

Carmen closed her eyes and rocked her daughter back and forth, murmuring soothing nonsense. I am going to go mad very soon, she thought. Gonzalo had said nothing to reproach his niece since his return home but he had not helped to comfort her either. For all Carmen knew, the two of them passed their days in total silence. Gonzalo either brooded or took insane risks. And now even the tenuous normality of life in the del Valle household was gone. Tomorrow her daily routine would be gone. Tomorrow, she thought, Aleja has to go to school. I'll take her myself. Get Aleja out of the house first. Then I can see about work. She shuddered. There was no work. There were the women in front of the soldiers' barracks, who put up with the jeers. *Puta roja.* Red whore. But they ate. She wasn't that hungry yet. But if Aleja began complaining. . . . Carmen turned abruptly to her brother, determined to shut out the thought. "I've heard you can buy things in the Plaza de la Cebada."

Gonzalo, who had been ignoring his sister and niece, was unaware that she was talking to him for a moment. "Cheaper, you mean?" he asked stupidly, when she repeated her comment.

"No." Carmen's voice was dry. "More expensive things. What you were asking about."

"Oh." Gonzalo turned. He hesitated a moment and then said, "Will you be all right if I go out now?"

The knot in his sister's chest loosened almost imperceptibly. It was not all right, and he would go anyway, but at least he was asking. "I'll be all right if you come back," she said, trying to smile.

He nodded. "I'll have to say I forgot my identity card, if they ask," he said.

She nodded. They both knew that he would not survive a meeting with soldiers without papers. But at least he was trying. Gonzalo took a cap that had belonged to his brother-in-law and tried to make sure that it shadowed his face as much as possible. It was not much of a disguise. He set out for the Plaza de la Cebada, hoping that he would meet no one he knew. As far as he could tell, his luck held. It was a fine evening, and people were beginning to come out again. There was enough traffic in the streets to make him inconspicuous, but he saw no one he recognized.

The Plaza de la Cebada was not far away, and Gonzalo was disturbed by how much the walk tired him. Carmen had given him a hot drink in the morning, which, against all sensory evidence, she had insisted was coffee. He had eaten the night before. It hardly counted as fasting. He crossed the Calle de Toledo with his head down, and then jumped as a streetcar clanged its bell. It was bearing down on him, and the driver was cursing and gesticulating. Gonzalo managed a shuffling run to get out of the way. He leaned against a building on the other side of the street, to recover from the surprise, he told himself, although narrowly avoiding a streetcar should not have been enough to make his temples pound as if he were about to faint.

The plaza was crowded with people. They stood in pairs and groups of three, muttering and glancing over their shoulders.

Everyone tried to look casual. No one succeeded. Many people here seemed to be heavily dressed, although the weather was not cold. Occasionally, someone suddenly became thinner as something slid out from under a jacket or shirt. Gonzalo caught a glimpse of a tortilla and found himself salivating. He hesitated, uncertain what to do. A woman, apparently heavily pregnant, was propped against one of the buildings. He wandered over to her.

She met his eyes, and then raised her eyebrows. "You looking for something?"

"I might be." Gonzalo kept his hands in his pockets.

"I only take Franco's bills. None of the Republic's stuff." She was brisk.

Gonzalo stared. "How do you know I'm not a guardia?"

"You?" the woman laughed. "*Hombre*, the guardia eat. It's easy to see you don't." She tapped her swollen belly. "I've got potatoes here, fresh, and some lentils."

"What about meat?" Gonzalo asked, thinking of what Manuela had told him.

She shook her head. "No. The potatoes are a better value, though."

Gonzalo's hand closed on the scrap of silver foil in his pocket. "I'm looking for someone who sells meat," he said firmly. "And, better than that, chocolate."

"Chocolate!" She laughed again. "You don't want much, *hombre*. How about a private yacht, while you're at it?"

"There must be someone here who sells it," Gonzalo persisted.

Her eyes narrowed. "You want the chocolate, or you want to find the person who's selling it?"

"What's it to you?"

She clasped her hands below the bulge on her stomach, and the bundle shifted in a most un-fetuslike fashion. "You want chocolate, you have to deal with the soldiers."

Gonzalo felt his pulse beginning to pound in his temples. Count to five, he reminded himself. "Soldiers?" he asked, keeping his voice as nonchalant as possible.

It was no use. The smuggler turned away from him to a woman with a leather purse and a shawl over her head. "You looking for something, Señora?"

"How much would a kilo of potatoes be?" Like Gonzalo, the woman tried to sound nonchalant, but the pleading in her voice was painful to hear.

Gonzalo drifted away, cursing himself for a fool. Information wasn't free. And he had nothing with which to pay for it. He wandered along the edge of the plaza, wondering if he would dare approach a soldier. None seemed to be in evidence. Did that mean the Plaza de la Cebada was not the place for chocolates?

"For the love of God, it's my engagement ring!" The voice flashed suddenly out of an archway—angry, desperate, and louder than it was intended to be. "The diamond alone is worth thousands of pesetas!"

There was a low murmur in reply. Gonzalo turned. The voice belonged to a middle-aged woman. She wore a hat and a coat that, although ancient and tattered, was undeniably fur. He loitered closer. The woman's voice had dropped again, but he heard her protesting and heard someone else steadily denying her pleas. After a few minutes, she passed by him, clutching something under her coat. He wondered for a moment if the smell of meat was only a phantom born of his own desires, and then marched through the archway. Two men lounged there, with a pair of well-worn suitcases in front of them.

"Where would I find chocolate?" Gonzalo asked quickly, before the men could take in his appearance.

"In Switzerland," one replied promptly.

Gonzalo gritted his teeth. "How many times have you told that joke today?"

The other man laughed. "Only once today. Not many people bother to ask anymore." He inspected Gonzalo. "Why are you asking anyway? It looks like you need more than that."

"Someone told me I should ask the soldiers," Gonzalo fenced.

The first man spat between his teeth. "Someone shoots off his mouth a lot."

"Taking cheap shots?" Gonzalo tried to keep his voice light.

"Any shot at the army's expensive, buddy," the smuggler replied.

Gonzalo had kept his hands in his pockets. He fingered the silver foil for a moment. Then he drew it out. "Suppose I was looking for something like this?"

One of the men leaned forward and looked at the wrapper. Then he said, "You'd pay?"

"Sure," Gonzalo lied. "I can't until I know who to pay, though."

The two men exchanged glances. Then one of them said, "You know the Guardia Civil station up along the Calle Alcalá?"

"Sure." Gonzalo was afraid of uttering more than the monosyllable. It was an effort to hide his excitement even then.

"You know the entrance to the park, a little ways from it?"

"Sure."

"Meet me there tomorrow, at around five. I'm not making promises. But I might be able to help you."

Gonzalo considered how to explain that he was really more interested in information than in chocolate. No good idea occurred to him. "See you tomorrow," he said, and turned to go.

"One thing." The man's voice stopped him.

"Yes?"

The two men exchanged glances again, and then one of them said, "Bring an identity card. Our supplier has been a little touchy lately."

"Got it." Gonzalo left, wondering how he would justify not bringing an identity card, and whether it would be worth his effort to bring a gun.

Chapter 8

Although his visit to Toledo, with its various ghosts, should have left him brooding and wakeful, Tejada slept the sleep of the just when he returned to Madrid that evening. That was as well. He was scheduled for the morning shift the following day, and he was barely dressed when Lieutenant Ramos sent for him.

"We've got a problem," the lieutenant said, looking, in Tejada's opinion, disgustingly alert and enthusiastic given the hour. "And solving it may take some discretion. At ease," he added. "And pull up a chair, Tejada."

Tejada, who had no objection to standing at attention but would have dearly loved five minutes to finish shaving, sat without comment. "I wanted you here because I'm expecting a phone call from Captain Morales at any minute," Ramos continued. "And I think it would be a good idea for you to hear part of it." He glanced at his watch and frowned. "He was supposed to call five minutes ago."

"It's not eight-thirty yet, sir," Tejada pointed out, struggling for a moment to place Captain Morales. Then he remembered: the commander of Paco's post.

"I know," said the lieutenant, with the sublime incomprehension of a naturally early riser. "He said he'd call at eight-fifteen. The thing is"— he lowered his voice—"we're losing rations. Someone in the quartermaster's office is on the take."

In Tejada's considered opinion, this was one of those statements like "Anarchists burn churches" that were not worth the
breath expended in saying them. "Surely that's not unusual,
sir," he suggested.

Ramos shook his head. "If you mean that they always skim
a little, of course. This is more than that. And it's affecting all
the posts in our company. And you know the saying 'An army
travels on its stomach.' A general who understands that will
never be defeated."

"Napoleon said that, sir," said Tejada, feeling that his commander deserved something for interrupting his shave. "And
he didn't do so well in Spain."

Perhaps fortunately, the telephone rang at this point. The
lieutenant picked it up. "Guardia Civil, Ramos. . . . Good morning, Captain. . . . Yes . . . yes, the man I mentioned is here. Yes,
Tejada Alonso y León." He gestured to Tejada, with one hand
over the mouthpiece. "Listen," he mouthed.

Tejada rose and walked around the desk so that he could
lean over the phone as well. Ramos held out the receiver, and
then spoke into it. "Yes, Captain, go ahead."

"I've spoken with the colonel," Morales's voice echoed
oddly from the phone, but it was perfectly understandable.
"He says that the company's rations are inspected and that they
leave as they should." Ramos made an eloquent face at Tejada.
"I've also questioned a number of guardias, and their estimates
of their meat rations agree with yours."

Ramos pulled the receiver away from Tejada for a moment.
"That's fine then." He glared at the sergeant, and gestured his
skepticism again. "At your orders, Captain."

"Nothing further about the rations then," Morales said.
"But you might send Sergeant Tejada to me about that other
matter."

"Other matter?" Ramos blinked. "Oh, yes, of course. Right
away, Captain."

Tejada spared a moment to hope that "right away" was a flexible concept that included breakfast.

"Yes, Captain. *Arriba España*." Ramos put down the phone. "Morales is worried too."

"I gathered," Tejada resumed his position on the other side of the desk. "What are your estimates of the meat rations that leave the quartermaster as they should, sir?"

"Two hundred and fifty grams per man," said the lieutenant.

Tejada raised his eyebrows. "*Exactly* two hundred and fifty grams?" he asked.

Ramos snorted. "It's very regular," he said grimly. "A number of the men told me not to worry, because they were sure it was the correct amount. It's a round number, and it's nearly twice civilian rations, you know."

"Someone's being clever then," Tejada commented. "Have you found any evidence of hoarding?"

"Jesus, Tejada, you know what this place is like. Do *you* think someone's hoarding?"

The sergeant shook his head. "I suppose you want me to find out what's going on at Alcalá?"

"Yes," Ramos sighed. "Ten to one you don't find hoarding there either. My guess is that it's going straight to the black market."

Tejada nodded, thinking of the shuttered stores and the crowds surrounding the post begging for food. "When are civilian provisions supposed to arrive for the city, sir?"

"Officially? Yesterday. Tomorrow, if we're lucky."

Tejada winced. "So it looks like the Reds will be fasting on Good Friday, like it or not."

The lieutenant snorted briefly. "Good for their souls, but bad for us. When this is settled, we'll try to shut down the black market once and for all. But for now, I don't want our provisions going to them. Understood?"

"Yes, sir. You'll wish me to report to Captain Morales, sir?"

Ramos nodded. "Yes. The problem has affected the whole company, but it's been worst at the Alcalá station. Morales will give you the details there. And Tejada—"

"Sir?"

"Be discreet."

When Tejada presented himself at the Alcalá station, a little over an hour later, he announced only that he had come to collect the personal effects of the late Corporal López. He stated, with an assurance that cowed the corporal on duty, that of course Captain Morales would need to see him and approve the transfer. Captain Morales, who initially looked slightly puzzled when the corporal announced Tejada, was suddenly enlightened when the sergeant said meaningfully, "Lieutenant Ramos sent me, sir. He thought that since I was a personal friend of Corporal López's I might be able to tell *if anything was missing.* I believe he spoke to you by telephone, early this morning."

"Oh, yes." Morales signaled to the corporal. "Thank you, dismissed." Then, when the door had closed, he said quietly, "At ease, Sergeant. Congratulations on your excuse, by the way. Would you like to tell me the real reason you're here?"

"Thank you, Captain. I believe you wished to communicate something about rations to Lieutenant Ramos that was too delicate for the telephone?" Tejada observed the man in front of him as he spoke. Morales was a burly man of perhaps forty. Unlike Ramos, he did not look like a paper-pusher, although his job involved as much desk work as that of Tejada's own superior. His desk, Tejada noted, was a real desk as well, and it was possible to see the surface. An organized man, Tejada thought, wondering who had first noted the disappearance of rations.

The captain quickly summarized his findings. As Ramos had predicted, they tallied exactly with the information Tejada already had. He took notes, although it was difficult to see how the notes would be helpful. When the captain had finished, Tejada said carefully, "Do you have any suspicions about any of the men here or at our post, Captain?"

"No," Morales said curtly. "I wish I did. Or rather"—he smiled briefly—"I don't really want to find out that one of my own men is behind this. You'd know Ramos's post better than I would."

The sergeant noted that Morales had quickly taken advantage of the slim opportunity offered to shift the blame. Ramos, Tejada reflected, had said that the Alcalá post was worse affected. But that might be an attempt to shift blame as well. No commander liked thinking ill of his own men. None of these thoughts showed in his voice as he said, "Lieutenant Ramos has asked me to try to find out who's responsible. If I find something, how should I contact you?"

Morales hesitated. Then he said, "By phone. Alcalá-2136."

"Is that secure, sir?"

The captain nodded. "Admirable discretion, Sergeant. But if you find out anything, I'd like to know as soon as possible. And this is a private line. Ask to speak to me personally and say simply that you have information."

"Very good, sir. Alcalá-2136." Tejada saluted. "At your orders, Captain."

"Question the guardias," Morales said. "I've already spoken to my officers but I don't have time to talk to all of the men."

"Yes, sir." Tejada hesitated for a moment. He had once met a lieutenant experienced in prisoner interrogation who had insisted that questioning was an art form. He added doubtfully, "But you must realize, Captain, I'm not trained as an interrogator."

"Your commander speaks very highly of you, and I have every confidence in your ability," Morales said. "And frankly, there is no one else available."

"Yes, sir." There was, Tejada felt, nothing else to say in the face of such a flattering analysis. He doubted that he would find anything useful, but Lieutenant Ramos clearly expected him to do something, though he had no good idea where to start. Captain Morales escorted him to the door and handed him into the care of the guardia on duty. "Take the sergeant to the dormitories," he ordered.

The Alcalá post had been a barracks before the war and was arranged with considerably more convenience than the one Tejada was accustomed to since the quarters for the guardias had actually been built for that purpose. Tejada spent the rest of the morning interviewing guardias. Some were confiding, some were openly hostile, and most were cautiously reserved. None of them, so far as the sergeant could tell, revealed anything important. If they were guilty, this was to be expected. If they were innocent, they might have nothing to reveal. Or they might know that revealing information is dangerous, he thought, and filed the idea away. He waited until lunchtime when a new set of men came off patrol duty and interviewed them, without success. It was well into the afternoon when he reported again to Captain Morales's office. The captain heard him out, and then shrugged. "Perhaps you'll have better luck at your own post."

"Yes, sir." There was nothing in Tejada's expression to show that he resented the slur. He played his last card. "Permission to collect Corporal López's things now, sir?"

Captain Morales looked dubious. "You mean you're really interested in doing that?"

"Yes, sir," Tejada chose his words carefully. "I *was* a friend of López's, sir, and I would like to send his effects to his mother. But . . . no doubt you've already thought of the implications, sir."

"Implications?" Morales looked blank.

"You don't think that Corporal López's death might have something to do with the disappearance of provisions, Captain?" Tejada asked. "After all, it's a surprising coincidence."

"No, of course not." Morales sounded surprised. "I thought López was killed by a Red." He laughed. "I could be wrong, but I believe that's based on the report that *you* filed, Sergeant."

"Yes," Tejada said slowly. "But of course you've considered that if the black market is involved, there's probably someone outside the guardia civil who knows about it." Something Paco found out, he thought, as two mental notes neatly combined themselves into one entry. Perhaps something based on what that little girl saw—a guardia civil selling something to a Red, maybe? I have to find that child this afternoon, if only to rule it out.

"Possibly." Morales shrugged. "But it seems to me that you took care of poor López's murder very efficiently. Good work, that."

Tejada was beginning to think that it had been extremely sloppy work, but he kept his opinion to himself. "I may look through his things, though, sir?" he asked patiently.

"Oh, I suppose, if you like. He was a friend of yours, you said? I'm sorry to hear that."

"Fortunes of war, sir."

"Well spoken." Morales clapped him on the shoulder and opened the door. "Guardia! Send me Sergeant de Rota, right away."

The guardia on duty outside the door saluted and disappeared, returning shortly afterward with a thin, stooping man in a sergeant's uniform. "Captain!" The man's shoulders sloped even when he stood at attention.

"Sergeant de Rota." Morales introduced the thin man. "Sergeant Tejada, Manzanares post. He's here to pick up López's things."

Sergeant de Rota's face took on an expression that Tejada recognized as a variant on the "I-am-not-arguing-with-a-superior-officer-even-though-he-is-insane" look. "Yes, Captain," he agreed. "At your service, Sergeant Tejada." Tejada acknowledged the salutation and wondered idly why his counterpart seemed so surprised by the command.

Sergeant de Rota led him past the dormitory where he had spent the morning, down a hallway, and to a small room, with two sets of bunk beds. Three of the beds were neatly made. The fourth one was occupied by a snoring man. Tejada glanced at the snorer and raised his eyebrows. Sergeant de Rota looked sullen. "Corporal García is on the night shift," he said stiffly. "There's the stuff you want."

He was pointing at the bunk bed below the sleeper. Tejada now saw that a soldier's pack was sitting in the center of the bed. He crossed the room, sat down, and opened the pack.

"What the hell do you think you're doing?" Sergeant de Rota's voice was far from friendly. "You want his kit. It's there. Take it and get out."

Had Rota been a superior, Tejada would have obeyed. As it was, he ignored his fellow sergeant, and upended the pack onto the bed. Few of the articles that tumbled out could have been called personal. They were standard issue, like the pack itself. But Tejada recognized some of them. A ribbon denoting bravery under fire, awarded by Colonel Moscardó. A leather-bound Bible, much worn. A penknife with a damascene handle. And—Tejada blinked suddenly prickling eyes— a fragile paperback copy of Azorín's *Castilla*. He carefully opened the creased book, afraid that bending back the cover one more time would detach it completely. His own handwriting looked back at him from the first page: *16/9/36 For Paco, who loves Castile—Carlos.*

Very gently, Tejada thumbed the little book. Something stiff had been placed between the cracking pages, perhaps as a bookmark. He let the book fall open to the beginning of "The Fragrance of the Vase," and discovered a photograph, carefully trimmed with pinking shears. Surprised, he took it between two fingers and examined it more closely. It was a portrait of a girl, apparently a candid shot, taken out-of-doors. She was looking over her shoulder, hatless, and her bouncy blond curls matched the ruffles of her light dress. She seemed to be laughing at the camera.

The picture was not of either of Paco's sisters. The entire López family had taken refuge in the alcázar during the siege, and Tejada had known both of the López daughters. They had been the objects of extravagant gallantry during the early days of the siege, but that was only because they were young ladies in an environment where young ladies were rare. Neither of them had possessed the startling beauty of the girl in the picture. Nor, Tejada thought, was it the kind of picture that one kept of a sister. He was not an expert on women's fashion, but it occurred to him that the ruffled neckline of the dress would probably be thought rather daring by Doña Clara—or by his own mother and sister-in-law. He looked at the back of the photograph. The pencil writing was faint and blurred, but still legible: *Dearest, Here is your "souvenir of a happy time." Love, Isabel.* Tejada inspected the laughing girl again. Doña Clara had been harsh. She did not look like a painted hussy. He looked up at Sergeant de Rota, who was still standing disapprovingly by the door. "Who's she?" he asked, holding out the picture. "Do you know?"

"No," said the thin man without moving.

"It would help if you looked at the photograph," Tejada said mildly. He had a certain sympathy for Rota. He himself would have resented being questioned by a stranger who did not outrank him. But it seemed to him that the sergeant of Alcalá was being needlessly uncooperative. He wondered why Rota was so resentful. Was the man's attitude a sort of proprietary response to his partner's death? Or did he dislike Tejada's investigation of the disappearance of rations? Morales had said that he had already spoken to all of his officers but Tejada found himself wishing that he could question Sergeant de Rota.

Tejada was considering whether and how to put Paco's sergeant at ease when there was a squeak of bedsprings and weight shifted over his head. Then a head appeared upside down and regarded Tejada with a mixture of curiosity and annoyance.

"What's all the noise?" asked the man who had been occupying the top bunk, with a jaw-splitting yawn.

"*I'm* sorry to disturb you, Corporal García," said Sergeant de Rota, with unnecessary emphasis. "This is Sergeant Tejada, from the Manzanares post. He was just leaving."

"I'm sorry to break in on your rest," Tejada said, mindful of his own feelings earlier in the day. "I'm here to collect Corporal López's personal effects. I found this, and wondered if you knew who it was." He held up the photograph.

Corporal García shoved himself farther over the edge of the bed, and hung downward. "Huh!" he said. "That must be Isabel. What a looker!"

Tejada suddenly remembered that he had identified himself as Paco's friend only to Captain Morales. He decided to indulge his curiosity. "Was she his wife?" he asked.

"Not officially." García's tone spoke volumes.

"Fiancée?" Tejada suggested, deliberately tone-deaf.

"I don't know what she was, *hombre*," García laughed. "But I know he sent her half his pay every month."

"*What?*" Tejada and Rota spoke at the same time. Rota subsided into silence, glowering at Tejada. Tejada turned his attention back to García. "How do you know this?"

García heaved himself upright and then slid off the bunk bed. "About six months ago we were out on patrol together and he asked me if I'd mail something for him," he said, studying the photo in Tejada's hand. "I asked him why he couldn't mail it himself and he said it was to a girl he wasn't supposed to see, that he had promised not to write to her *himself*, but . . . the letter, not the spirit, eh, Sergeant? I tried to kid him about it a little but he clammed up. He wasn't the confiding type." A few weeks ago, Tejada would have disagreed with this assessment. But now, in light of Isabel, he wondered how much Paco had confided in him. "I got the impression Isabel wasn't the sort of girl he could bring home to Mama," García continued, still looking at the photograph. "So that's her, huh? Well, she looks worth the pay. Do you suppose that blond is natural?"

"How do you know he was sending her his pay?" Tejada asked, ignoring the superfluities.

"When a man hands you a roll of bills at the end of each month, the day after we all get paid, you usually assume it's pay," García pointed out logically.

"García, this is ridiculous," Sergeant de Rota broke in emphatically. "Corporal López sent his pay to his parents, as do all unmarried officers."

"No, sir." García shook his head. "He sent gifts to his parents. Food and suchlike. I know, because he used to tell me about them when he wrapped them up. But half his wages went to this girl, Isabel, regular."

Tejada's mind was reeling under the onslaught of information. It seemed that Doña Clara's confidence that her son was free of romantic entanglements had been misplaced. "What is Isabel's full name?" he asked.

García shrugged. "Toledano, I think."

"You think?" Tejada echoed. "But if you mailed things to her. . . ."

"Not to her," García corrected. "The address was *poste restante* to some little town in Cantabria."

"But it must have been addressed to someone," Tejada protested.

"Well, he told me the address was care of Señora Toledano," García explained. "But the way he talked, Isabel was a señorita, not a señora."

"Corporal, I remind you that you are speaking of a dead man," Sergeant de Rota said, through clenched teeth. "And any dramatic touches are in extremely poor taste. Whatever his . . . liaison . . . with this girl, there was absolutely no reason for López to send her half his salary."

"Very good, sir, just as you say," García agreed, pulling himself to attention and stamping. He relaxed again immediately and cast Tejada a glance that clearly expressed his opinion of his commanding officer.

Tejada did not normally encourage insubordination but he flashed an amused glance back. He had already sensed the tension between Sergeant de Rota and Corporal García. Given his own dislike of Rota, he was inclined to trust the corporal. He was also curious about Rota's vehement denials that Paco was sending his pay to a girl. "Can you think of any reason for him to send this girl money, Corporal?" he asked coolly.

"Really, Sergeant—" Rota began angrily.

"Sir!" García saluted appreciatively. "I thought, sir, that there might be a child involved."

"You won't cast slurs upon the dead, Corporal!" Sergeant de Rota's sharp voice cut across Tejada's meditations. "And that's an order. Or do you care to face charges of insubordination?"

"I beg your pardon, Sergeant. He was obliged to answer my question." Tejada's voice was still cool and unconcerned but he had moved to stand in front of Corporal García. "Thank you, Corporal," he added over his shoulder. "I'm sorry to have disturbed your rest."

Corporal García, who knew when not to push his luck, remained silent. He was wishing that he had caught the unknown sergeant's name and wondering what the chances were of being transferred to the Manzanares post.

Sergeant de Rota's mustache flattened slightly as he flared his nostrils. "Do you have any other questions, Sergeant?" he asked ominously.

"Only one." Tejada had at least ten more questions but he too knew how far he could push his luck. He sat down on the bed and began to repack Paco's things. "You seem to think that it's highly unlikely that Corporal López sent this girl regular payments, Sergeant. May I ask why?"

"I assume you're aware of the salary a corporal earns, Sergeant." Rota's voice was blistering. "I think it highly unlikely that López would have devoted so much of it to an affair like this. And he had no other source of income."

A suspicion had presented itself to Tejada while García was talking. He did his best to ignore it, but it was now jumping up and down on the threshold of his brain and banging the knocker. "Are you sure he had no other source of income?" he asked. "Corporal García suggested that his parents might have objected to this girl. He wasn't from a wealthy family, perhaps?"

"I suppose it's *possible*." Rota's voice was tight. "But I doubt it. And that's more than one question, Sergeant."

"Indeed." Tejada stood up. "Thank you."

Sergeant de Rota saw him to the door of the post and bid him a sullen farewell. Tejada hardly noticed. His mind was working frantically. For all his hostility Rota had managed to suggest a suspect for the post's link to the black market. Given García's unexpected disclosure and Rota's insistence that Paco could not have afforded to make payments to Isabel, the obvious inference was that Paco had found some clandestine source of income. Then Rota had practically insisted that Paco did not come from a wealthy family. Tejada walked slowly along the Calle Alcalá, frowning heavily. Paco had been a proud Falangist. And he had never boasted, of course. It was just within the bounds of possibility that someone who did not know him well might imagine that he came from a humble background. Possible, Tejada thought, but not likely. But if Rota had been talking to someone who'd never met Paco, he'd have set up a nice suspect: a man sending off sums of money he couldn't afford to an unexpected destination. A very neat little piece of character assassination. "Oh, no, he *couldn't* have had any other source of income." And all the while knowing that I'm looking for someone with precisely that.

He reached the end of the Calle Alcalá. The Puerta del Sol stretched in front of him, an elongated diamond shape, pockmarked by bombardment and now enlivened by the soldiers on parade. The logical thing would be to continue back to the post and make a report. Lieutenant Ramos, he knew, would be waiting for him, probably cursing impatiently, with a list of other tasks. But Ramos had insisted that the theft of rations was important, too. And Captain Morales had agreed. Tejada skirted the Puerta del Sol and bore leftward, heading for the Calle Tres Peces. It was time to seek out María Alejandra Palomino.

If Tejada had not been preoccupied with his thoughts as he crossed the Calle Atocha he might have noticed the gaunt man in ill-fitting civilian clothes and a cap that partially hid his face, who cast a stricken look at him and shrank into a doorway. Even if he had noticed the man and marked his behavior as suspicious, he would have had no way of knowing that he had just crossed paths with the uncle of the little girl he intended to see.

Chapter 9

Gonzalo was early for his appointment with the smugglers. With the help of a few sections of orange, Carmen had persuaded her unwilling daughter to go to school that morning. Aleja had agreed under protest, and only with the assurance that her mother would walk with her. Gonzalo, who had taken to sleeping late, had awakened hearing the argument, but feigned unconsciousness.

He was still lying on the couch, willing time to move faster, when Carmen returned several hours later. "Did she go to school?" he asked.

"Yes." Carmen sank into a chair and rubbed her temples. "I believe I've had a headache for the last six months."

"Only one?" Gonzalo asked, without opening his eyes. His sister snorted, but did not reply. "Did you find work?" he asked.

"I only just got back from the school," Carmen said wearily.

Gonzalo sat up. "The school's barely a mile away," he protested. "You've been gone over three hours!"

"I rested a little on the way back," she snapped. "Anything wrong with that?"

Gonzalo bit his tongue. He wondered for a moment whether it was worth hoarding pennies for impossibly expensive food or if it was more practical to save energy by spending them on streetcars. He remembered his own struggle to get to the Plaza de la Cebada. "Aleja make the walk all right?" he asked.

"I carried her part of the way. And I said that she shouldn't come home for lunch."

Gonzalo did not ask where Carmen had found the strength to carry her daughter. It was, he assumed, one of those things that mothers were able to do. "Do you know where there might be work?" he asked, aware that he was irritating her, but unable to stop himself.

"No." To his surprise, she did not snap at him.

The unspoken whisper, *red whore*, danced in the silence, and each hoped that the other did not hear it. Carmen had seen more of the women in the street than Gonzalo so the whisper was louder in her ears. To drown it out she said aloud, "Perhaps I can take in sewing."

Gonzalo winced as a clear voice said in his memory, "Your sister hates to sew, and, really, I don't mind it." Viviana had always claimed to enjoy sewing. And he had teased her, telling her she sounded like a good Catholic girl who prayed for General Franco's health every night. "If . . . Viviana . . . were here she could help," he managed to force out the words.

"Well, she's not." Carmen had no energy for gentleness.

She doesn't know what it's like, Gonzalo thought, shocked by her cruelty, forgetting how Carmen had reacted to the news of her husband's death. He subsided into silence. Carmen sat silently also. Gonzalo was not sure if he dozed or simply if his mind went blank for a period of time. He was roused a little before three, when Carmen said, "I'm going to go see Manuela. Aleja will want supper."

He nodded, determined to say nothing, knowing that if he spoke he would say that he was hungry too. When the clock struck three-thirty, his patience ran out. He pushed himself off the sofa and went into the bedroom. Much of the closet was empty. His brother-in-law's clothes, and many of his sister's as well, had long since been cut up to make clothing for Aleja. But there, behind Carmen's dresses, as he had hoped, was the revolver he had received when he had joined the carbineros. He took it and pulled an oversized coat from the closet as well. When he was satisfied that the gun did not show under the coat, he slipped out of the apartment and down the stairs. It would not, he knew, take anywhere near an hour to walk to the Calle Alcalá. But he told himself that there was no harm in resting along the way, as Carmen had. And the smugglers might not wait for him if he was late. They were weak arguments, but anything was better than lying on the sofa doing nothing.

Gonzalo walked slowly, carefully gauging which was the most direct route, to save his steps. The little alleys around Tres Peces were comfortingly familiar. The buildings pressing in on either side offered friendly shadows and promised solid walls to support him if he needed to rest. The windswept width of the Calle Atocha made him feel unpleasantly exposed. The lack of cars made the street seem bare, and the rubble-filled lots where shells had hit gaped like a prizefighter's shattered teeth. He paused before stepping out into the open, telling himself that he was only looking for streetcars. The guardia civil crossing in the opposite direction shattered this comfortable illusion. Gonzalo froze against the shutters of what had once been a café and watched as the guardia walked past him, and then stopped.

Heart pounding, Gonzalo wondered if he was about to be challenged. The gun hidden in the folds of the coat pocket felt heavy. The guardia did not turn around. Instead, he dug in a pocket and pulled out a piece of paper. He read for a moment. Then he shaded his eyes with one hand and studied the street sign.

The tension pounding in Gonzalo's stomach released itself as fury: first at himself for being stupidly afraid, then at the guardia for walking so coolly and easily into unknown streets, then at the streets themselves for allowing this invasion, and finally once more at himself, for being powerless to stop the guardia from going where he wished. Had Gonzalo been able to see the slip of paper in the guardia's hand, with his own address written on it, he would probably have used his weapon. Since he could not see the paper, he raised his head and marched across the street with steps kept firm by pride and adrenalin.

He was walking with his head high and his thoughts elsewhere when a voice said, "Hello, Gonzalo! How are you?"

Gonzalo started and found himself facing a stooped man with several days of gray stubble on his furrowed throat. The man was smiling, apparently very pleased at having caught Gonzalo's attention. "And your sister?" the old man continued. "How's she? Did she ever marry that young carpenter fellow?"

"Errr . . ." Gonzalo tried desperately to place the man. He was vaguely familiar but Gonzalo had no idea from where. Who on earth, he wondered, still remembered Pedro Palomino as a carpenter's apprentice? "Err . . . fine. Yes, actually. She's fine."

The man coughed and spat between a gap in his teeth. "Good, good. Glad to hear it. No good will come of this war, I said. But I remember you and that carpenter boy, all dressed up and proud of yourselves. . . ."

"And how are you, sir?" Gonzalo interrupted desperately.

"Oh, don't worry, son. Old Tacho knows when to keep his mouth shut," the old man grinned benevolently.

Something swam out of the depths of Gonzalo's memory. Summer evenings in the Plaza Tirso de Molina, endless games of tag among the strolling couples, then later becoming part of a strolling couple himself. Through it all, the smell of burnt sugar and the cries: "Tacho, here's ten centimos," "Tacho, give me a *churro*," "Tacho, a chocolate for the young lady." He superimposed the face of the man behind the fragrant cart of hot pastry onto the face of the man in front of him. The image fit. But surely Old Tacho had been fatter?

"How are you, sir?" Gonzalo asked again, more gently. He had never called Tacho "sir" before.

"Oh, times are bad, times are bad." The old man shook his head. "But it's good to see you."

"Likewise," Gonzalo agreed.

He started to walk again, and Old Tacho shuffled along beside him. "I don't suppose you'd have any bread, Gonzalo? For old times' sake."

The wheedling note in the man's voice made Gonzalo blush with shame. "No," he said, staring at the ground and feeling like a hypocrite, although he was speaking the simple truth. "No, I'm sorry."

"Ah, well. God bless."

"Thanks. And you." Gonzalo wondered, as he walked away, if Old Tacho believed in God. Maybe he thought heaven was a crowded square on a summer evening, with the smell of *churros* and hot chocolate hanging between the buildings like the colored lights and streamers. Maybe he was right: The concept had the fuzzy, implausible quality of a Sunday-school fable.

Gonzalo's mind slipped away from the faded memories of a life without war and focused on his appointment once again. He could not afford to buy information. But he could threaten. The black marketeers, he told himself nervously, were not soldiers. They might bear him a grudge afterward, but they would tell him what he needed to know if he pointed a gun at them. If a guardia civil was involved, as the smuggler had hinted, it would be best not to threaten. It occurred to Gonzalo that he might actually be on his way to meet Viviana's murderer. For a moment, he was elated at the idea that it might be that simple. Then he remembered that he had left without telling his sister he was taking the gun and that she would probably be waiting anxiously for his return. I should have told her that I might not be coming back, he thought. I don't want her to lose sleep. He regretted the oversight but only in the way a man who has just watched the train station fade into the distance regrets forgetting to bring a toothbrush. It was a minor annoyance but it would not change his course.

He reached the Calle Alcalá, and began to walk alongside the park. Although he had confidently claimed the day before that he knew the spot meant, he realized that there were two possible gates, neither of them directly opposite the Guardia Civil post. He settled for the nearer one, willing to rest for a few minutes before walking farther. A nearby clock began to chime. It was still only four-thirty. Gonzalo settled onto a bench near the entrance and pulled at the collar of his coat. He was cold, and the encounter with Old Tacho had reminded him that it was best to hide his face. He buried his hands in his pockets for warmth.

The wind blew scraps of paper and dead pine needles along the walkways of the park. It passed easily through Gonzalo's coat, making him shiver and making the gun he was clutching seem ice-cold. The clock struck four-forty-five. The park was empty, except for a few old women in black. "It's the waiting that drives men mad," the young milicianos had told each other sagely. "The waiting's the worst part of combat." They had told each other this in the tense autumn of '36, proud of their maturity, until an old soldier who had fought in Morocco had laughed at them. "Shit, boys, the worst part of combat is combat. Enjoy the waiting while you can!" The clock struck five. Gonzalo stood up, trying to look nonchalant, and began to make his way toward the other entrance. He had clearly mistaken the directions.

The other entrance was similarly deserted. Gonzalo hesitated, wondering if perhaps he should head back to his original spot or whether he ought to rest a while here. Perhaps the men had forgotten the appointment. Perhaps they had been unavoidably detained. Perhaps the whole thing was a trap. Gonzalo began to walk back the way he had come, as rapidly as possible. At his original bench, he paused again. It might be worth waiting another few minutes.

At five-fifteen Gonzalo was about to leave his bench when he heard voices coming from the entrance of the park and saw a man in the uniform of Franco's army heading toward his bench. The man wore the fasces of the Falange in his lapel. Gonzalo froze and then saw that the Falangist's companion was a girl. The couple passed him without acknowledging his presence. The young soldier had one arm around the girl's waist and was gesturing expansively with the other to illustrate some point. Gonzalo watched them until they were out of sight, his hand trembling from the effort of not raising his weapon.

Another person entering the park distracted him. This time it was a man with a suitcase who walked briskly. He was dressed as a businessman might dress if there had been any prosperous businessmen left in Madrid. He carried the suitcase lightly, with one hand, as if it were a briefcase and his coat was belted tightly around him. He checked at the sight of Gonzalo. "Good afternoon, sir." He touched his hat. "Fancy meeting you here. Are you heading toward the lake?"

It was the man Gonzalo had spoken to the previous day. "Yes," he said cautiously.

"So am I," the man with the suitcase said easily. "Care to walk with me?"

"A pleasure." As they strolled along the gravel walkway, Gonzalo lowered his voice. "You're late."

"Business matters," the other replied, hardly moving his lips.

They turned onto a narrower walkway, under what was intended as a canopy of ornamental trees, trimmed in the French style. But the trees had grown wild for the last few years and now there were only bare and gnarled branches that rattled in the wind. Gonzalo glanced around. "You're on your own today?"

"Yes. My . . . colleague had other business."

Gonzalo hesitated. One man would be easier to deal with, if it came to that, but he was unsure how to broach the subject that interested him. He kept silent, hoping that the other man would make the opening gambit. He was not disappointed.

"I can get what you want." The man's voice was pitched so low that the crunch of gravel nearly drowned it out. "But I'll need an advance."

"Why?" Gonzalo demanded, keeping to his role of suspicious customer.

"It's not the sort of thing you buy on credit, friend. Fifty pesetas."

"Fifty!" Gonzalo choked, forgetting his mission. He wondered for a moment if anyone in the city had that kind of money to waste. "You're joking."

"Fifty in advance. Twenty-five when I get you the goods. Burgos currency, of course."

Gonzalo reminded himself that it was a waste of time to bargain over money that he did not have anyway. "How do I know you won't just take the fifty and disappear?" he demanded.

"You take my word for it."

"And why shouldn't I just buy directly from your . . . supplier?" Gonzalo asked carefully.

"If you want to deal directly, friend, no one's stopping you." The man's voice held a note of triumph.

Gonzalo took a deep breath. The time had come to take a plunge. He could use the gun. Or he could play a hunch that was almost as risky. He glanced around. Ahead of them, he could see the path broadening out by the side of the lake where the trees ended. But the walkway was deserted. The gun or the guess. "You're lying," he said softly.

"Think what you like." The man shrugged, and picked up his pace a little.

"Your supplier is dead," Gonzalo continued, matching his stride. "He was killed last week, wasn't he? In the Calle Amor de Dios. That's why you can't get me the stuff now."

"I don't know what you're talking about!" The smuggler's voice shook. He stopped and turned to face Gonzalo.

"Right," Gonzalo said, pleased at the man's reaction. "So you weren't buying from a guardia civil and you didn't kill him last week? Why didn't you kill him, by the way? Weren't you having an argument about the profits?"

"No!" The smuggler's self-control crumbled. "I never killed anyone. I didn't even know he was dead until . . ." He stopped, his face blanched above his dark coat. "Why the hell do you care anyway? Oh, shit, are you a guardia?"

In answer, Gonzalo drew his gun and held it against the other man's ribs. "Didn't know he was dead until when?" he asked.

"Until you told me!" The smuggler stared at the gun, seemingly fascinated.

Gonzalo mentally cursed himself for giving the man time to recover from his slip. "Was he demanding too high a price?" he asked again.

"No." The smuggler held his hands a little away from his sides and seemed to be sucking in his stomach to break its contact with the gun. "No, he never gave a damn about the profits. Sent them all to some girl. We had no quarrel with him. And that's the truth, I swear. For the love of God, I *swear.* He did his part, and we did ours but I never killed him. None of us did!"

"Who did, then?"

"I don't know." The man's voice had a ragged edge. "A Red sniper, I thought." He gasped as the gun burrowed into his rib cage again.

"Who told you that?"

"Our new supplier. He said it was a coincidence."

Gonzalo's voice was tense. "What happened to the sniper?"

"I don't know! I swear, I don't know. I heard he was dead. But it wasn't any of us! It was the guardias civiles on patrol from another post."

"Which other post?"

"Manzanares, I think." The smuggler gulped. "But it wasn't anything to do with the goods. A Red killed Paco, and then someone from Manzanares killed the Red. That's all!"

"Isn't this mystery man from Manzanares your new supplier?" Gonzalo asked.

"No. Honestly! This guardia—a sergeant, I think—he's straight as an arrow. That's what señor . . . that's what our supplier says. To watch out for him!"

"A sergeant, from the Manzanares post," Gonzalo repeated slowly. "You're sure?"

The man's eyes narrowed. "Say, what are you interested in anyway? First it's the goods, and then it's Paco, and now it's this sergeant. Who are you and what are you after?"

Gonzalo realized that he had better end the interview quickly. There were a few people around the lake in the distance and while it was unlikely that any of them had noticed the figures on the walkway, the longer he delayed, the more chance there was of discovery. Besides, the smuggler seemed to be losing some of his initial fear. He might yell for help, or simply flee, at any moment. "You're lucky I'm not like them," Gonzalo said. "Or you'd be a dead man by now." He hesitated a moment. "Put down the suitcase. Now turn around. Keep your hands where I can see them." He pressed the gun into the small of the smuggler's back, then withdrew it a little. Now for the tricky part. He bent his knees and picked up the suitcase. It was heavy for him to lift with one hand, and his other arm was starting to ache from the weight of the gun. "Start walking," he ordered, hoping that none of his nervousness showed in his voice. "I'll be right behind you."

Very slowly, the man began to walk, hands still held a few inches from his sides. Gonzalo kept a pace behind, doing his best to move silently over the gravel. Slowly, he allowed himself to fall farther and farther behind the smuggler. A little way from the lake, a smaller, dirt-covered path crossed the main walkway. Gonzalo waited until he reached the cross path, then hastily slipped the gun into his pocket and ducked down the narrow path, lugging the suitcase with both hands. In summertime, the high shrubs would have rendered him invisible. As it was, he hoped that the brown and tangled bushes would provide sufficient cover for him to get well away. He pounded down the path, heading for what had once been the rose gardens. He was tempted to abandon the suitcase but its weight promised food, and to give it up now after risking so much seemed cowardly.

The smuggler, Gonzalo hoped, would not rouse the guardia civil. Gonzalo had not absolutely denied that he was a member of the guardia and it would be difficult for the man to avoid awkward questions about the contents of the suitcase in any case. Still, he did not breathe easily again until he was well out of the park and back in the shelter of the streets. Then he leaned against a gray stone apartment house, pockmarked with shells, and allowed his pounding pulse to return to something resembling its normal rate. Bracing himself against the building, he realized that he was dizzy, and sank down onto the suitcase between his knees, and then leaned over, so that his hair nearly brushed the cobblestones.

A sergeant from the Manzanares post, he repeated, as he slowly forced himself into a sitting, and then a standing position. It wasn't wasted time. A sergeant from the Manzanares post. The walk home took him a long time. The suitcase was heavy and his flight through the park had weakened him. Nevertheless, by the time he reached home, breathless and sweating, he was closer to happiness than he had been since the day he had learned that Viviana was dead. He dragged the suitcase into the dim living room. "Carmen?" he called.

"Gonzalo?" She appeared from the kitchen. "Gonzalo! Oh, thank God! Thank God!" She rushed at him and hugged him fiercely, gasping with dry sobs.

"I'm glad you're glad to see me," he said, bemused. He remembered how he had calmly contemplated the possibility of dying without telling her, and felt a flicker of remorse. "But look what I've brought." He pushed her away, and bent to open the suitcase.

It fell open with a thud, and a few roundish objects bounced out. Carmen dropped to her knees and picked one up. "Potatoes," she whispered. "And . . . meat! Gonzalo, how . . .?"

"It's a long story." He watched the tears spilling freely over her cheeks now and felt something approaching contentment. "I'll tell you while you cook."

She nodded, and carefully placed the packages back in the suitcase, holding it to her chest as if it were an infant. "Of course." She smiled at him. "Of course, Gonzalo. Oh, thank God."

"Now why were you so worried?" he asked, trying to smile at her as they headed for the kitchen. "Don't you have any faith in your brother?"

To his surprise, she did not rally under his teasing. "It wasn't that." She set the suitcase on the kitchen table. "There was a guardia civil here while you were gone. Asking all kinds of questions. I think he suspects that I'm hiding a carbinero."

A day earlier, Gonzalo would have accepted her statement with fatalistic calm. Now, with his search for Viviana's killer so close to its goal and the pleasurable feeling of having found food for the family flooding over him, it stirred him to action. "We'll talk about it over dinner," he said firmly. "There must be a way out."

Chapter 10

Tejada had found his way as far south as Atocha fairly easily but finding the Calle Tres Peces presented some difficulty. He had visited the capital as a student and was acquainted with the major streets, and he had gained some more recent knowledge from studying maps but the twisting and ill-marked pathways of the inner city were unfamiliar to him. The fact that shells appeared to have hit many of the street signs (if there had ever been street signs) did not make his quest easier. He finally stopped an old man and demanded directions. His demand was brusquer than he realized, for he was annoyed by the unaccustomed feeling of incompetence and the stink of the streets depressed him. Looking at the chipped and peeling facades, and the houses unsteadily propped up by planks where neighboring buildings had decayed or been destroyed, Tejada found himself longing for a bulldozer and a decent architect. A grid, he thought. Modified, designed to radiate around the central boulevards. You could finish knocking down these relics and rebuild the streets wide enough for a jeep to pass, if you added a few stories on to make up for lost depth. The street he had been following merged seamlessly with another, without bothering to change its name. Definitely a grid, Tejada thought with disgust, wondering if the directions he had received were still accurate.

By the time he found the Calle Tres Peces, he was in no mood to search for nonexistent numbers. He selected a building at random, marched up to it, and pounded on the first available door. There was a long pause, and then a voice said hesitantly, "Who's there?"

"Guardia civil. Open up." Tejada considered adding a further threat, and then decided that he probably would not be able to make it good alone.

The door swung open and a woman with a shawl over her head faced him. "We've done nothing wrong." Her voice trembled, and Tejada wondered for a moment what she had on her conscience.

He dismissed her probable sins as irrelevant. "Can you tell me where number 25 is?"

She stared at him, open-mouthed for a moment, and then slumped against the doorjamb in relief. "Yes, Señor Guardia. Yes, of course. It's across the street and three doors down."

"Thank you." Tejada turned on his heel and marched away. Behind him he heard the door slam shut.

When he reached the building indicated, he realized that he did not have an apartment number. Clearly numbered buildings, he thought, expanding his urban planning instincts. With a reliable concierge who has an up-to-date list of who is in which apartment. He stifled a sigh and pounded on the door of the first floor. "Guardia civil! Open up!" Whoever lived in the first-floor apartment was either not at home or trusted that he would not break down the door.

Tejada considered for a moment. It was possible that this was the apartment he was interested in. If it was, then several other possibilities presented themselves. If the miliciana who had killed Paco was Carmen Llorente, Maria Alejandra's mother, then the apartment might well be locked and deserted. On the other hand, even if the miliciana who had killed Paco had no connection to Alejandra aside from a carelessly dropped notebook, the Palomino family might have its own reasons for avoiding the guardia civil. Or whoever lived in the apartment might simply be away. Or it might be the wrong apartment entirely. The simplest way to find out was to talk to someone. He moved on to the apartment in the rear of the building, and knocked again. "Guardia Civil! Open up!"

This time the door opened after only a few moments of hammering on it. "Yes?" Again, it was a woman who answered. Tejada wondered briefly if there were no men left in Madrid. If there were, they seemed to hide behind their women. Typical of the Reds.

"Do you know a little girl named Maria Alejandra Palomino?" Tejada asked. "About seven years old. She lives in this building, I believe."

The woman gaped at him. "Alejandra? Why yes. But why . . .?" She shut her mouth abruptly, suddenly realizing that questioning a guardia civil was the worse part of valor.

"She lives with her mother?" Tejada asked.

"Yes. Her mother and—" The woman stopped.

"And?" Tejada raised his eyebrows, remembering that Alejandra's mother was supposed to be a widow.

"And . . . and she lived with her . . . aunt." The woman gulped slightly. "But her aunt . . . passed away a few days ago."

If she was not lying, Tejada thought, then obviously she was trying to conceal something. But she was frightened and a poor liar. It might be worth questioning her further, instead of merely asking for the correct apartment number. At that point, however, he was distracted by the sound of footsteps behind him and the rhythmic thump of someone trudging up the stairs. The woman glanced past him and gasped with relief. "There she is," she babbled. "You can talk to her yourself. Carmen! Carmen, this officer's been asking for you."

Tejada turned and looked upward. A woman with a shawl tied over her hair and a dark coat wrapped tightly around her was standing on the staircase, as if frozen. As he came nearer, he saw that she was squarely built, with broad shoulders that formed a strange contrast to her extreme thinness. "Señora Llorente?" he asked.

He saw her lips move and guessed from her faint nod that she had spoken. But her whisper was inaudible.

"I'm glad I caught you." It did not occur to Tejada that this was not the happiest of phrases. "I have a few questions."

She bowed her head. "What do you want to know?"

"There's no need to stand in the hallway," Tejada said easily, rounding the banister and beginning to climb toward her. "We can go upstairs and talk in private." He had not pitched his voice particularly loudly, but it carried clearly in the silent hall, and Carmen's neighbor rapidly shut her door.

Tejada had continued advancing on Carmen and she had no choice but to turn and begin climbing the stairs again. "What do you want to know?" she repeated, a little breathlessly.

"I'm actually looking for one of your relatives," Tejada said. "Careful," he added, as she tripped on one of the steps and plunged forward. "Your daughter, I believe. Alejandra."

"Alejandra?" The blood pounding in Carmen's ears subsided somewhat. She hoped that the guardia could not tell that her voice was unusually high and quavering. "Why?"

"She may have some information of interest to the Guardia Civil," Tejada replied as they reached the landing.

Carmen hurried ahead of him and unlocked the door. "I don't understand, Señor Guardia." She raised her voice as much as she dared. "Why should the Guardia Civil be interested in Aleja? She's only a little girl."

The door swung open. Carmen did her best to take off her coat slowly and noisily, praying that the guardia would not push past her. He stood quietly, apparently unaware of her delaying tactics. "She may have witnessed a murder," he said. "Speaking of which, your neighbor tells me that you are recently bereaved. My condolences."

"What?" Carmen stared, bewildered. In her experience, the Guardia Civil did not offer condolences.

"Your sister," Tejada said. "I understand she lived with you. Or would this be your sister-in-law?"

"My sister," Carmen said quickly, internally damning her downstairs neighbor for being a bitch and a gossip. Perhaps the guardia did not know of Gonzalo's existence. "She was my sister." Judging that it was impossible to delay any longer, Carmen led her unwelcome guest into the living room. To her profound relief, it was empty. She wondered whether it would be wise to say that she and Viviana had lived alone. But if someone in the building had told him about Gonzalo . . . "I'm afraid Aleja's at school," she said hastily. "But if there's anything I can tell you?"

Tejada had been inspecting the living room. It displayed no signs of wealth. It was barely furnished. And Carmen Llorente's hunger-pinched features did not suggest that she had access to the black market. He was inclined to think that if Alejandra had been a witness, she had been an accidental one. Alejandra's mother radiated fear, but so had everyone else he had spoken to in the neighborhood. "When will she be home?" he asked.

Carmen realized with horror that the guardia must intend to wait for her daughter. If Gonzalo was already in hiding, that was fine. But if he came back unexpectedly . . . "I don't know," she said automatically, then thought it best to explain. "I mean, Aleja's school is some distance from here. I gave her permission to go home with a friend who lives closer to the school today and she may stay the night there."

"Where is that, Señora?" Tejada wondered if it was worth a trek north to try to find Alejandra.

Carmen was prepared for the question. "Along San Mateo," she lied glibly, carefully not specifying whether she meant the Calle San Mateo or the Travesía San Mateo.

Tejada did not notice the omission but the idea of searching through another set of winding and unmarked streets was not appealing. Lieutenant Ramos expected his report, and delaying further would be irresponsible. Tejada decided to share his suspicions with the lieutenant and wait for further orders. He stifled a sigh. "Very well, Señora. I will try to come back tomorrow. You understand that your daughter's information may be of vital importance to the Guardia Civil. I will expect to find her at home tomorrow."

"Yes, sir." Carmen's mouth was dry.

Tejada had the feeling that he was overlooking something important. But he was tired, and he wanted a chance to file the information he had gathered. He left the white-faced Señora Llorente, wondering how much of what she had told him was the truth. Alejandra was proving surprisingly elusive. *If her mother knows she saw something, she might be trying to keep her out of the way,* he thought. *There's no reason they would stop at killing a child. Easier really than to kill Paco unless they only knew that there was a witness and didn't know who the witness was.* He realized, with a not entirely pleasant sensation, that he was now carrying with him the notebook his friend had been killed for. *No one knows that except Jiménez though,* he reassured himself. All the same, he was glad when he reached the end of the winding alleys and gained a broader and better patrolled thoroughfare.

By the time Tejada had finished making his report to the lieutenant, it was well after five. A lingering worry over the information contained in Alejandra's notebook made him look for Jiménez. To his disgust, Guardia Jiménez had gone on a twenty-four-hour leave three hours previously. Resigned to the inevitable, Tejada headed for the tiny room that served as both his bedroom and office. He sat down and stared at his notes. They swam in front of his eyes. *It isn't fair* he thought, leaning forward slightly and propping his elbows on the table. *We've won, and we work twice as hard now that we're at peace. Paco had time to get involved with that Isabel during the war, but now he wouldn't have a moment. Or did he meet her* before the war? I wonder how, if she was in Cantabria. . . . I've heard Cantabria's beautiful. Next to the Basque country. . . . Filled with rain. . . . But Paco hated rain. . . .

A thunderclap interrupted his thoughts. He started, and realized that the thunder was in fact the stamp of Guardia Vásquez's booted foot. Vásquez was standing at attention, looking embarrassed. "Sergeant Tejada, sir!" he said, staring forward and doing a poor job of not noticing that Tejada's head had been resting on the desk.

Tejada silently cursed himself for wasting time and then added a brief imprecation in the direction of Lieutenant Ramos for waking him at an ungodly hour. "Yes, Guardia, what is it?" he asked, trying not to sound irritated.

Vásquez's posture remained rigid. "A lady to see you, sir!"

Tejada winced. Female hysteria ranked high on his list of work-related annoyances, and he felt he had dealt with enough white-faced and terrified women for one day. "What time is it?" he snapped.

Vásquez checked his watch. "Twenty hours, thirty-two minutes, sir," he said, doing his best to make the military phrasing disguise his opinion that the sergeant could perfectly well have looked at his own watch.

"Then she's here to see Sergeant González," said Tejada grimly. "I went off a twelve-hour shift two minutes ago."

"Err . . . she asked to speak to you specifically, sir. By name." The guardia had lost much of his rigidity and almost all of his assurance.

"What?" Random guesses whirled through Tejada's brain like the paper on Lieutenant Ramos's desk during a crisis. With a sudden sinking feeling he remembered his final words to Doña Clara: "I am always at home to you." It was inconceivable that Clara Pérez should make a social call at a post but . . . "A dignified older lady, gray hair, wearing a black dress?" he hazarded, desperately shuffling through his thoughts.

"No, sir." Vásquez's embarrassment increased. "A younger lady, with a blue skirt and dark braids."

The guardia's words snagged a piece of useless knowledge from Tejada's hasty and ill-assorted pile of civilian memories. "*Ce doit être Micaëla,*" he said automatically.

Vásquez blinked. "I'm sorry, sir?"

"Never mind." Tejada remembered enough French to understand the gist of the quote, but he had no idea where he had pulled it from. "Is Lieutenant Ramos still in his office?"

"No, sir. He went off duty half an hour ago."

"Then bring her to the lieutenant's office," Tejada said. "I'll meet you there."

He headed for the office, still trying to figure out who the lady asking for him might be. He could think of no friends of the family who still lived in Madrid. And no one in their right mind would travel to the capital now. Perhaps a friend of a friend? But what young lady would call at a guardia civil post to see someone she did not know? He reached the office and automatically began to tidy the papers on the desk, scanning them to make sure that no sensitive material had been left out for prying eyes. Who in Madrid—outside of fellow officers— even knew his name? "Micaëla," obviously, he thought with disgust. Whoever that is. He tapped a stack of papers on the table to align their edges, and then turned them face downward, idly pursuing the smaller enigma: Where had the quote come from? Something about a blue skirt and dark braids, with an inane little tune attached, probably for mnemonic purposes. He hummed, trying to remember. The door swung open, and he heard Vásquez's voice saying, "This way, Señora."

"Thank you." A woman in a light blue skirt, with dark, unfashionably long hair wound in a crown around her head stepped into the room. "Good evening, Sergeant Tejada," she said in a clear voice, and he recognized Alejandra's teacher.

Chapter 11

Vásquez withdrew, tactfully closing the door behind him. Tejada did his best to stand up straight, woefully aware that he had sleep in his eyes, stubble on his chin, and cobwebs in his brain. "Good evening, Señorita—" He reached for her name for a moment. "Fernández," he finished, after a barely perceptible pause. Some remnant of inculcated manners made him add, "What an unexpected pleasure."

"You are very kind." She formed the words carefully, enunciating each syllable with such clarity that Tejada was surprised to realize that she had spoken very softly. She stood motionless, her coat folded over her crossed arms. She looked perfectly composed but apparently had nothing more to say.

"Won't you sit down?" Tejada asked before the silence became too awkward. "And please, tell me why you're here."

She sat down slowly on the edge of the chair he had indicated, and set her feet parallel on the floor with the same precise economy of movement that marked her speech. Her back was very straight, and that, combined with the masses of hair pinned to her head, reminded Tejada obscurely of a ballerina. He took the chair behind the desk, wondering irrelevantly if her hair was really black or if it only seemed so in the artificial light, its darkness accentuated by her pale face. "I hope"—she hesitated for a moment—"that I was not wrong to ask to speak to you personally, Sergeant. But I thought. . . ."

"Yes?" Tejada said, as encouragingly as he could.

"You asked me a number of questions about Aleja Palomino's notebook." The teacher seemed to reach a decision. "May I ask if your interest in it stems from the death of one of your colleagues last Friday?"

Tejada had been unsuccessfully trying to guess why Señorita Fernández had sought him out. She might, of course, have come on behalf of a prisoner but he did not think that she was one of those who would stoop to attempting to use personal influence, and he disliked the idea that she might be associated with any of the prisoners. It had seemed impossible that she would have any further information to give him. Now she seemed uncommonly well informed. He leaned forward. "May I ask what suggested that idea, Señorita?"

"Alejandra was back in school today," she said. "She was very upset about the loss of her notebook, and she confided in me." She hesitated. "I am, perhaps, breaking her confidence by coming here."

Tejada took a deep breath and made sure that his voice would be calm before he spoke. "I appreciate your coming," he said truthfully. "And I assure you that I have no interest in harming Alejandra. In fact, she may be safer if I know all that she has to tell."

"That did occur to me." A smile flickered across the woman's face. "But I appreciate your reassurance. Aleja explained to me that she lost her notebook last week, on her way home from school. She says that a guardia civil passed her, and that a little while later she heard gunshots. She was frightened and hid. She says she saw a guardia civil come past her hiding place right after that. At first she thought it was the same one but when she went on, she found the body of the man who had passed her in the street. She realized that the other guardia must have killed him, and she fled. I know that you probably don't want to look for one of your own, Sergeant. But Aleja's a truthful child."

Tejada frowned, skeptical. "And the notebook?"

"She dropped it when she saw the dead man and ran for home. She was frightened, Sergeant."

Tejada's first impulse was to believe that this was a story concocted to mislead him. Elena Fernández knew of his interest in the notebook, and therefore was the perfect person to come forward with the information. But if the notebook was linked to the black market, it was an incredible coincidence for her to be part of the same ring of smugglers. Or was it? Under what circumstances had Alejandra seen . . . whatever she had seen? He felt a certain disappointment. He had admired the teacher for her composure. He did not really want to believe that she was a criminal. And yet . . . "Alejandra's notebook was not found by Corporal López's body," he said, narrowly observing her.

She looked grieved, but not guilty. "Oh, dear. Had Tía Viviana already found it, then?"

The sergeant stifled a gasp. Nerve was one thing. This casual naming of a murderous criminal was another. He considered the possibility that Señorita Fernández was telling the truth. "Tía Viviana?" he asked.

She smiled, but her voice was sad as she replied. "That is what Aleja calls her. I never knew her full name, or even if she was a blood relation or simply an aunt by marriage, or something like that. That's really why Aleja was so upset about losing her notebook, of course. Viviana promised she would get it back for her."

"What?" Tejada said, feeling slightly dizzy.

"Aleja found out that she had lost the book when she got home. She says that Tía Viviana agreed to go and get it back for her. Apparently. . . ." the teacher hesitated. "Well, naturally, the guardia civil were still acting under wartime orders, and. . . ."

"Oh, my"—Tejada remembered, barely in time, that there was a lady present, and rapidly swallowed several of the curses he was thinking—"goodness," he finished, with a vehemence that did not match the words. "So you're saying that Corporal López never had the notebook in his possession *at all*?"

"In his possession?" If Elena Fernández's surprise was not genuine, she was a very good actress. "Of course not, why would he?"

Tejada choked on another swallowed curse. "And you came here to tell me?"

"That Alejandra may have been the witness to a murder," the teacher said quietly. "That was why I asked to speak to you, instead of another guardia. Her testimony implicates a guardia civil, you understand, and I wanted to protect her." She flushed faintly. "I assumed that *you* would not be guilty of the murder, Sergeant."

Tejada put his head in his hands, hardly sensible of the compliment. "Did you ever meet this aunt of Alejandra's?" he asked, without much hope. "Viviana?"

"Once or twice."

"Could you describe her?" Tejada felt his last hopes that the teacher was lying fade away and die under her hesitant description. It would have fit many people, but the height, age, and coloring all matched what he remembered of the miliciana. As he strained to remember the woman he had taken the notebook from, he suddenly remembered that she had denied killing Paco. "Who did kill him then? One of your friends?" he had asked. "One of *your* friends, more likely!" she had retorted. If Alejandra had told her that a guardia civil had been responsible for the killing . . . "I *hope* there's a special Providence for fools," he said when Señorita Fernández had finished her description.

"Sergeant?" She sounded a little puzzled.

He raised his head and smiled bitterly. "Señorita, before you came forward with this information I was positive that I knew who had killed Pa—Corporal López, and fairly sure why he had been killed. Now I have no idea who killed him or why, and I have just spent the last week working on a false lead." He opened the pouch designed for spare cartridges, where he had been keeping the notebook, and tossed it onto the table. "Here. Give this to Alejandra, with my compliments. I'm sorry she has missed it for so long."

She hesitated for a moment. "That's very kind of you, Sergeant. . . ."

"I doubt she would think so," he retorted, thinking that if he and Jiménez had been five minutes slower Alejandra would have had her notebook without delay.

"If you would be so kind as to give me Aleja's address I will gladly return it to her."

Something in Elena's tone caught the sergeant's attention. "Give you her address?" he repeated. "It's in the school records. And surely you'll see her after the Easter break?"

"I do hope that Aleja will return to school after the vacation." Her voice was colorless. "But unfortunately, I will not."

It occurred to Tejada that Señorita Fernández was twisting her hands in her lap, and that this was the first unnecessary motion he had ever seen her make. "Why?" he asked.

For a moment he thought she would not respond. Then she said, reluctantly, "Today was my last day of employment at the Leopoldo Alas School."

"Isn't that rather sudden?" Tejada said with surprise.

She stared at her lap. "Señor Herrera thought it would be best for the school if I resigned."

Tejada remembered the fussy little man. "He thinks you're a Red because I asked to talk to you, and he's afraid that we'll close the place and arrest all the staff," he translated.

She made no reply. Bravo, Tejada thought. So far in this investigation you've killed a woman looking for her niece's notebook and thrown another one out of a job. "You've been very helpful," he said. "Would you like me to speak to Señor Herrera?"

"No." She smiled at him, and her voice had regained its calm. "No, thank you. He deserves to be left in peace."

At another time, Tejada would have quarreled both with Señor Herrera's merits and with the implication that the Guardia Civil harassed people. At the moment he was preoccupied. "What will you do?" he asked.

She shrugged. "Go home, probably. My parents are in Salamanca."

"Salamanca? Your people are Nationalists then." Tejada was irrationally pleased. Paco might still have been killed because he knew something about the disappearing provisions, he thought. It just means that they did it themselves. And now I know what to look for, I can find the bastard who killed him. He smiled at the teacher, certain now that she was telling the truth. "I'm very much in your debt, Señorita," he said, standing and holding out his hand.

He had risen rapidly and the movement caught Elena unprepared. She stood up more quickly than she had intended and, to Tejada's surprise, leaned her palms on the table as if to balance herself. The shaky furniture shifted under her weight, and she swayed unsteadily for a moment. "Are you all right?" Tejada leaned across the table to steady her and found that his hand easily spanned her arm.

"Yes, thank you." She put her free hand up to her head for a moment. "It's nothing, just a touch of dizziness. I'll be fine."

Her blouse was cream-colored, with long tapered sleeves. They were designed to cling to the forearms, but as she raised her arm one sleeve sagged, and Tejada saw the bones of her wrist and arm clearly defined against the skin. He wondered if the train with foodstuffs for the civilian population had arrived as scheduled. "Have dinner with me," he said abruptly, releasing her arm.

"What? Oh, thank you, but I couldn't possibly. . . ."

"Consider it a payment of the debt," Tejada suggested. "It wouldn't be anything too elaborate. Just the officers' canteen. It would be my pleasure."

Elena looked distressed. "Thank you. But I'm not . . . accustomed to eating much in the evenings."

Tejada, who correctly guessed that she had intended to say "not hungry," was pleased by this further evidence of veracity. "Then come and have a drink with me," he said, taking her elbow and guiding her out of the office.

The dormitory housing the Manzanares post had been selected partly because it contained a large cafeteria with adjacent kitchen, originally intended for students, suitable for adaptation to a mess hall. Lieutenant Ramos had designated one of the nearby common rooms as a canteen. Tejada escorted his guest past the cafeteria with as much haste as possible and ushered her into the canteen. It was empty when they entered, except for Ramos, who was eating with the single-minded intensity of a man who has things to do and does not wish to waste time on supper. He looked up as the door opened and then gaped, with unaesthetic results.

Tejada saluted, wishing that his superior officer would close his mouth. "Permission to bring a guest, sir?"

"Restricted to family members, Tejada." The lieutenant swallowed hastily, and then stood, brushing crumbs from his uniform. "Is the young lady . . .?"

"My cousin, sir," Tejada said firmly.

"Then of course." One of the maddening things about Tejada, Ramos reflected, was his capacity to tell barefaced lies with absolute assurance. Still, he had never abused the privilege before, and it would be a shame to embarrass the girl. Ramos held out his hand. "Your servant, Señorita," he said, making a mental note to have a discussion with his sergeant about the definition of family members. He finished his supper and left, still wondering about Tejada's guest.

As Tejada had expected, Señorita Fernández did not protest when food was set in front of her. She took a few deep breaths and then began to eat. Tejada, watching her carefully take tiny bites and chew each one with painstaking thoroughness, marveled that she had still had sufficient pride to make a token protest earlier. She was clearly well past the kind of hunger that made people gobble and into the region where a morsel of food was slowly treasured. He sat and watched her eat. After a few minutes she looked up, aware of his silent scrutiny. She blushed. "I'm sorry, Sergeant. Did you say something?"

"I asked how long you'd been in Madrid," Tejada said, quickly picking the first question that came to mind.

"Almost eight years now. Since I started university."

"You didn't want to study at Salamanca?" Tejada asked.

She smiled. "I grew up at the university in Salamanca. I wanted to see the capital."

She would, Tejada thought, have arrived in Madrid just around the time the Second Republic was proclaimed. He found that he did not want to probe her political convictions. "I got to Salamanca a few years before you left," he said, to avoid asking another question. "Perhaps we have acquaintances in common."

"Perhaps," she agreed politely. "It's a small world. Do you have family from there?"

"No," Tejada laughed. "I have a law degree from there. A souvenir of the last time I let myself be guided by my father."

She set down her fork, and her eyes widened. "You're a university graduate?" There was something very like horror in her voice. "But you're a guardia civil. I mean . . . I thought they came from their own academy?"

Tejada snorted. "It's a long story. When I was eighteen I wanted to do my military service. My father wanted me to buy a substitute and continue my education. He finally told me that he would support me at university and pay for a substitute, and that if I still wanted to go into the army when I graduated he would see about a commission but that otherwise I'd be disinherited. I agreed to study law and planned to spend four years sulking."

"And did you?" the teacher asked, reflecting that she had never thought about why someone might wish to become a guardia civil. They were born, or perhaps sprang fully grown from the head of some general.

"Well, I did become interested in criminal law but I'd wanted to be a soldier for as long as I could remember. The Guardia Civil seemed like an obvious compromise." Tejada grinned. "My mother says that I shortened my father's life by years when I told him."

Elena laughed, as she was supposed to. She had a pleasant laugh, Tejada thought. Unaffected. "What did Señor Tejada want you to become?"

The sergeant shrugged. "How would I know? He certainly had no need for me at home. My brother's more than able to manage the farm."

"The farm?" Elena raised her eyebrows, wondering where the sergeant was from. He spoke, she realized, like an educated man, without strong regional accent.

"Mostly grain," Tejada explained. "Although we do have a few vineyards. It's . . . oh, maybe five thousand acres . . . my brother could tell you the exact number. Outside Granada."

"You grew up there?"

"In the summers. We have a house in Granada as well." Perhaps in an attempt to put Elena at her ease, and perhaps because she seemed genuinely interested, Tejada talked about himself far more than he had intended to over dinner. He talked about his childhood, about the academy, and then, somewhat against his better judgment, about meeting Paco.

Aware that he was monopolizing the conversation, he tried a few times to draw her out but many subjects seemed taboo. He did not wish to ask her what she had done in Madrid during the war. Nor would it be courteous to press her for the details of her background.

Elena, who was as tense as a crouching cat, had been acutely aware of his earlier questions, and relieved by his willingness to let her remain silent. She ate steadily, at first with a desperation that precluded shame and then with increasing embarrassment. The sergeant ate little. He had placed a loaf of bread on the table between them and seemed to expect that she would eat it all. She ate, hating herself at first for accepting his charity, fearful of the payment he might demand. As he continued speaking, her fear dulled to a bearable level, but she found she was more ashamed of showing weakness in front of him. She made some attempts to respond to him, or at least to make comments, partly to prolong the meal, and partly to prove that she had some manners. "So," she said, a little awkwardly, during a pause in the conversation, "you . . . you've been a Falangist for some years now?"

"I first became interested in the Falange at the end of my university courses." Tejada saw her raise her eyebrows and realized that she had sensed his evasion about when he had actually joined the party. "It seemed like a party that had a lot of answers to questions I was interested in."

"Oh." Elena felt her smile freeze on her face, remembering the blue-shirted youths who had roamed the streets during the last years of the Republic, wielding coshes and bicycle chains. She concentrated on chewing, although the food tasted like sawdust in her mouth.

The sergeant took her silence as a further question. "I didn't actually join the movement until General Franco took command, when the war started," he said, somewhat embarrassed.

The teacher gave a little gasp of relief. Tejada, mis-interpreting the smothered gesture, hastily expanded his explanation. "It wasn't just a question of expediency," he justified himself. "I'd been very interested in the Falange's land redistribution programs for some years. It's just that they might affect my family quite directly, and. . . ." He paused, uncertain how to explain that he had been unwilling to strain his parents' patience further by coming home wearing not only a guardia's uniform but a fasces in his lapel.

"Your parents wish to retain the title to their family home?" To Tejada's surprise, Señorita Fernández helped him finish the awkward sentence. Her eyes were twinkling slightly.

He laughed. "Shall we say that my grandfather was a rather prominent Carlist?" he said, relieved that she seemed to be sympathetic.

"Understood." Elena nodded firmly, although she really did not understand at all. She could see why the sergeant's family had no love for the Falange. For all his pointed self-deprecation, his voice and manners belied his uniform; he was clearly a member of one of the old landowning families who formed the monarchist Carlist party. But she could not understand why the sergeant would disoblige his parents by abandoning the Carlists for the radical populism of the Falange. He did not seem like the type of man who enjoyed gratuitous brutality, or one of those who were overly concerned with making sure that Spain was as European as possible. He would not have been attracted to the Falange simply because there were successful Fascist par-ties elsewhere in Europe. Surely he could not have been impressed by the Falange's pretended concern for peasant laborers? If he were a little brighter he might have turned into a Socialist, she thought. She looked at the uniform in front of her and brushed away the idea. It was ridiculous. He was sim-ply a gentleman who enjoyed playing at being a policeman.

Tejada, sensing that his guest was uncomfortable with the extended discussion of politics, cast about for a change of subject. "Do you enjoy teaching?" he asked finally, and then kicked himself, remembering that she had just lost her job.

"Oh, yes!" Her enthusiasm was obvious, and untempered by resentment. The school was, at least, a safe subject. "I love working with children. It's so fascinating to watch them grow and change. And they're so generous!"

"Generous?" Tejada asked.

There was a long pause. Then she said slowly, "Well . . . for instance . . . most of the children, if they come to school at all now, they don't go home for lunch—to save the extra walking, you know—and, well . . . of course, the rule is that we share anything that's brought to class. And it's terribly hard for the little ones, never being full, but they *always* share. They've even offered to share with me." She blushed. "Of course I couldn't take food from them."

Tejada, who had watched her eat, wondered about the "of course" and privately thought that if her students were generous it was because their teacher set them the example. "I'm surprised you've never married," he said. "You ought to have children of your own to raise."

"It's never come up." Her voice was unembarrassed, but Tejada was suddenly ashamed of the comment. The only men she would have met in Madrid would have been the Reds, who did not marry their women anyway, and the liberal apologists for the Republic. It was inconceivable that she would have lived in sin with some grubby miliciano, and as for the so-called better classes—Cowards, Tejada thought. Pasty little half-men like that Herrera. Probably fairies anyway, most of them. They haven't got half her strength and they couldn't appreciate her. And how could she respect them?

Señorita Fernández could not guess his thoughts, but she saw that he was looking grave. Since she much preferred it when he was smiling, she said lightly, and as jokingly as possible, "I suppose it's a distinction to be the living embodiment of a proverb."

"Which one?" Tejada asked, noticing her forced gaiety and thinking that she would never pity herself for having no shoes when there were others with no feet.

"Oh, you know. A girl who studies Latin . . ."

Tejada had in fact forgotten the saying, possibly because it was one of his mother's favorites. *A girl who studies Latin will never wear white satin.* He mentally clothed Elena Fernández in his sister-in-law's wedding gown. It was an attractive picture, and startlingly easy to visualize. "Surely you don't actually know Latin?" he suggested.

"I'm afraid I do." Elena returned his smile. "My father is a"—she remembered to whom she spoke, and caught herself quickly—"very devoted admirer of classical literature. He taught me, at home."

"He's also a teacher?" The sergeant's question was casual, but Elena knew it was dangerous.

"He was," she answered carefully. "But I don't know. I haven't seen my parents since the war started."

"I'm sorry."

Elena bit her lip, remembering her mother's last letter.

> Your father has been arrested, because they say he is a Marxist. He told them the truth—that he was a friend and colleague of Don Miguel's for years, and that he had felt compelled to protest what had happened to him, but that he is no revolutionary. I'm sure this will all be settled soon, and I'll write again as soon as I have news.

"At least I never learned Greek." She spoke because she knew that silence would betray her. "That's where my impossible name comes from."

Tejada frowned. "Elena? Helena? Oh, Helen of Troy?" Then as she nodded and rolled her eyes, he added, "It suits you."

"A fickle adulteress? Thank you!"

"I've never thought of Helen like that," said Tejada, who had not thought of Helen at all since his last final exam in literature. "I think . . . I think she was just very young and . . . impressionable. Very idealistic. And Paris came along and he was handsome and spoke well, and she was too innocent to know that he had made an infernal bargain to seduce her. And when she found out it was too late."

"That's an interesting interpretation. Have you ever read—" Elena Fernández choked, as she realized that she was about to ask a self-confessed Fascist if he had read Jean Giraudoux. "Racine?" she finished hastily, wondering what on earth had possessed her.

"Not to remember," Tejada admitted. "Are you fond of French literature?"

As it happened, Señorita Fernández *was* fond of French literature, but she had the distinct impression that the Guardia Civil would disapprove of most of the modern authors she liked. She returned a noncommittal and modest reply. To her surprise, the sergeant said, "I don't suppose you can remember any character named Micaëla?"

She frowned. "I don't think so. Why?"

"Someone said something to me earlier that reminded me of a quote: '*Ce doit être Micaëla*,'" Tejada explained, somewhat embarrassed. "I've been trying to place it. And there's a piece of a song that goes with it." He thought a moment, and then hummed the melody.

"I don't think I . . . no, wait!" Elena set down her fork, and began to laugh. "May I ask if you. . . ." She paused and inspected Tejada. He was looking politely puzzled, but her eyes passed over his face quickly and dropped to his hands, steepled below his chin. They were ringless. "If you are an opera lover?" she finished, her courage failing her.

"My mother is." Tejada was unaware of his own grimace. "I've seen a few."

"It's Bizet." Elena stifled another laugh. "From *Carmen*. Micaëla is the soprano role. The good, virtuous heroine." It was Elena's turn to grimace unconsciously. She wanted to ask the sergeant what had called the quote to mind, but did not quite dare.

Tejada noticed her expression, but misinterpreted it as agreement with his own opinion of *Carmen*. His French tutor had forced him to memorize some of the opera, and although he had not objected to the music, he had thought the plot an unparalleled piece of idiocy. Impressed by Señorita Fernández's erudition, and pleased by her good taste, he allowed the subject to drop, and instead asked her about her favorite authors.

By dint of not mentioning anyone who had written in the last hundred years, Elena managed to have a pleasant and uncontroversial conversation with the sergeant. "Coffee?" Tejada asked at the end of a friendly argument about Lope de Vega.

Señorita Fernández's eyes widened. "Coffee!" she repeated, stunned. "Really?"

"It's a flexible term," Tejada admitted with a smile. "But one can't say to a guest after dinner, 'hot brown liquid?'"

Elena laughed. "If you will drink also."

"Of course," Tejada agreed. He rose and returned shortly with two carefully balanced cups. She thanked him and sipped at the bitter liquid without complaint. He raised his own cup and tasted the contents. "Swill, isn't it?" he commented cheerfully.

"From what I have seen, the guardia civil have no cause for complaint." She spoke quietly, but with absolute assurance.

Sergeant Tejada was abashed. "We're not starving," he agreed gravely. "But even we don't have real coffee often." His voice slowed and dropped almost to a whisper as he spoke. When he set down the cup it clattered and a little of the liquid slopped over the edge.

Elena was surprised by her own rush of sympathy. The man was . . . whatever he was. But he had been very kind to her, and he looked as if he had seen a ghost. "What's the matter?" she asked, and her voice was the voice she used to comfort a student who had lost a treasured possession.

"Nothing," Tejada lied automatically. "I'm fine."

There was nothing she could reply. She sipped at her drink in silence. He drank silently as well, frowning heavily, and a little of her fear returned. He's a guardia, Elena thought. Better educated, and maybe brighter than most, but one of Them. They can be human, off duty, even pleasant, but they're . . . Them. She drained her cup and set it down. He was on his feet before she realized he had moved. "I'll take you home."

"No!" The vehemence of the single word startled Tejada, returning him to the present. "I mean"—Señorita Fernández was flushing—"I don't want to put you to the trouble. You've been so kind . . . please don't."

Tejada had enjoyed much of the evening more than he had intended. Fifteen minutes earlier he would have been puzzled by Señorita Fernández's distress, and would have demanded an explanation. Now, his certainty had peeled away like a strip of ill-hung wallpaper, leaving bare cynicism beneath it. He remembered his doubts about her truthfulness when she had first come, and the pauses in the conversation that he had tried so hard to ignore. She obviously did not want him to know where she lived. He could think of only one possible explanation. "As you wish," he said formally. "I'll show you out then."

Elena heard the change in his tone, and was sorry for it, even though she was grateful for his acquiescence. She almost regretted her words, and then her stomach clenched in terror and disgust. He might be the best of his kind, but she would not willingly take him home. In the courtyard of the post she put out her hand. "Thank you." She knew the words were insufficient. "I wish . . . thank you."

"It's nothing," Tejada said dryly. He shook her hand because she would suspect that something was wrong if he did not, and then watched her cross the street and head east.

Then, as silently as possible, he followed her. He did not know what had pulled Paco into the sordid world of the black market but he knew that only that world could have produced the coffee that Doña Clara had given him in Toledo. If Paco could lie to him, then there was no reason why a Red schoolteacher would not. And if Señorita Fernández had gone to the risk and trouble of trying to throw him off the trail of a killer, then he was very anxious to see where she was going, and who—if anyone—she was going to meet.

Chapter 12

Gonzalo sketched his meeting with the smuggler for Carmen as she cleaned the potatoes. She, in turn, described Tejada's visit as best she could while she cooked. There was no oil for the potatoes, but the meat was some unidentifiable ground mixture and Carmen happily dumped it into the frying pan, trusting the fat to provide grease. Scalding a pan was a small price to pay for food, in any case. Aleja, who had returned home only a few minutes after Tejada's departure, was lured to the kitchen by the smell, and danced up and down with impatience until Carmen finally gave her a small slice of raw potato. The surviving members of the Llorente-Palomino family sniffed the air with a mixture of desire and fear. It was impossible not to fall in love with the aroma, even saltless and dry as it was. But their joy in the rapidly blackening meat and potatoes was tempered by jealousy. If the fragrance penetrated too far it would bring the neighbors down on them.

Gonzalo realized, as he told his story, that he had just robbed a man at gunpoint, and was ready to laugh with joy at the results. Some feeble prewar self hammered at the ice crystal that imprisoned it, and tried to protest this immoral behavior but its cries and gesticulations remained safely locked away. Carmen, as she listened to the story, feared for Gonzalo's safety, but not his scruples. Food was food. "We can't eat it all," she said firmly, as she set the lid over the frying pan to imprison the treacherous smell. "We'll just each take a little, and save some for tomorrow. And don't eat too fast, Aleja. You don't want to get sick."

This praiseworthy restraint proved impossible. Aleja obediently savored her portion, as did Carmen and Gonzalo. But the mass of fried meat and potatoes seemed hardly smaller when they had finished, and surely a *little* more could not hurt. The second helpings disappeared more quickly, and then there was so little left that it seemed silly to try to keep it, when it could be appreciated right away.

After dinner, Aleja went over to Gonzalo and put her arms around his waist. "Thank you, Tío." She hugged him. "I'm glad you're here."

Gonzalo stroked her hair. It was, he found, easier now to forgive his niece for the carelessness that had cost Viviana her life. Perhaps it was being almost able to identify Viviana's real murderer. Perhaps it was only being less hungry. "You're welcome, sweetie."

Aleja raised her head. "I haven't told *anyone* you're here," she said seriously. "Not even Señorita Fernández."

"That's good, sweetheart."

"I had to tell Señorita Fernández I lost my notebook, though."

Carmen, watching her brother intently, could not see any change in his expression as he said quietly, "Of course."

"Aleja," Carmen broke into the little silence that followed. "You know there was a guardia civil here before you got home from school. He's going to come back tomorrow. What will you tell *him* if he asks about Tío Gonzalo?"

"That I haven't seen him since he went into the hospital," Aleja said stoutly.

"What if he says that good little girls tell the truth?"

"That I haven't seen him," the child repeated.

"What if he threatens to take you to prison?"

Aleja clung to Gonzalo a little more tightly. "Candela's father went to the stadium in Chamartín, like they told all the carbineros to, when you were in the hospital," she said in a small voice. "Candela says her mother won't take her to the prison, because they don't allow children there. So I'll say I haven't seen you."

"What if he asks about your notebook, Aleja?" Carmen suggested.

Aleja paused. "Can I tell him I lost it?" she asked doubtfully. "He might ask Señorita Fernández."

"He may already have the notebook," Gonzalo interjected. He looked at his sister with sudden hope. "Did you find out his rank? What post he's from?"

Carmen reviewed the interview in her head. "I don't think so." She saw the direction her brother's thoughts were headed, and added quickly, "It's time for you to be in bed, Aleja."

"I'm not sleepy," the child said automatically.

Carmen began her nightly argument with her daughter. It was briefer than usual tonight, because the unaccustomed feeling of a warm, full stomach had made the child drowsy. When Aleja was safely asleep, Carmen returned to her brother. He was still sitting at the kitchen table, looking contemplative. "I don't know what you're planning," she said quietly. "But you can't do it. It's too dangerous."

"For God's sake, Carmen, you said that this guardia came to the house alone." Gonzalo's voice was low but intense. "And that he asked for *Aleja*. How would he even know she exists if he didn't have her notebook? And how would he have that unless he found it? He may be the one who killed Viviana. And if he *is*, then what better time to catch him alone and off guard?"

"And kill my daughter in the crossfire?" Carmen hissed back. "And then what? Shall we wait until the Guardia miss him and come here to find him dead on our floor?"

"I'll be gone by then," Gonzalo promised.

"Wonderful!" Carmen blew out the lamp, leaving them in darkness. Her whisper could have cut diamonds. "And what do *I* tell them then? 'Yes, the officer came to ask my daughter some questions and then was mysteriously shot by a stranger who climbed out through the window?' I'm sure they'll believe that!"

The meal had sharpened Gonzalo's senses and his satisfaction at a task successfully carried out had dulled his paralyzing grief. He realized, as his sister spoke, that she was leaving a good deal unsaid. She had tacitly accepted that he did not particularly care if he lived or died after carrying out his vengeance, and that acceptance alone showed some generosity. But she had done more than that: His plan placed little value on his own survival, but none at all on hers. She had not openly reproached him for that, and had spoken only of Aleja's safety. It occurred to Gonzalo that Carmen was already risking prison for his sake and that to kill a guardia in her home would be almost to insure her death. He felt a twinge of horrified compunction from his amputated conscience, as if it were a phantom limb. "I won't do anything to hurt you or Aleja," he said quietly. "I won't do anything in the house. But if I can hide, and then follow him somehow. . . ."

For a moment, his voice reminded Carmen of the little brother who had plunged into fistfights with boys twice his size for insulting her. Tears started to her eyes as she realized how infrequently she thought of him that way anymore. Loving him had become a habit, and a duty, but the man who had come home to her house after Viviana's death had been a stranger. "What will you do after that?" she whispered.

He shrugged, a useless gesture in the darkness.

"No." Carmen's voice was choked. "No, Gonzalo. You can't just commit suicide. If you follow him afterward, try to slip away. You can flee."

"To where?" he asked, and his voice was still gentle.

"Out of the city. If you could get away for a time . . ." Carmen knew that she was speaking nonsense. There was no safe place in Spain for Gonzalo now. If he killed a guardia, the unsafe places would become even more dangerous. "France," she whispered.

"Might as well be the moon." He was speaking the simple truth.

"What about that English boy, Miguel, who was Pedro's friend?" She was clutching at straws. "He left us his address. I've been thinking since you came home that if I could write to him . . ."

Gonzalo, who knew that it cost her something to say Pedro's name, made the useless effort of recalling the young volunteer she had mentioned: red-haired, snub-nosed, friendly as a puppy, a boy who had taken the trouble to learn some Spanish before coming to Madrid, but spoke with a bizarre and barely comprehensible accent and idiom. "He was American, I think," Gonzalo said absently, recalling the accent. "Remember, he said his teacher was from Cuba, or Santo Domingo, or somewhere."

"Yes, of course," Carmen agreed eagerly, hoping against hope. "If I could send him a letter, I'm sure he'd help. You would just need to lie low until the papers came through."

"A letter would never get through," Gonzalo reminded his sister, as gently as possible. "It would only put them onto *your* trail. You can't risk that, for Aleja's sake. Besides . . . I don't want to run."

"But . . ."

"I don't want to run," Gonzalo repeated softly.

Carmen was still for a moment. Then she put her arms around him and wept silently in the darkness. "It was always a risk," Gonzalo said, although he knew that was cold comfort. "You knew, ever since the war started. . . ."

"Not like a rat in a trap."

"At least I'll bite the rat catcher one last time," Gonzalo said.

Carmen went to bed soon after that. Gonzalo curled up on the couch and reviewed the day's events. He felt strangely emotionless, not with the numbness of his by-now familiar grief for Viviana, but with a dreamlike calm. Suspicious of his serenity, he stuck a cautious toe into the sea of memory. Freezing turbulent waves did not sweep him off his feet. The best parts of the past lapped gently around him, like ripples on a summer lake: the park on summer Sundays; his first paycheck; the reading room at the union headquarters, where he had discovered Marx and Dickens and Freud and Galdós, whom he had secretly loved best of all; nights in the plaza, when he and Pedro had flirted with the passing girls; the night he had realized that Pedro no longer flirted and the evening his best friend had come to him and said, "Carmen and I wanted you to know . . . it's serious . . . you don't object?" and it had not occurred to him to object, because he was not jealous of his sister's honor, only—a little—of her happiness. Gonzalo took a deep breath, and immersed himself in more recent memories. They, too, lacked sting: the way the bells had rung the day the Second Republic was proclaimed, and it had seemed as if the April flowers would bloom forever. Aleja's birth, the May Day parades, and a thousand fists raised together. The tense first days of the militias and the shock of having women training beside them. The shock of one woman, who had always been the loudest and most beautiful of the group: "Why should you pay the streetcar fare for me, Gonzalo? We're comrades. Equals." And he had been surprised into the truth: "Because I love you." By all logic, the memories of Viviana, and the unmoving front, and the slow, bitter losses should have hurt. But Gonzalo found himself dwelling on moments of calm: on the incomprehensible songs and battle cries the foreign volunteers had taught them and the impromptu language classes (frequently devoted to swear words) they had given the volunteers; on the days when he and Viviana had planned out impossible futures; on the jokes that had made the milicianos roar with laughter not because they were funny but because it was so good to still be alive. Good memories, Gonzalo thought. A good life. I can't complain.

It felt late, but Gonzalo was still not sleepy. He had no way of telling the time. The church bells were silenced for Good Friday. They would not ring again until Easter. The city was dark and still, with the stillness that usually only came in the hour before dawn. After a while, he rose and walked softly to the window. The usual ragged black curtains covered it. He pulled one of them back and looked out. It was a small risk. An observer was unlikely to see him in a darkened window. He could make out the bulk of the opposite buildings, their lights all extinguished for the night. The sky was cloud-streaked, and the moon hung like a gigantic streetlight, pale and full, just above the buildings. It extinguished the stars around it as effectively as real streetlights would have. Gonzalo stared upward for a while. He had never particularly enjoyed watching the night sky. He was a city dweller and he believed in watching the lighted streets. But when he had gone to the front he had learned to be grateful for moonlight and starlight. The moon was a comrade from the front. He was glad of the opportunity to say good-bye to her.

Chapter 13

Tejada damned the full moon to seven kinds of hell as he slid past the gates of the post. The streets were deserted, but without the flood of moonlight it would have been easy to follow Señorita Fernández without her knowledge. Relatively easy, at least. Most of the streetlights were still out, and she was not expecting pursuit. On the other hand, she knew both the city and her destination and he did not. And she's an intelligent woman, he thought, with a bitterness that seemed disproportionate to the offense.

He kept well behind her, so that she would not be alerted by the click of his boots on the cobblestones. She was walking quickly and showed no tendency to glance back. Tejada allowed her to draw ahead at first, fairly certain that she would head toward the center of the city. It would, he knew, be more difficult to follow her once she reached the heart of Madrid. As he had expected, she hurried east, but he was unprepared for her sharp turn to the north immediately afterward, and he almost lost her. Fortunately, there were streetlights up ahead and the lone female figure was readily visible. As he drew nearer to the lights, he heard the sound of the anthem being sung loudly, and not very tunefully, by a couple of voices. They were, he realized, near a barracks. That explained the light, and the unusual noise. Tejada felt himself relax slightly. He was quite competent to handle Señorita Fernández and anyone she might be meeting, but it was still comforting to know that he would have support, if he required it. He kept to the shadows, aware that his khaki uniform would be conspicuous among the dark uniforms of the soldiers. He was not, he saw, the only loiterer in the darkness. The spaces outside the puddles of light were populated with both men and women—usually in pairs. They were generally anxious to be ignored and perfectly willing to be politely blind to him.

He passed the main gate of the barracks. Señorita Fernández had pulled ahead of him again, and he did not want to lose her in the darkness. The sound of the anthem got louder, covering his footsteps, as a pair of young soldiers stumbled out of a side street ahead of him and his quarry, and made toward the barracks. They were singing with the slurred enthusiasm of the moderately drunk. Tejada cast a glance at them and decided that they would be wiser and sadder men at the next reveille. Boys, rather. Neither of them looked much older than Jiménez or Moscoso.

One of them attempted a whistle as Señorita Fernández approached. "Hey, beautiful!" She kept walking. "I said *hello.*" He weaved away from his companion, nearly blocking the sidewalk in front of her. It was difficult to tell if the maneuver was deliberate or if he was simply unsteady on his feet.

"Hey, Little Red," the other boy spoke. "Why're you in such a hurry?"

"Little Red!" The first one roared with laughter. "Li'l Red without a hood!" They were walking along on either side of her now, giggling at their own wit. The sergeant felt a twinge of irritation. If she was in fact heading for a place where Reds were in hiding, she was unlikely to lead two drunken Falangists to it.

One of them grabbed at her arm. "How 'bout a kiss, Little Red?"

They were well up the street and away from the lights by now. By moonlight, Tejada saw Señorita Fernández shake the soldier's hand off her arm. She said something, too softly for him to catch, and attempted to go forward. The other man caught her around the waist and propelled her toward him. "Don't be shy, sweetheart!" He inclined his face toward hers, and then suddenly recoiled, thrusting her backward at his companion. "You bitch!" The echoes of the oath drowned out the sound of his knuckles as he backhanded her. His companion caught her as she stumbled, and threw her to the ground.

Without thinking, Tejada broke into a run. "Guardia Civil! Hands up!"

The two soldiers heard the cry but ignored it, assuming that it was addressed to some criminal. Tejada realized that they would not respond to threats, even at gunpoint, and grabbed the nearer boy, dragging his arms behind him more by force than by finesse.

"That was an order, soldier!" he snapped, twisting one arm until he heard the boy whimper in pain. "I don't like repeating myself. You!" He addressed his captive's colleague. "What the hell do you think you're doing?"

The second soldier straightened and tripped over Elena as he stepped clear of her, looking somewhat befuddled. "I-I don't know, sir." His gaze took in Tejada's uniform. "Hey, you're one of the Guardia."

"We hold military rank," Tejada snarled, obscurely annoyed that his prisoner was not struggling. It would have given him great satisfaction to smash the boy's head into the cobblestones. "Do you want to be court-martialed for insubordination?"

"N-no, sir." The soldier managed a sloppy salute.

"Good. We'll settle for drunk and disorderly conduct then." He released the boy he had been holding with some reluctance. "Unless you care to beg the lady's pardon, in which case it's her choice."

"But she's just a Red wh—," one of them began, and then stopped, as he felt the guardia civil's pistol make contact with his forehead. "She *spat* at me," he finished, with some petulance and considerably more courage than he knew.

"She had ample provocation. Now, are you going to apologize?"

One of the boys turned (still cradling one arm, Tejada noticed with vicious satisfaction) and looked down at Elena. She was sprawled on the cobblestones, her face turned away from the three men, her shoulders hunched, shivering. "Sorry, Señorita," he muttered.

"Sorry," the other one added. And then, to Tejada, "Can we go now?"

Tejada would have liked to make good his threat of arrest and court-martial, but the fact that Elena had not risen from the pavement worried him. "Get out of here," he said. "And don't go attacking decent women. The whole damn city is full of whores, if you need them."

The soldiers might have argued, but Tejada had not holstered his weapon, and something in the casual way he held it suggested even to their slightly muddled brains that he would not be averse to using it. They stumbled off, muttering together. Tejada turned his attention to Señorita Fernández. She was, he realized with relief, not actually lying but sitting, propped on her hands, and curled forward. "Are you—," he began, kneeling, and putting his hands on her shoulders.

"DON'T TOUCH ME!" The force of the words threw him backward a pace.

He dropped to one knee again and allowed one hand to hover over her back, carefully not touching her. "Are you hurt?" Her hair had come down during her struggles. The dark braid lay like a gash across the light fabric of her blouse. She remained hunched over and twisted away from him, but did not reply. "Can you stand up?" he asked, with the cold consciousness that if she was injured it was his fault for not intervening sooner.

"Get me my coat, please." Her voice was shaking.

Grateful for any reply, he searched for her coat, glad of the moon for the first time. He found it in a crumpled heap in the gutter and shook it out as best he could. She had not moved. He hesitated a moment beside her. "It's filthy."

"So am I."

She pushed herself unsteadily to her feet, and Tejada reached for her elbow. "Let me help—"

"Keep away." He froze.

On her feet, she crossed her arms over her chest, head bent, in the attitude of a penitent. Tejada realized that her blouse was torn. "Your coat." He held it out, staring at the ground. She snatched it with one hand and draped it around her clumsily.

"I'm sorry," Tejada said to the ground. "They're . . . just kids."

Her silence could have drowned out a marching band.

"Drunk, stupid kids, who don't know any better," Tejada said, wondering why he felt compelled to defend the boys whom he would have cheerfully murdered five minutes earlier. "They thought you were a Re . . . publican," he finished carefully, unwilling to add unnecessary insult to injury.

"So I am, Sergeant. Hadn't you guessed?" He could not know that the loathing and mockery in her voice were mostly self-directed.

"No, I mean they thought you were—" Tejada stopped, realizing that there was no way to finish the sentence without offending a lady.

Elena was past suffering from excessive sensibility. "A Red whore. Most of us are, nowadays, for food."

The edge in her voice suddenly explained to Tejada why she had refused his escort. "I . . .," he stumbled. "That wasn't why I wanted to see you home."

She was quiet long enough for a treacherous voice in the sergeant's head to say, Wasn't it? Would you have refused, if she had offered? He felt himself flushing, and was glad that the darkness obscured his face.

"Why did you follow me?" she asked finally.

Circumstances suggested a convenient lie. "I was worried about you," Tejada said. "A young woman alone . . . at night . . . in a city."

"This is the first time I've had trouble." Elena realized that she was trying to provoke the sergeant. Had she been calmer, she would have realized why. She trusted him, and trusting one of the Guardia Civil was dangerous. He should *act* like a guardia civil.

Tejada recognized her implication but was more grieved than angered by it. "I'll see you home," he said quietly. "To the doorstep. Understood?"

Elena fought an impulse to burst into tears. "Understood," she whispered. She licked her upper lip, tasted salt, and then fumbled in her pockets. "Do you have a handkerchief? I think my nose is bleeding."

"Here." Tejada held one out. "It looks like it's stopped, actually." He inspected her critically. "You'll probably have quite a black eye tomorrow, though."

"Thank you." She turned and started up the street.

Tejada followed her. She was walking more slowly now, and he wondered if she had been hurrying from fear before or if she was simply exhausted now. "Is it far?" he asked, for the sake of saying something.

"No. Near Cuatro Caminos."

They walked in silence for a little while. The moon was setting and the buildings blotted it out, casting the streets into total darkness. Here and there, a streetlamp glowed at an intersection, like a train's headlight in a tunnel. Tejada saw that she was shivering as they passed under one. He wondered if she was in shock or simply cold. "You're sure you're all right?" He risked putting an arm around her. She flinched, but did not actually pull away.

"Yes." Elena spoke automatically. I stink, she thought, marveling that the sergeant was not revolted by the smell. She wanted to be at home, to peel off her clothes and bathe, and to vomit the dinner that she had eaten so gratefully, and purge herself inside and out of everything that had happened this evening.

If Elena had relaxed into the curve of his arm, Tejada would have been happy to share the quiet with her. Words would have marred the peaceful notes of the whistling breeze and muffled footsteps. But she remained rigid with tension, trembling slightly. He sought for something comforting to say. "You mustn't think, because there are a few bad apples, that . . . things like tonight . . . happen often," he said at last. She did not noticeably relax. "I mean . . . the army is disciplined. If those boys had been Reds, they would never have listened to a commanding officer."

If they were loyalists, their comrades wouldn't have let them attack me. Elena was tempted to say the words aloud. Instead she said stiffly, "Perhaps."

"Well"—Tejada abandoned his attempt to defend the regular army—"the Guardia Civil would never—our mission is to protect people and property. To keep the streets safe. We—"

Elena pulled away from him. "Spare me a recital of your charter, Sergeant."

Tejada had seen a few women who had been raped but they had all been dead or unconscious. He had never before dealt with a victim of attempted rape. He had the vague idea that women were supposed to cry, or faint, or have hysterics in such a situation. He had not expected this brittle hostility. By rights, it should have irritated him. But he had the illogical feeling that

Señorita Fernández was clinging to her composure the way a man clings to the edge of a cliff with his fingernails, and he wanted to throw her a rope. "You know that I would never hurt you," he said, and it was half a statement and half a question.

Elena felt her eyes starting to tear, and ducked her head, hoping he would not notice in the darkness. He was a guardia civil. The son of a Carlist landowner. The friend of Falangists. A symbol of everything that was wrong with Spain. But she had trusted him enough to tell him something she thought would protect Alejandra, and now she found herself biting her lip to keep from saying, "Yes. I know. I believe you." To her profound relief, they reached a familiar dark intersection. "This way," she pointed and began to walk as quickly as possible. "Here." She stopped in the arch of an unlit entrance that looked exactly like every other unlit entrance to Tejada. "Good night. And . . . thank you."

"It's nothing," Tejada said absently. "When will I see you again?"

"You know where I live," Elena pointed out. "You can send for me at any time."

Tejada shook his head, annoyed. "No. I meant . . . socially. What parish is this? When does the Easter service end? If you are still in Madrid, I could pick you up afterward."

"No, you can't." Elena's voice was shaking.

"But why?" Tejada spoke before he could stop himself.

Elena's self-control snapped. "Because I won't be in church."

"What?"

"I won't be there," Elena repeated more loudly. "I'm a Socialist, Sergeant. A dirty Red." Her voice rose steadily, gaining an edge of hysteria. "I was *glad* when they burned the churches and executed the priests! Glad!"

"Shut up," Tejada said quietly, wondering who might be listening behind the darkened windows.

"Why? Go ahead and arrest me!"

Tejada knew some of the basics of how to elicit a confession but he had never tried to stop one before. Señorita Fernández's clear voice rang through the empty street. "You don't believe me, Sergeant? *Viva la República!* I'm a member of—"

Tejada grabbed her arms and kissed her. He waited until her lips stopped frantically moving and then reluctantly pulled away. "You're hysterical," he said hoarsely. "And I didn't hear any of that."

"Traitor," Elena whispered, hating him for his perceptiveness and for deliberately allowing his hands to rest lightly on her shoulders so that she could easily pull away. "Fascist, parasite, Carlist." Her tongue tripped over the last accusation, possibly because she was crying.

He kissed her again, and allowed his arms to close around her with slightly more force. After a few moments, her fingers lightly touched the back of his head.

"You said . . . the doorstep," Elena reminded him, a little while later.

"I know," he agreed softly. He could feel a pulse pounding at the base of her jaw. "Do you want me to go?"

"I think . . . I do." Elena knew that her voice was trembling.

"Jesus, love, answer yes or no, at least!"

"Then . . . yes, I want you to go." Elena pushed him away, while a part of her mind shouted that she was making a huge mistake. "It's . . . it's not you, Carlos. . . . I can't . . . it's not you."

"What, then?" Tejada froze. "You have a lover."

"No! No, of course not! No, I just . . . what I said, before. . . . I'm . . . you're . . . a guardia civil." The despair in her voice was painful.

Tejada drew a long, ragged breath. "All right," he said quietly. "But, Elena, listen, just for a second." He reached toward her shape in the darkness, and very carefully embraced her. She sighed and finally relaxed against him, and his doubts about her feelings vanished. "Listen," he repeated soothingly, twining his fingers in her hair and thinking rapidly. "Remember, at dinner, you said you were named for a fickle adulteress?"

He felt her nod against his shoulder.

"And I told you that you were wrong. Helen of Troy wasn't that. She was seduced into believing in someone who wasn't worthy of her, and that *wasn't* her fault. But I think there was more than that. I think she stayed in Troy long after she knew she had made a mistake because she was noble. I think . . . she understood about honor, and sacrifice, and things that Paris couldn't even begin to comprehend. So she stayed, even after she knew that he wasn't worthy of her . . . even after she knew the Greeks would win." He felt Elena stir, and tightened his grip a little. "I think she stayed because she felt responsible. Because she wanted to help the Trojans who were suffering in a war not of their own making . . . perhaps, especially, the children." Elena was rigid in his arms now, and he spoke more quickly. "I think she was too proud to beg for mercy when the city fell. She had too much honor for that. She might have perished, or become a slave, when the Greeks finally won back Troy. Perhaps, even, she believed she deserved that. And some of the Greeks believed it too, because they saw only her defiance, and didn't understand it. But. . . ." Elena made a faint effort to break free, and he held her a little harder. "But . . . her husband . . . who loved her . . . understood why she had stayed. And he sought her out in the ruins, and asked her . . . . begged her . . . to return with him. To start over again, to be the wife of a man who could match her bravery. To let him take her away to a place where she would be honored and loved and protected, as she deserved."

Elena heaved a long sigh. Tejada loosened his grip, and she raised her head and kissed him on the cheek. It was rough with stubble. "That's a very interesting interpretation," she whispered. "But I think . . . if it were true . . . she would be known as Helen of Sparta, not Helen of Troy." She disengaged herself from his suddenly nerveless arms. "And I think perhaps you underestimate Prince Hector." She took a deep breath and put all of her energy into making sure that her voice did not quaver. "Good night, Sergeant Tejada." She made it all the way to her room before bursting into tears.

Tejada had a considerably longer trip home. He got lost in the darkened streets a few times, but hardly noticed the extra steps. It was several hours past midnight when he finally reached the post. Sergeant González, the ranking officer on the night shift, greeted him with some surprise. "Tejada! Something happening? Do we need backup?"

"No, it's nothing." Tejada did not break stride.

"You been out on the town?" González asked sociably. "The lieutenant told me you had dinner with a girl. Thin, he said, but not bad looking. Did you enjoy yourself?"

Tejada froze, halfway up the stairs, and for an instant his knuckles gleamed white on the banister. "Go to hell, González!" he said quietly. Then he was up the stairs and away.

Chapter 14

Good Friday dawned, clear and brilliantly sunny. Gonzalo had just finished shaving and Carmen was scrubbing Aleja's face when someone pounded violently on the door. Brother and sister exchanged glances. Then Gonzalo snatched his razor and headed for the bedroom. The knocking continued. "Who is it?" Carmen called, as loudly as possible. The closet door swung shut behind Gonzalo.

"Me," said a voice faintly. "Carmen, *mujer*, let me in, it's important."

Carmen warily opened the door, and discovered Manuela Arcé on the threshold, breathing heavily. She gave a sigh of relief. Manuela pushed her way hastily into the apartment and closed the door carefully behind her. Then she shepherded her friend into the living room. "Where's Gonzalo?" she said in a low voice.

"Gonzalo?" Carmen repeated, disconcerted. "I don't know." She would not have grudged the knowledge to Manuela, but it was not the sort of question one answered lightly.

Manuela heaved a sigh of relief. "He got away already then. That's good. Never mind. Sorry to disturb you so early."

She turned as if to go, but Carmen laid a hand on her arm. "What do you mean, already? Why did you come?"

"You don't know?" Manuela lowered her voice, and then spoke very quickly. "A friend of Javier's said he saw Old Tacho last night. You know, the *churro* vendor. He said Tacho was drunk as a skunk and blubbering into his wine about how thirty pieces of silver ought to buy more bread."

"What?" Carmen went white.

"Javier's friend finally managed to get out of him that he'd run into Gonzalo yesterday. Tacho's ratted on him for the reward. The guardia civil know about Gonzalo. They could be here any minute." Manuela turned to leave again.

"Why didn't you tell me sooner?" Carmen protested.

"I only just found out," Manuela snapped. "I was hoping for news of Javier, if you must know."

"Who is this friend?" Carmen demanded.

"A friend. Someone you can trust." Manuela was already in the foyer.

Carmen's mind was working frantically. "Did he tell you anything about Javier?"

Manuela shook her head, her face bitter. "*Nitchevó.*"

The Russian word confirmed Carmen's half-formed suspicion. "Manuela!" She seized her friend's arm and held it. "Gonzalo's still here. If this *friend* of yours can help him . . ."

Manuela hesitated. "I'll ask," she said. "But I don't know. And it won't come free."

"Where can they meet?"

"Try the Cathedral of San Isidro," Manuela said quickly. "Sometime this afternoon. The burial chapel, and look below the undamaged window. Someone will ask him if he's seen anything of Isabel lately. He should just say, 'Not since she was married.' But I'm not making promises."

"Bless you!"

Carmen embraced Manuela, who quickly disengaged herself. "Let me get out of here, you idiot. The Guardia are probably already on their way."

She slipped out, and Carmen ran for the bedroom. She yanked open the closet door and hastily told her brother what

Manuela had said. Gonzalo, swearing softly, reached for his coat and slid his gun into the pocket once more. "No point taking any bags," he said. "I'm trying to stay inconspicuous."

Carmen felt her eyes beginning to tear. "Manuela said they might want money. But maybe if you can persuade them . . ."

"We'll see," Gonzalo said, although he was not optimistic.

His sister was rummaging frantically through the top of the chest of drawers. "If that officer comes back today, to speak to Aleja, I'll try to find out who he is," she promised.

"Thanks." Gonzalo found himself oddly touched by the useless gesture.

"Here." Carmen held up a scrap of paper, triumphant. "Here's that American boy's address. Take it. Maybe it'll be useful."

Gonzalo obediently slipped the scrap of paper into his pocket.

"And here's some money." She held out a handful of bills. "Manuela's friends might take it."

Carmen knew as well as Gonzalo did that this was nonsense. No one in the city took Republican currency anymore. But he slipped it into his coat pocket as well. Then he hugged his sister. "Now, you take good care of Aleja," he ordered.

"I will," she choked.

Aleja, who had watched the proceedings, wide-eyed, from the doorway piped up. "Be careful, Tío."

Gonzalo knelt and hugged her as well. "I will, sweetheart. You listen to your mother and be a good girl."

He rose, rumpled his niece's hair, and headed for the door. Carmen heard it swing shut and waited, heart in mouth, for the shout of the guardia civil or the sounds of struggle in the stairs. There was nothing. Five minutes later, there was still no sound and she began to hope that he had gotten away. Carefully, she began to go over the apartment to make sure that there were no recent traces of Gonzalo's presence.

An hour passed. Nothing happened. Carmen's hasty attempt to remove traces of Gonzalo expanded into a thorough housecleaning. Aleja helped her, singing the chorus of some silly tune that Viviana had taught her. "Remember," Carmen cautioned her, "when was the last time you saw Tío Gonzalo?"

"When he went into the hospital," Aleja replied obediently.

"Good girl," Carmen smiled.

It was nearly noon. Aleja was dusting, and Carmen was on her knees scrubbing the kitchen floor. The window had been thrown open to air out the apartment, and the noises of the street filtered in. Aleja was still singing, "*Three little ducks went out one day, over the hills and far away. . . .*" The pounding on the door was distinct from Manuela's knocks. This time it was made not by fists but by rifle butts. "Guardia Civil!" The shout carried clearly through the thick wood. "Open up!"

Carmen dropped her sponge, and all of the fears she had scrubbed out of darkened corners and out from under chairs, along with the cobwebs, came rushing back. She rose and headed for the door of the apartment where the tattoo of blows suggested that the guardias were breaking down the door. Aleja, who had laid down the dust rag she had been using, trailed her mother into the hallway, hands clasped behind her back. She had stopped singing.

Carmen opened the door and looked down the barrels of a set of guns. There were four guardias there. "Hands up!" one yelled. "All of you, hands above your heads! Turn around!"

Carmen turned, hands raised, and felt one of the men poke her in the back with his gun. Aleja shrank against the wall, her hands obediently stretched above her head. Carmen allowed the guardia to shepherd her into the living room. Aleja tailed her, lips pressed tightly together, eyes wide.

"Where is he?" It was the one who had yelled before. Carmen had lived the scene over in her nightmares so often that she felt as if she were performing a rehearsed script. The rehearsals did not save her from stage fright, though.

"Who?"

"You know damn well. Gonzalo Llorente Cardenas, first corporal, of the carbineros." The voice was grim. "He's charged with treason."

"My brother." Carmen's voice sounded like a bad recording: scratchy and breathy. "My brother," she repeated, trying to adjust the volume, "isn't here."

"We'll see about that." The one who had spoken was obviously the ranking officer. "Gómez, you keep her and the brat covered. The rest of you, search. Start with the bedroom." The men under his command moved to obey him. Carmen, sitting on the couch and facing the man called Gómez, heard the sound of the closet door being yanked open and then a scraping noise, as the guardias prodded under the bed with their rifles. Then a series of crashes, as the dresser drawers were methodically yanked out, one by one, and their contents dumped onto the floor. The officer paced toward the open window. "Did he get out this way?" He leaned suspiciously out the window, as if Gonzalo might be clinging to the brickwork. Then he headed for the kitchen.

"That's just been washed!" Carmen protested, years of habit overriding even terror.

"Tough luck." He strode into the kitchen, and then swore as he slipped on the wet floor. Carmen bit back a smile.

The guardias were chillingly thorough and Carmen spent the next few minutes silently thanking Manuela over and over again. Their commanding officer finally stood in front of Carmen again. "Who tipped him off?" he demanded.

"What?" Carmen knew that "I don't know what you're talking about" would be more convincing than the monosyllable but her throat was closed and forcing the air through it even for a single word was an effort.

"Who tipped him off?" the guardia repeated menacingly. "We know he was here."

"My brother," Carmen swallowed, "was hospitalized some months ago. I haven't seen him . . . since the end of the war."

"Bullshit," he said succinctly. He gestured to one of the other men, who reached out, grabbed Carmen's arm, and yanked her to her feet. Aleja, who had been tightly clutching one of her mother's hands with both of her small ones, was dislodged by the sudden movement and began to whimper. "Come on, then. You can think over when you last saw him—in prison."

Carmen had not struggled as the guardia pulled her arms behind her back, but as they began to march her to the door she twisted. "Wait! What about my daughter?"

The march paused. "Where's her uncle?"

"I don't know!"

"Then let him take care of her."

"Look, just let me take her downstairs to a neighbor," Carmen begged. "It'll just take a minute. Please!"

Aleja, who had listened intently rushed at her mother and clung to her. "I want to go with you!"

"No, Aleja," Carmen struggled for a moment to free her arms so that she could comfort her daughter, but her captor was uncompromising. "No, don't worry, sweetheart. I'll be back soon. But. . . ."

"Nooooo!" Aleja's voice became a wordless wail.

"You're making it harder on the kid, Señora," suggested one of the men who had not spoken until now. "Just tell us where Llorente is. Save yourself some grief."

"I don't know," Carmen repeated, profoundly thankful that she was telling the truth, trying to forget that Gonzalo might be at the Cathedral of San Isidro in a few hours. She realized with sudden cold clarity that if they threatened to hurt Aleja she would probably tell them anything and everything they wanted to know. "Please," she repeated, trying to keep her voice from shaking. "Just let me drop her off with a neighbor. Just let me tell someone what's happened, so they can come for her! Please!"

Aleja heard the rising note of panic in her mother's voice, and screamed. The guardias civiles were taking her mother away. The same guardias who had made Tía Viviana and Tío Gonzalo go away, too. She clung to her mother as far as the stairs in the hallway, screaming and crying, and heard her mother crying as well, and then the officer commanding the guardias snarled a command, and a rifle butt came down on her head, and then the world exploded and went black.

Chapter 15

Tejada had passed a nearly sleepless night. He finally fell into an uneasy doze shortly before dawn and dreamed that Paco was being shot before his eyes. He killed the sniper as Paco fell, and when he reached the bodies he realized that the Red was a miliciana with Elena's face, and then Paco's corpse clapped him on the shoulder and said, "Don't feel badly, buddy. She's just a Red whore," and he turned on the corpse with ferocity and beat it until it lay still again as dead people were supposed to. He woke up sweating.

Tejada spent the morning doing paperwork and trying not to think about Elena. He tried to focus on what he had learned about Paco's death instead, carefully avoiding any thought about the source of his latest information. He almost decided against going to question Alejandra Palomino. If Paco had never had her notebook in the first place, it was unlikely that she knew anything about what or who had drawn him into the black market. But Tejada was forced to admit to himself that if Alejandra had actually seen Paco's killer, she might be in a position to give valuable information. After arguing with himself all morning, the sergeant finally set out for the Calle Tres Peces.

His first thought when he reached the top of the stairs and found Aleja in a crumpled heap was that Paco's killer had struck again, to silence a witness. A quick inspection revealed that the child was still breathing. The door to her apartment was ajar, as if someone had left hastily without bothering to close it. Tejada picked up the unconscious girl and deposited her on the couch in the living room.

Aleja's injury was fairly obvious. One side of her head was bloody. Tejada headed for the kitchen, searching for water to clean the girl's wound, and found a sponge, lying by a pail of soapy water, in the middle of the well-worn tiles. Near the pail was a set of footprints, brown outlines against the newly washed floor. The heel of one of the prints was smudged, as if someone had slipped. Tejada looked at the footprints for a moment, and then raised the sole of his own shoe and inspected it. The outline matched the footprints too closely for comfort.

He washed Aleja's face and, in the absence of ice, left a cool rag on her head to help reduce the swelling. Then he wondered what he should do next. The terrified woman whom he had interviewed the day before was not present. A quick tour of the apartment revealed that it had been searched. In the sergeant's judgment, the searchers had been professionals. He thought about the footprints, which could so easily have matched his own soles, and unwillingly remembered Elena Fernández's voice saying, "Her testimony implicates a guardia civil." Elena would not lie to him. He winced away from the painful spot in his own brain and focused once more on Aleja's. It occurred to him that whoever had visited the apartment earlier could certainly have made sure that Alejandra was dead. The blow she had received might easily have been fatal, and might still be, but a second blow would have finished her off and could have been delivered easily. Whoever had hit the girl must not have cared greatly whether she lived or died. Which made no sense whatsoever, if she had been attacked to prevent her from revealing a secret. But then the search and Señora Llorente's absence made no sense either.

Tejada tried to recall what he knew about head injuries. The longer a man was unconscious the worse the injury, he knew, but he had no way of telling when the little girl had been struck. He was just resolving to take Aleja to the nearest hospital to ask for a professional opinion, when he heard her speak.

When she woke up, she was lying on the sofa and someone had placed a damp rag on her forehead. Her head hurt, worse than it had when she had had the flu a year ago. She tossed restlessly, trying to remember why her head hurt. "Mama?"

"Thank God!" It was a man's voice, not one she knew. A face appeared, bending over the top of the sofa. Aleja blinked at him. Her vision seemed fuzzy, and he swam in and out of focus. She did not know him. She shut her eyes again. "I want Mama!"

"Ssh-ssh. Just lie quietly." The man came around and sat on the sofa by her feet. He sounded like a teacher. Or maybe a doctor. Or like Señor del Valle, whom Mama had worked for.

"My head hurts," Aleja told him, in case he was a doctor and wanted to know what was wrong with her.

"I'm not surprised." Aleja had no word for irony, but she recognized the tone of voice. When the man spoke again he sounded grave. "Can you tell me your name?"

"I'm Aleja."

"And what's that short for, Aleja?"

"Maria Alejandra."

"Have you learned to count yet, Aleja?"

"Of course!" Aleja had the feeling that he was making fun of her. "I'm not a baby!" She opened her eyes and glared at him.

He smiled. "Good. Can you tell me how many fingers I'm holding up?"

She squinted. "Three."

"*Very* good." He seemed as pleased as if she were a tiny baby who couldn't be expected to count to three. "Have you studied geography, too? Can you tell me the capital of Spain?"

"Madrid, of course!" He was definitely treating her as if she were a baby. "It's *always* been Madrid."

"Close enough, I guess." To her annoyance, the man sounded as if he thought she had said something funny.

Aleja decided that he asked silly questions. She asked one of more importance. "Where's Mama?"

The man frowned. Then he asked another question. "Do you remember what happened before you . . . woke up here?"

Aleja strained to remember. Tío Gonzalo had left that morning, but she wasn't supposed to say that to anyone, even a doctor. She knew that his leaving was important, though. After he had gone, Mama had been careful to put away all his things. Then they had cleaned the house. "I was dusting," she said, fairly certain that it was all right to say that. "Mama was washing the kitchen floor."

"Did you finish dusting?" the man asked gravely.

Aleja still had a headache, but it was receding now and no longer made her eyes swim when she opened them. She was able to focus more on the man's face. It did not seem like a scary face. She wondered why she had been frightened, for a moment, when she had first seen him. "Someone knocked on the door," she said slowly.

"What happened then?" The man had a red collar, and a khaki coat.

Something bad had happened, something to do with Tío Gonzalo, but Aleja stared at the khaki coat, and knew that she could not tell him about Tío Gonzalo, without knowing why. "I—I'm thirsty," she said, because it was true.

"I'll get you a glass of water." The man stood up. Standing, he was very tall, and she saw that his coat and trousers matched, and that he was wearing a cartridge belt, and pistol.

The past came roaring back to Aleja, and as she remembered what had happened to her, she recognized the man's uniform, and began to scream.

For a moment, Tejada had hoped that Aleja would be able to make sense of her situation for him. Then, at the crucial point in the story, she suddenly became hysterical. The sergeant was surprised, and somewhat concerned, by her transformation. She had been confused, and a bit wary before. Now she was clearly terrified and hostile. The maddening thing was that he had the feeling that she *could* have told him something, but that she was no longer willing to. After unsuccessfully trying to comfort her for a few nightmare minutes when he was unable to hear himself think, Tejada decided that she might need a doctor after all. He was, he realized, unsure of the way to the nearest hospital, and unwilling to leave Aleja alone to search for it. The idea of wandering through the labyrinthine streets carrying a screaming child to an uncertain destination was not attractive. It would be simpler to take her back to the post and telephone for a doctor from there.

Tejada realized, as soon as he scooped Aleja up, that he had been wrong to think he would have to negotiate the winding streets carrying a screaming child. He was going to have to negotiate them carrying a screaming and kicking and scratching child. With a definite sense of distaste, and a fervent wish that he had thought to bring along a subordinate, the sergeant started down the stairs, doing his best to cradle Aleja's injured head in one elbow and keep his other arm clamped under her knees. She was too large to carry this way easily, but Tejada had a feeling that other means of transporting children involved their active cooperation.

A number of people were on their way home for the siesta and Tejada caught a few startled glances from them. The glances always darted away as soon as he was aware of them. Walking was tiring. Aleja was not much heavier than the regulation backpack of a guardia civil on mountain patrol but Tejada's grip on her was awkward, and backpacks neither squirmed nor screamed. The streetcar on the way down the

Calle de Toledo looked like the answer to the sergeant's prayers. He hailed it, and shoved his way on board. It was crowded, but the other riders melted into each other to give him and his noisy bundle room. The stares here were more concentrated, and Tejada began to feel as if he were standing in a very bright spotlight, surrounded by accusing eyes. He could feel the expressions of sympathy being muttered under the cover of Aleja's sobbing. "Poor little thing." "It's a real shame." "She looks hurt." "Poor dear." He found himself wanting to catch someone's—anyone's—eye and say confidentially (but loudly enough to be heard by everyone around him), "I found her with this bump on her head. I'm taking her to the doctor." But no one met his eyes and he faced row upon row of faces as shuttered as the city's stores.

Tejada reached the post with relief. Aleja's protests had subsided to dry, moaning sobs by this time. The sergeant found himself wondering how long children could scream before they went hoarse. Apparently quite a long time. Moscoso and a young man Tejada did not recognize were on guard duty. They saluted smartly when they saw Tejada and eyed the sergeant's armful with some curiosity.

"Here." Tejada thrust the child at Moscoso. "Be careful of her head. And follow me."

"B-but, sir—" Moscoso stammered, and then clutched desperately at Aleja, who had revived enough to kick savagely while being transferred. "She seems kind of upset. Don't you think maybe a woman would be . . . ow! . . . maybe better?"

"No doubt," said the sergeant, heading for the infirmary. "But I don't see one available, and I've carried her all the way from Tres Peces. She won't hurt you, Guardia."

Moscoso's grunt of pain as Alejandra bit his hand seemed to contradict his commanding officer but Tejada paid him no attention. The guardia's last comment had pulled away the dressing on a thought Tejada had been tending like a wound: Elena would know how to deal with her. When they reached the infirmary, Moscoso set the girl down on a cot with relief and backed away. Alejandra, realizing that she was free for the time being, made a spirited attempt to get up and flee. Her legs folded under her and she slid onto the floor. The two guardias civiles watched her from a safe distance.

"Call a doctor, Moscoso," the sergeant ordered. "Tell him we have a girl, about seven years old, with a slight concussion and a bad case of hysteria. And ask Corporal Ventura if we have anything that will quiet her down."

"Yes, sir." Moscoso inspected his hand. A few drops of blood had beaded on it, and the palm bore a set of little teeth marks. "Umm . . . sir?"

"Yes, Guardia?"

"Umm . . . she's not rabid, is she?"

"Not to the best of my knowledge, Guardia." Tejada smiled slightly. "I'll know more when you bring me a doctor."

"Yes, sir. Right away." Moscoso made a rapid exit.

Tejada inspected the sobbing lump of misery that composed his main witness to murder and wondered again what had provoked such a sudden and violent reaction. Was it something he had done or some private demon that she had remembered? She was wailing pitifully for her mother now. Where was her mother? Had the reticent Señora Llorente also seen more than was good for her? He was interrupted in his meditations by Corporal Ventura, a balding, cheerful little man, in charge of the post's rudimentary pharmacy.

"Moscoso says you've got a rabid kid there, sir," he said, pulling on a pair of dark leather gloves that contrasted oddly with the white jacket he wore over his uniform.

"Moscoso exaggerates," the sergeant said absently, thinking, as he always did, that the white jacket looked silly.

"Oh, well." Ventura cast a regretful look at the gloves, a side-wise one at the officer, and then left them on. "Anything I can do, Sergeant?"

"Would morphine calm her down?" Tejada asked.

Ventura cast a professional glance at the little girl, and then knelt beside her. "Oh, sure. Put her out like a light. But so would a shot of brandy, probably." He gently picked up Aleja holding her upright but cradling her head. Tejada realized that it was a much more workable position than the one he had tried to carry her in. "All right, sweetie. All right," Ventura murmured. "All right, I know. I know you want Mama. You just calm down, honey." He gently set her down on the cot and this time she remained there, staring up at him, wild-eyed but relatively quiet.

"Well done," Tejada commented softly.

The corporal shrugged. "She's about my second boy's age. Why'd you bring her in, Sergeant?"

"I found her unconscious in an apartment that had been ransacked," Tejada replied, without mentioning that he had been looking for her. "She'd been given a tap on the head."

"Mmm." Ventura prodded one side of Aleja's head with interest, and she whimpered. "You don't want to add morphine to this then, sir. Not if you want her to wake up afterward."

Moscoso returned at a run, managed to slow himself to a quick march, and stamped for decorum's sake before speaking. "Sorry it took so long, sir. I had to call three posts. Dr. Villalba's over at Coruña Road. I told him it was an emergency, sir, and he said he'd be here in half an hour."

"Thank you, Guardia." Tejada spoke without the hint of a smile. "Perhaps Ventura can clean your wounds and then you can go back on duty." He thought a moment. "And send me Jiménez, if he's on duty."

"Yes, sir." Moscoso happily gave himself into Corporal Ventura's care.

As the corporal left, Alejandra pushed herself onto one elbow and followed him with her eyes. Tejada's mouth twisted with annoyance. Somehow he was the villain, even though he'd nursed her back to consciousness, and Ventura had become a hero. It didn't seem logical. The tramp of marching boots distracted his thoughts. "Sir!" Guardia Jiménez's voice bounced off the walls of the infirmary like a bugle call. "Reporting for duty, sir!" The young guardia's stamp could have crushed marble to powder beneath his heel. His arm was ramrod straight when he saluted. Even for Jiménez, he was formal.

Tejada turned from Aleja to inspect the young man. "What's that you're wearing, Jiménez?" he asked mildly.

"A sweater, sir!" Jiménez stood rigidly at attention.

"At ease. May I ask why?"

Jiménez obediently clasped his hands behind his back but he could not have been said to be at ease. "I was told your orders were to report immediately, sir. I have just returned from leave, sir."

Tejada inspected the recruit. The boy was wearing dark and unremarkable trousers and a rather baggy sweater, knit according to the most basic pattern possible. The front and back panels were a yellow wool that would have been loud under any circumstances. In contrast with bright red sleeves, they were an abomination. Jiménez looked like a walking fire engine.

"I see," Tejada said, expressionless.

"The sweater was a gift from my grandmother, sir." Jiménez' face matched his sleeves.

"I see." Tejada's face and voice were absolutely serious. Mentally, he thanked his patron saints personally and by name that his own grandmothers limited themselves to crocheting lace.

"It's supposed to be a Spanish flag, sir," Jiménez explained, with a hint of pleading in his tone. "She's very patriotic."

Tejada nodded slowly, not trusting himself to speak. Fortunately, there was an interruption at this point. "The Spanish flag has purple, too." The sergeant realized, to his amazement, that Aleja had spoken. "But it's a pretty sweater," she added politely.

Jiménez gasped with relief, and turned to the little girl. "Who's this, sir?" he asked, smiling. "She's young to be a Red."

Tejada smiled, but did not risk laughter, afraid that Jiménez would misinterpret—or rather, interpret correctly—the cause of his amusement. "Let her tell you herself."

Jiménez squatted, to be at eye level with the cot. "What's your name?"

Aleja stared past him to Tejada, eyes brimming with terror. She said nothing. Tejada leaned over Jiménez's shoulder, concerned. "Don't you remember? You told me this morning." Aleja slid sideways and put out one hand to grab Jiménez's sweater with a little squeak of unhappiness.

The guardia glanced up over his shoulder. "Don't be afraid of the sergeant, sweetheart. He won't hurt you."

Aleja's lip trembled, but she remained stubbornly silent. She is young to be a Red, Tejada thought. But she's tough. In ten years she'll be able to withstand torture, I bet. The Reds start training their young ones early. The sergeant looked down at Jiménez's brilliant sweater, and suddenly remembered Ventura's white coat. "Jiménez," he said, "leave her alone for a moment." When they had withdrawn a few paces, the sergeant said quietly, "Do you have any other civilian clothes?"

"No, sir." Jiménez looked puzzled. "Well, not a complete outfit anyway. Why?"

Tejada inspected the guardia narrowly, and without particular enthusiasm. They were about the same height and build although Jiménez still retained traces of a gawky adolescence. "Then I'd like to borrow those. You should be in uniform now, anyway."

"Sir?" Jiménez was not unwilling, but he was amazed. Sergeant Tejada was the only person on the post who had not grinned broadly at the sight of his sweater. This, in Adolfo Jiménez's opinion, merely showed that Tejada was a kind and considerate gentleman. Sergeant Tejada was, in Jiménez's opinion, as close to a perfect officer as it was possible to be. But this request was a test of faith.

"I think she's frightened of the uniform," Tejada explained. "And I need to ask her some questions without having her too scared to answer. Call Ventura, tell him to sit with her until I get back, and then bring me your clothes, when you've changed."

"Yes, sir." Jiménez beamed, pleased at being taken into the sergeant's confidence, and once again convinced of Tejada's judgment and sanity.

"Oh, and Jiménez—" The sergeant's voice was casual.

"Sir?"

"Your . . . grandmother's gift is a personal keepsake. I understand it must have great sentimental value. There's no need to lend it to me."

"Understood, sir," Jiménez agreed. Then, because he was grateful for the sergeant's tact, he added, "I have a jacket that might fit you, sir. I'll bring that instead."

Tejada waited until Corporal Ventura was settled beside Aleja, ordered him not to leave her under any circumstances, and went to change his clothes.

Chapter 16

Gonzalo, hurrying north with a hat pulled over his face, was extremely grateful he had eaten a large dinner the night before. At least he was feeling rested and relatively strong. He realized that he had no idea what to do or where to spend the next eight hours. Manuela had specifically said not to get to the cathedral until the afternoon. Wandering aimlessly was a sure way to attract attention and probably to encounter more people who would know him. The trick was to look purposeful. Where could he go?

He had headed toward the center of the city unthinkingly, the way an injured animal seeks its den. He could not have said whether this was the wisest or the most foolish place to go. But it was likely to be the most crowded place, and all of his instincts and experience told Gonzalo that safety lay in crowds. He deliberately took the little streets, where the houses leaned against each other like wounded comrades, avoiding the broad avenues where bombs had opened holes between the buildings.

He stopped when he reached the Puerta del Sol, no longer sure where to hurry. This was the center of the labyrinth: the heart of Madrid. But the labyrinth had been penetrated. The balconies of the buildings were draped with the red and yellow flags of the Nationalists and the red and black of the Falange. The city's heart was pierced. Gonzalo, staring across the expanse, remembered why he had avoided the Puerta del

Sol until now. The gaping hole in the cobblestones where a German bomb had ripped an obscene parody of a building's foundation was still there. It still hurt to look at it. He had seen the hole for the first time with Viviana on his arm. It was the first time he had seen her cry. My love, my dear one, my precious, how could they have done this to you? And how could I have let them? He did not know if the lament was addressed to his lover or his city. Perhaps both.

On the other side of the square, a battered metal signpost proclaimed the entrance to the Metro. Gonzalo looked at the proud blue *M* inside the red and white diamond, and the sign above it: OPEN TO THE PUBLIC. No one had bothered to take the signs down, although there was no longer any need for bomb shelters. The Metro had sheltered madrileños throughout the war. It could shelter him now. He fumbled in his pocket for the bills Carmen had given him. Perhaps one would still be good for a ticket.

The stench of sweat and urine hit Gonzalo like a slap as he descended into the Metro, and with the smell came the memories of the last time he taken the train. He had kissed Viviana and squeezed onto a train that was ready to burst at the seams. And voices had been roaring the *Internationale,* and he had tried to roar it too, although his face was practically smashed into someone else's armpit. And thank God it had been a short ride because he wouldn't have been able to stand the smell much longer. It was a good thing the front wasn't more than ten minutes away. But no, that was not actually the last time he had taken the Metro. He vaguely remembered Jorge yelling, "Shit, Gonzalo, are you hit? Medic! Medic!" and then being lifted onto a stretcher with a jolt, and swimming in and out of consciousness as he was bumped down an endless stairwell, filled with curses. "Goddamn it, watch him, he's slipping. Move it, move it, there's a train coming to evacuate them. . . . I don't fucking care if this train's full, he's been fucking gut shot, he needs to be moved *now!*" He did not remember the last ride back, in the hospital train, and he was grateful that he did not.

There were a pair of guardias civiles at the foot of the staircase, apparently on patrol. Gonzalo caught sight of them and almost stopped. If he were caught passing the Republic's money he might well be asked for an identity card. Admitting that he didn't have one would be fatal. But he could not enter the Metro without a ticket and to turn around and go back up the stairs now that the guardias had seen him would invite attention. He walked slowly toward the ticket counter, trying to decide what to do. He could fumble in his pocket, and then say something like, "Oh, sorry, I thought I had my wallet. Drat, I'll have to go back and get it." But even that would mean passing by the guardias a second time. And what if they—or the ticket agent—were solicitous? "Check your other pockets, Señor," they might suggest. And then how would he explain the presence of the carbinero's weapon?

Heart thudding in his throat, Gonzalo approached the ticket counter. There was no line at this early morning hour. "One. Round-trip. To Cuatro Caminos, please," he managed, picking the station farthest away. He had meant to make his voice sound imperious, or at least absentminded, but it sounded pathetically choked and guilty to his own ears.

"Five centimos," the girl behind the grill said.

"Sorry, I don't have change." He handed her a bill at random, hoping that she would not inspect it any more closely than he had.

She glanced at the bill, a note for five pesetas, and then up at him. Then she looked more closely at the serial number on the bill. His heart sank. "This isn't valid," she said softly. And then, more loudly, "Do you have a one-peseta note, Señor? I could make change more easily for that."

Gonzalo stared at her, uncertain of what she meant. "I . . . I'm not sure," he muttered.

"You have any Burgos currency?" she muttered back.

"I'm not sure." Gonzalo felt himself flushing, and wished that he was a better liar.

"Thank you, sir." Her voice was once again loud and bright. In a rapid undertone she added, "I won't give you change. Carbineros should ride free, comrade." She slid a ticket under the grill.

Gonzalo stared at her. No one had called him comrade since before his fever. She winked. Suddenly overjoyed, he winked back. The Metro was still the Metro: still madrileño to the core. "Thank you, Señorita," he said loudly, and took the ticket. The smell of the tunnels did not bother him after that. Madrileños had taken refuge in the Metro when there was nowhere else to go, and this was their smell: the smell of those who chose to take refuge—not in a foreign camp but in the depths of their own city. It was what he was doing, after all.

Gonzalo strolled down to the platform, not loitering, but not rushing either. Most of the posters proclaiming DEFEND MADRID and VIVA LA REPÚBLICA had been ripped down. A few still clung to the tunnel walls, their edges peeling, with swastikas or giant black Xs painted across them, or obscenities scrawled in red. He had expected crowds. He remembered the platforms filled with homeless empty-eyed refugees sitting on ragged rolls of blankets that held all their possessions. The platform was empty now except for a few early morning commuters. He wondered where the refugees had gone.

The train was late although not late enough for Gonzalo. The ride to Cuatro Caminos was all too short. But he had a stroke of luck. Few ticket collectors were on duty and no one demanded his ticket. The round-trip ticket would still be good for two more trips. As he left the train, he realized that the wisest thing to do would be to transfer to the number two line, which also terminated at Cuatro Caminos. It was the longest route and he could ride it back past the Puerta del Sol and then back to Cuatro Caminos again. That would take up about an hour. It was another hour and a half's walk back to the Cathedral of San Isidro. He glanced at the station clock. It was just past nine-fifteen. There was still too much time to kill.

He left the station, wondering if there was any place around Cuatro Caminos where he could rest for a while. But the streets around the station were silent and dead. Cuatro Caminos had been built as a shiny new suburb, along with the Metro line. The streets were broad and paved. But shelling along the northern front had shattered the windows of the once-luxurious apartment buildings, and stray bombs had hit a few. The buildings were dark and silent, and grass grew between the cracks in the sidewalk. Birds were singing loudly, as if making up for the silence of the buildings. Soon, Gonzalo knew, the buildings would fall away into the vast, dry emptiness of the Castilian plains and he would be in the country. It would be impossible to hide in that flat, barren land and impossible to find his way in the uncharted, featureless desert. He turned and headed back toward the Metro as quickly as possible.

The station was deserted although it was after nine-thirty now. Before the war the platforms would have been jammed with commuters. Gonzalo realized, as a train pulled into the station, that he could easily let it pass and wait for the next one, as long as no one saw him waiting. He turned and stepped into the empty stairwell, where he would be out of sight of the train's conductors. He waited in the stairwell for over an hour, allowing several trains to pass. Finally, the presence of a ticket agent forced him to get on the next train.

At the other end of the line, Gonzalo repeated his actions: He left the station, wandered aimlessly for a time, and then returned, allowing as many trains as possible to pass him by before boarding one. It was nearly one o'clock when he once again got out at Cuatro Caminos. This time he began to walk with more purpose, back toward the city center, toward the

Cathedral of San Isidro. He took an indirect route and tried to walk slowly. It was unexpectedly difficult. He would not have admitted to being nervous but he had a goal and it seemed stupid not to get there as quickly as possible.

It was a little before three when he reached the cathedral. It was a flame-blackened, seventeenth-century building, impressive despite the smashed panes that had once held stained glass. Gonzalo's steps slowed as he approached it. It had been a long time since he had entered a church. He took off his hat as he stepped into the shadowy space, hoping that the dim light would hide his face. To his surprise, the church was almost full. Then he remembered: Good Friday. And aren't we all devout, now? he thought bitterly. Cross yourself and pray to Franco, Son, and Holy Ghost. He wondered, as he slid into a half-empty pew at the back of the church, how many of the people kneeling around him had hurled stones at the colored windows and the black-clad priests at the beginning of the war.

At least the multitudes of the faithful hid him. Gonzalo had been confirmed when he was eleven because his mother had wanted it. He had stopped going to church the following year, the same year he left school, because he was the man of the house and it wasn't right to make Carmen and his mother struggle on alone any longer. At twelve, he had regretted giving up neither the classroom nor the confessional. He had regretted leaving school later, but never leaving the church. He had all but forgotten the words and ceremonies, first from carelessness and later from principle, but he moved his lips when the rest of the parishioners spoke, and he rose and knelt with them. They moved jerkily up and down, and Gonzalo followed as if he were a marionette.

When the cross had been revealed and the service was over, the crowd slunk out the door, talking very little. Do the priests think we're repenting our sins? Gonzalo wondered as he shuffled out among the others. Do they really believe that we're silent and sorry because an innocent man died nearly two thousand years ago? As if we had no other problems! He began to move sideways through the parishioners, edging his way toward the chapel at one side of the nave. Candles were burning and guttering here. He waited until the church had emptied out. A little hesitantly, he knelt in front of the image of the Virgin, uneasily aware that he was early and wondering how long one could plausibly remain lost in prayer.

After what felt like an eternity but was really less than ten minutes, he heard footsteps behind him. He bent his head, heart pounding, not sure whether he most hoped or feared that the person behind him would stop. The footsteps paused and then came closer. There was a creak as a bearded man knelt on the wooden bench beside Gonzalo. "Seen anything of Isabel lately?" he asked quietly.

Gonzalo swallowed. "Not since she was married," he breathed.

"A shame," the man said. There was silence for a few moments, and then the man said softly, "Turn right when you go out and walk slowly toward the Plaza Mayor."

Gonzalo bowed his head, mumbled a prayer that had stuck with him from childhood, crossed himself, and rose. The man remained, apparently absorbed, in front of the candles.

Gonzalo was only a few yards from the entrance to the Plaza Mayor, wondering what he should do next, when someone touched his arm. "We meet again," said a familiar voice. Gonzalo blinked in surprise, and then recognized the bearded man from the church. He was wearing a pair of thick glasses now. "Are you Gonzalo?"

Gonzalo felt something clench in the pit of his stomach. He did not want to give his name into the keeping of this stranger. And yet . . . "Who are you?" he asked.

"Just call me Juan. Come on, the others are waiting." The bearded man began to walk briskly across the plaza, apparently blind to the guardias civiles circling the perimeter.

"Others?" Gonzalo asked, falling into step beside him.

"Do you play soccer?" the stranger called Juan asked, apparently deaf.

"Not since I was a kid."

"Me neither, but you should see my nephew. There's not a goalie born who he can't get past. He'll be famous one day, I swear! I knew it years ago."

"Oh." Gonzalo felt idiotic. "How old is he?"

"Just nine, but even the teenagers want him on their team. Why, you know what he did last week?" Juan launched into an involved anecdote, which lasted until the two men were north of the Gran Vía. He stopped in front of a nondescript row house, took out a key, and entered, drawing Gonzalo in behind him. "Come on, it's down the stairs." He headed down a flight of ill-lit steps, too narrow to need a banister, which creaked ominously under his tramping feet. Gonzalo followed, aware that his life was in the hands of a rather eccentric stranger and wondering if he was making a fatal mistake. Juan was hurrying down the basement hallway now, apparently by feel, since it was completely dark. He stopped abruptly and knocked. Gonzalo, who had been following closely, bumped into him.

"Who's there?"

"Andrés, with news of Isabel."

Gonzalo blinked, shocked at the casual way that Juan had lied. Then he realized that it was far more likely that the bearded man had lied to him, and that "Juan" was really "Andrés." Or, more likely, someone else entirely. The door opened and he was pulled into a smallish room that he realized was intended as a kitchen. It opened onto a garden sandwiched between buildings. There were two people already in the room. One was a man, probably in his late fifties, with a white mustache. The other was a woman, dressed in black and wearing a black veil that obscured her features. Both of them stood as Gonzalo and Andrés (or Juan) entered. The man spoke first.

"Comrades." He clenched one fist but raised it only to the level of his face, making the greeting almost furtive.

"Comrade." Gonzalo's companion returned the salute, but bowed his head deferentially. "Everything quiet?"

"Yes." The older man turned his attention to Gonzalo. "You're a friend of Javier Arcé's?"

"Yes." Gonzalo nodded, uncertain what was expected of him. How the hell did Javier know these people? he wondered. And who are they? He felt that he was being measured but was not certain for what. Anxious to break the tense silence he added, "I got quite a shock when I heard he'd been arrested."

"So did we all," the older man said dryly, and the tension in the room lessened slightly. "Why are the guardia civil looking for you?" In this atmosphere of passwords and secrecy the question was startlingly direct.

Gonzalo paused. This was not the question he had expected. The answer seemed too obvious to warrant the risk of saying it aloud. But the man with the white mustache was waiting for an answer. "I am . . . I was . . . a carbinero," Gonzalo said slowly. "I've been in hiding since they told us to report to Chamartín stadium." Too late, it occurred to him that the question might be a trap.

"And that's *all?*" the man asked, with emphasis.

"Yes," Gonzalo said, surprised. His curiosity got the better of his fear. "Why do you want to know?"

"We need to know who else is affected." The woman spoke for the first time. Her voice did not match her appearance. It sounded young, unexpectedly ragged, and tear-choked. "We can't afford to lose anyone else."

"I'm afraid I can't help," Gonzalo said. He was remembering his last conversation with Manuela, and pieces of random information were rapidly falling into place: Javier's tendency to go for walks at strange hours, his unusual knowledge about the black market and the Guardia Civil. Gonzalo had wondered at the time how political a garbage collector could be. It had not occurred to him that Javier might have been arrested not merely as a city employee. "I only knew Javier socially." The past tense slipped out easily. If Javier had been arrested as a spy, the best one could hope was that he was dead.

The white-haired man raised his eyebrows. "We *have* spoken to Javier's wife." His voice suggested disbelief.

Gonzalo was puzzled. He had only known Javier through Carmen's friendship with Manuela. Manuela could have explained that better than anyone. So why hadn't she? "I don't understand," he ventured.

"She told us you seemed very anxious for information, the last time you spoke to her." The man's voice held the hint of a threat, and Gonzalo was aware that Juan (or Andrés) had moved to stand behind him. Then he felt something poke him gently in the back. He twisted and saw that the bearded man was holding a pistol.

"I suggest that you give some explanation, Señor Llorente," the man said quietly in Gonzalo's ear. "We've taken a considerable risk in bringing you here. Keep your hands where I can see them."

Gonzalo's hands, which had gone automatically to his coat pocket, froze, and then slowly moved away from his sides. The woman silently came forward and disarmed him with an efficiency that suggested she had done this before. Gonzalo's mind worked frantically, trying to find a plausible explanation, but all that occurred to him was the truth. "I asked Manuela about a murder," he said cautiously. "My . . . my wife . . . was killed the day before Javier was arrested. I wanted to find her killer." It was the first time he had called Viviana "my wife." But "friend" and "comrade" were too cold, among these frightening strangers, and the old, inaccurate term seemed to fit best.

"Why did you ask Javier's wife?" That was the woman. The man with the white mustache frowned at her, and Gonzalo guessed that she was not supposed to have a part in the interrogation.

"Manuela found her." Gonzalo winced. "And I knew a guardia civil had killed her. I wanted to find out which one, and. . . ." He stopped.

"Why was your wife killed?" That was the older man again.

Gonzalo hesitated, but the nudge of the gun against his kidneys was persuasive. "There was a guardia civil there, dead. They thought she'd killed him, I suppose."

The man with the white mustache frowned. "And this dead guardia. What was your interest in him?"

"None," Gonzalo said. "But I thought if I found his partner I might find . . . the man I was looking for."

"What does the name Diego Báez mean to you?" The question was sharp, as if the man hoped to catch Gonzalo off guard.

Gonzalo shook his head. "I've never heard of him," he said, wondering if he was going to come out of this alive, and also wondering a little what exactly "this" was.

"What about Paco López?"

"I don't know him either." Gonzalo was very aware of the gun pressed to his back. He knew that there was small chance his questioners would believe he was telling the truth. He swallowed, trying to muster saliva. "I came here for help," he said, as steadily as he could. "Because Manuela warned me that someone had tipped off the Guardia Civil about me. I don't know anything about any of this."

No one spoke for a moment, and Gonzalo had the impression that everyone was waiting for a sign from the white-mustached man. Finally, the old man spoke. "That being the case, comrade, you will not mind if we hold you here temporarily. You understand our position."

"Of course." Gonzalo did not trust himself to say more. It would be too embarrassing if his voice trembled.

"As a gesture of good faith, then . . . until we establish that you are what you say you are . . ." The man picked something up from the counter beside him. As he stepped forward, Gonzalo saw that the object was a coil of rope.

Gonzalo submitted to having his hands bound without resistance. In any case, it would have been difficult to resist. The older man's strength belied his white hair, and the younger man—Juan or Andrés—remained, pistol at the ready. Gonzalo was marched, firmly but not ungently, into a sort of pantry that adjoined the kitchen. It was more like a large closet than a room, windowless, with shelves set into its walls. The shelves were bare, but someone had placed a stool in one corner. "You can sit, if you like," said the older man. "We'll be back in a little while."

Gonzalo sat, aware that the younger man's pistol remained steadily trained on him. The older man backed out, and the man holding the gun followed. The door to the pantry swung shut, leaving Gonzalo in total darkness. He heard a key turn in the lock. There were muffled voices outside the door. Then there was only silence.

Chapter 17

Tejada was pensive as he changed out of his uniform and into the clothing that Jiménez brought him. The young recruit had thoughtfully provided not only a jacket but a clean ironed shirt. There was something odd about the fact that Jiménez had not only civilian clothing, but an actual change of shirts, while he had nothing but his uniform. Of course, Jiménez was new to the Guardia, and still probably had a lot of clothes from his life as a civilian. But this is what I wanted, the sergeant thought, to get away from being Señorito Carlos. To just be a member of the Guardia Civil, without all that damn nonsense. Well, now I'm a guardia civil. And girls scream at the sight of me. It was not, he knew, a little girl's shrieks that troubled him but the memory of an older one's choked whisper. He shrugged into the ill-fitting jacket and went downstairs to see Aleja.

The child was lying where he had left her, with Corporal Ventura squatting beside her. The pharmacist had bandaged her head, and placed a cold compress on it. She was looking more alert, and much calmer. "No," Ventura was saying, as the sergeant came within earshot. "I have a boy who is bigger than you are and two who are littler. But no little girls. Do you have any brothers?"

"No." Aleja seemed rational enough. "There's just me."

"Then your mama and papa must take extra-special care of you," Ventura observed.

Aleja's lip quivered. "My papa's dead. Mama takes care of me." A few tears leaked out. "I want Mama."

"Of course you do," Ventura murmured. He glanced over his shoulder, and rose. "Where's her mother, sir?" he asked in an undertone.

"I don't know," Tejada replied quietly. "I was just up to trying to find out when she got hysterical." He bent, to be at eye level with the girl. "Hello, Alejandra. How are you feeling now?"

Alejandra stared at him with wide, frightened eyes and he knew that she recognized him, even without his uniform. She said nothing. Tejada sighed. "I won't hurt you," he said. "If you tell me what happened to your mother, I can try to find her for you. Wouldn't you like me to find your mother?"

The little girl regarded him steadily for a moment. Then she said, in a very small voice, "They took her away."

"Who did?"

"You. The guardias."

Tejada exhaled slowly. He was not really surprised. The footprint, the search, the girl's irrational terror: They all suggested the same thing. But it was still not clear why Señora Llorente had disappeared. Had she been arrested? Or were the guardias acting for their own purposes? "Did they say where they were taking her?" he asked, without much hope.

"To prison," Aleja whispered. "And they wouldn't let me come with her. One of them hit me," she added, "when I wouldn't let go."

Tejada relaxed and realized that he had been tense out of fear for Alejandra's life. If the girl was telling the truth—and there was no reason he could think of for her to lie—then her injury had been accidental. That meant that Paco's killer still did not know she was a witness. He thought for a moment. She was coherent now but she did not trust him and it would be difficult to question her about Paco's murder. The easiest way to get her to trust him would be to find her mother. Tejada felt a certain relief that the guardias had spoken of jail rather than using the ominous euphemism "We're going for a stroll." "Why was your mother arrested, Alejandra?" he asked, while mentally composing a memo giving the prisoner's name, date of arrest, and charges against her, to be circulated to all posts.

Aleja buttoned her lips.

"Tell the sergeant, sweetheart," Ventura coaxed. "It'll be easier to find your mama if we know more about who we're looking for."

The child remained silent.

"What had she done?" Tejada tried again, to no response.

"Did the guardias read a charge?" Ventura asked gently. "Did they use big words that you didn't understand? Can you remember the words?"

Aleja maintained a stubborn silence. Tejada remembered that he was dealing not only with Elena's student, but with the niece of the miliciana he had found by Paco's body. So young to be a Red, he thought. Even a few days earlier the thought would have angered and disgusted him. Now, he found himself slipping into a vast puddle of melancholy for the minds and hearts irretrievably twisted by the Marxists. Ventura was still cajoling the child, without success. Tejada knew that his role was that of a bully.

"Tell the truth," he ordered, as harshly as it was possible to speak while leaning over a sickbed. "Why was she arrested? Black market? Theft? Prostitution?"

"Sir," the corporal interjected reproachfully, still in the role of mediator, "she's only a little girl."

"I'm sure she knows about all those things already," Tejada said dryly. His heart was not in the role. He knew that he was speaking the truth. But so was Ventura. Alejandra Palomino might not be an innocent but she *was* only a little girl. It didn't

seem fair that the two truths were compatible. Perhaps Aleja
sensed his lack of menace. Perhaps she was simply determined
not to speak. In any event, she said nothing and merely watched,
wide-eyed. He would have to try to convince Lieutenant Ramos
to trace Carmen Llorente's whereabouts without knowledge of
the charges against her. He decided that Alejandra's presence
would probably be his best argument. "Can she be moved safely?"
he asked Ventura.

The corporal nodded. "Yes, sir, if it's just over a short distance. But I wouldn't recommend it."

"Thank you." Tejada bent over Alejandra again. "I'm taking
her to see the lieutenant," he explained, as he picked her up.
"He should be able to find out where her mother is. Oh, don't
start crying again," he added to Aleja, with disgust. "We're
going to find your mother."

The sergeant had benefited from watching Ventura, and he
carried the girl with more assurance now. It helped that
although she was sniffling and whimpering, she was not
actively struggling. The guardia outside the Lieutenant's office
barred their way. "You can't—" he began.

"This requires the lieutenant's immediate attention,
Guardia," Tejada interrupted. "I'll take responsibility."

"Err, yes, sir." He looked doubtfully at Alejandra. "Errr . . .
why are you . . .?"

"As you were, Guardia," Tejada said pointedly, and pushed
open the door.

Ramos was, as usual, behind his rickety table, pounding furiously at his typewriter. He looked up as the door opened and
received a general impression of sports jacket and crying child.
"This room is off-limits to civilians," he snapped. "Who let you
. . . Tejada! What the hell's that?"

"I'm sorry, sir." Tejada raised his voice over the little girl's
sniffles, but spoke with his usual calm. "This is Maria Alejandra Palomino Llorente."

Ramos inspected the girl the sergeant was carrying. "So what?"

"She's the girl I told you about, sir," Tejada said, not mentioning that his information about Maria Alejandra had been considerably augmented since the last time he had spoken with Ramos. "The one who might have information about the matter you asked me about."

"Oh," Ramos digested this and took in the bandage on Alejandra's head. "Jesus, Tejada, did you have to hit her that hard?"

Tejada stiffened but his voice was colorless as he said, "No, sir. She was injured by accident, sir, in an unrelated matter. Her mother was arrested this morning, and she's been quite upset since then. I thought perhaps a few phone calls to trace Señora Llorente might help calm her down, so that I could ask her questions and get some answers."

"What's the charge against her mother?"

"I don't know, sir."

"Where's she being held?"

"I don't know, sir."

"Jesus!" Ramos glared at his subordinate. "And you think a few phone calls will help?"

Tejada had an answer ready. "The likeliest place is here or the Alcalá post, sir. But inquiries could radiate outward. I know the woman's name and when she was arrested. It shouldn't take too long."

"You can't waste the afternoon," the lieutenant protested. "You're scheduled for patrol."

"Yes, sir. At your orders," Tejada agreed. "What do you want me to do with the girl then?"

Too late, Ramos saw that he had been maneuvered into a trap. "Can't you just take her back where you found her?" he asked, without much hope.

"It's some distance, sir," Tejada informed him smugly. "As I mentioned in my report last night—"

"All right, don't take her back then!" Ramos said irritably. "Find some place to put her."

"Where, sir?"

The lieutenant gritted his teeth. "I'm not running a god-damn kindergarten," he said.

"No, sir," his subordinate agreed, meekly.

"She can't stay."

"No, sir."

Lieutenant Ramos rummaged on his desk, and finally came up with a grubby length of paper. "Here's the list of men on patrol this morning. You can ask any of them if they know this Llorente woman. After that you can make some phone calls."

"Thank you, sir."

"Can't you make her be quiet?"

"She doesn't like uniforms, sir," Tejada explained.

"So that's why you're in that getup." The Lieutenant grinned suddenly. "By the way, did you see that kid—what's his name?—Jiménez, when he came back this morning?"

Tejada grinned back. "Yes, sir. Very . . . vivid, sir."

Ramos snorted appreciatively. Whatever he planned to say next was interrupted by a quick rap on the door. Then the door opened, and a man with a neatly trimmed mustache, wearing the dark uniform of an army lieutenant, entered and saluted Ramos. Ramos returned the salute, and glanced at Tejada questioningly. The newcomer explained himself. "Dr. Villalba, at your service, Lieutenant. I understood there was a medical emergency at your post?"

"Here, sir," Tejada said, quickly deciding that any apology for Moscoso's exaggeration would be a waste of breath. "This child is the patient."

The doctor looked startled. "You do realize, Sergeant, that my services are intended to be put solely at the disposal of the Guardia Civil?"

"Yes, sir." Tejada was wooden. "With respect, sir, this child's health is of importance to an investigation undertaken by the Guardia."

Dr. Villalba was inclined to grumble but Ramos hastily supported Tejada and the doctor was finally persuaded to take Maria Alejandra downstairs and conduct a routine examination. Tejada thankfully surrendered Alejandra into his and the ever-helpful Corporal Ventura's care and began his search for Carmen Llorente.

None of the men at his own post knew anything about Carmen Llorente, and a quick phone call to the Alcalá post (where Captain Morales tactfully refrained from asking about progress in Tejada's investigation) was also fruitless. But a call to the post in Cuatro Caminos yielded a hasty consultation, and then a voice that said, "Sergeant Martínez speaking . . . Yes, Sergeant. María Carmen Llorente is being held in connection with the disappearance of her brother, Gonzalo."

"What's happened to him?" Tejada demanded.

"He's a Red. He didn't show at Chamartín, and he's been in hiding since. Someone gave information against him yesterday."

Shit, Tejada thought. No wonder Alejandra didn't want to tell us. Damn. This'll make it hard to get anything out of her. Aloud, he said, "I have Llorente's niece here, in connection with something else. Where's her mother being held? I'd like to drop her off."

There was a sound of rustling paper, and then the voice on the other end of the line confirmed that Carmen Llorente was being held at the new prison, just north of the Cuatro Caminos post. She was not in solitary confinement and had not yet been interrogated. "We're letting her cool her heels a bit," Sergeant Martínez explained. "That usually makes them more eager to cooperate."

"Good luck," Tejada said briefly. "Her daughter is stubborn as a mule."

"The women are always the worst," the other commiserated. "But listen, we're pretty crowded here. I don't know if the captain will approve a transfer."

"She's only seven," Tejada said, alarmed at the idea that his counterpart might saddle him permanently with Aleja. "She won't take up much space."

"Hold the line," Martínez said. After a few moments of consultation he returned. It was hard to tell tone of voice on the telephone but Tejada would have been willing to bet that the other man was reluctant. "All right. You can dump the brat on us."

"Thanks. I'll owe you one for this." The phone call ended on an amicable note.

Tejada looked at the information he had scribbled on the nearest available scrap of paper. So Carmen Llorente had a brother in hiding. He remembered the way Carmen's neighbor had said, "She lives with her—" and then hastily changed the sentence. Aleja was probably trying to protect her uncle. After a few moments' thought, Tejada headed downstairs. He met Dr. Villalba at the edge of the infirmary. "That's a very lucky little girl you have there, Sergeant," the doctor said, after accepting Tejada's salute.

"Lieutenant?" It occurred to Tejada that a child who had been clubbed while her mother was being arrested for treason could not perhaps be called entirely lucky, but Dr. Villalba was clearly pleased with his diagnosis.

"Children's skulls are more easily fractured than adults," the doctor explained. "A little harder and that blow would have broken the cranium. And that," concluded Villalba with a certain macabre enthusiasm, "could have been very messy."

"I see. Thank you, Doctor." Tejada risked a question. "She should make a full recovery, though?"

"Well, it's in God's hands," the doctor said, with a certain air of disappointment. "But I think it's likely. Keep her quiet for a while. And if she has any relatives, tell them to feed her up. She's suffering from malnutrition."

Tejada wondered briefly if medical training had the unintentional side effect of divorcing doctors' brains from their external surroundings. Since Villalba was a superior officer, he did not point out that most children in Madrid were probably suffering from malnutrition. He thanked Dr. Villalba, saw him out, and then returned to Alejandra. "Good news," he said carefully, sitting down beside her. "I think I've found your mother."

Aleja struggled to sit up. "Can we go see her now?" she asked.

Tejada had hoped for this reaction, but he found her eagerness oddly pathetic. "I'll take you to her in a little while," he said, reminding himself that he had done the child no harm, and in fact some good. "But I would like to ask you a few questions first."

"Then can I see Mama?"

"Yes, after you answer the questions."

Alejandra was silent for a little while, visibly digesting this information. "I can't see her first?" There was a hint of a whimper in her voice.

"I can't bring you to your mother until you've answered the questions," Tejada explained. "But there's no need to talk now, if you're tired. The doctor says you should rest, anyway."

Aleja's face twisted in agony. Tejada, watching her, saw that she had understood his gentle threat. It's not really cruelty, he reminded himself. She wouldn't even know where her mother was, if I hadn't found her. And it's necessary to learn if she has any information. Still he wished that her expression were more childlike and less like those of the adults he had seen interrogated. She was only a little girl.

"I want Mama," the child whispered. Tejada was about to speak again when she added, with heroic effort, "But I'm tired now. I don't want to talk."

The sergeant remembered again the specially trained inter-rogator he had met in Toledo. The man had been quite proud of his methods, and pleased to share trade secrets. Don't give them anything. Keep them on tenterhooks, guessing what you know and what you want to find out. Tejada sighed, and disregarded the advice. "It's not about your uncle Gonzalo," he said.

Aleja tensed, and looked at him with hunted eyes. "I'm tired now," she repeated uncertainly.

Dr. Villalba's last words gave the sergeant an idea. "All right then," he said. "Would you like something to eat?"

Aleja said nothing, but her eyes flickered. Tejada noticed and was encouraged. "You just rest," he said. "I'll come back in a little while. We can have a chat and then you can have a snack and go to see your mother."

He rose and walked away quickly before he could say some-thing that would ruin the lure he had tossed out. He was not quick enough to avoid hearing Aleja start quietly sobbing again.

Chapter 18

Gonzalo did not know how long he sat in the darkness. It's like being buried alive, he thought. The idea reminded him that he might shortly be buried, not alive. He wondered if he should have taken his chances with the Guardia Civil. He tried to think clearly but nothing made any sense.

He was roused by the sound of someone unlocking his prison. Then the door opened and the woman in black appeared. She had thrown back her veil, and he saw a long, angular face, framed by black curls. She still had Gonzalo's revolver. She kept it steadily trained on him as she advanced. "Stand up." To his surprise, her voice was almost friendly. "Turn around."

He turned and heard her withdraw a few paces. He wondered if he would hear the report before the bullet hit. Then he heard a few more steps and felt someone loosening his bonds. A moment later, his hands were free. He turned around slowly, massaging his wrists, and saw that the bearded Juan (or Andrés) had taken the weapon from the woman and was standing in the doorway. He was no longer aiming the revolver, though. "Manuela's vouched for you," the woman said.

"Which means we have to help you," the man added, ushering him back into the kitchen. Gonzalo sat down. The bearded man sat across from him, while the woman remained standing behind.

"Help?" Gonzalo repeated blankly.

The bearded man grinned suddenly. "I suppose we could start with an apology, comrade. You must have been scared shitless."

"Just about," Gonzalo admitted, thinking that the man's amusement was decidedly misplaced. "You might tell me what's going on, too."

"Sorry, my friend, I can't tell you that." Juan was brisk. "Now you'll need false papers, correct? And a reason to cross the border. Possibly a disguise, but I think we'll hope they don't have photographs of you." He inspected Gonzalo critically. "You don't have any distinguishing features. That's a plus."

Gonzalo stared, openmouthed. All of Carmen's plans seemed to be coming true. He felt that he should be wildly elated. They were offering him his life, and they had not even mentioned payment. "You mean . . . France?" he faltered, too confused to analyze his feelings.

"I don't know yet," Juan replied. "Maybe Portugal. We'll see about a boat from there. Or we could try to send you through Gibraltar." He shook his head. "The trouble with Madrid is that it's in the middle of goddamn nowhere."

Gonzalo stiffened at the insult to his home. He knew what the man *meant*, of course, but it made more sense to say that Portugal and France were nowhere. Madrid was the center of things. "I wasn't planning to leave," he said apologetically.

"You can't stay," Juan said. His voice held the calm conviction of someone stating the obvious.

"I don't want to leave," Gonzalo repeated, feeling a little ungracious. It seemed rude to refuse the help offered. Anxious to make his position clear, he added, "I know . . . I won't live. But I don't really care."

The bearded man's eyes narrowed. "It's not for your benefit, comrade. It's for ours. We're not safe as long as you're here."

Gonzalo knew the man was right. But his reason for living was linked to staying in the city, and some lingering stubbornness made him say slowly, "Then before I leave the man who killed my . . . wife . . . is a sergeant at the Manzanares Guardia Civil post. I'd like to find him. That was my plan."

"Are you crazy?" Juan demanded, just as the woman raised her voice to say with sudden intensity, "How do you know he's a sergeant at the Manzanares post?"

Gonzalo shrugged, uncertain which question to answer. Juan looked over Gonzalo's head at his companion, and then said slowly, "Good question. How do you know he's a sergeant at Manzanares?"

"It's a long story."

"We have time for it." Again, it was the woman who spoke.

Gonzalo shrugged again and did his best to summarize his investigations into the identity of Viviana's murderer as quickly as possible. They already knew about Manuela, and he saw the bearded man nod slightly at a few points and relax as Gonzalo told them what she had said. Encouraged, Gonzalo went on to describe his accidental discovery of the chocolate wrapper and his later dealings with the black market. The bearded man tensed again, and the woman moved around so that she could see Gonzalo's face. Gonzalo explained about Aleja's lost notebook, and added his plan of hiding and observing the guardia who was supposed to call on his sister. "But then Manuela came and warned us," he finished. "So I missed the chance. He's probably met with Carmen already. I hope she's all right," he added, aware that they did not care about Carmen's safety and somewhat ashamed that he had not thought of her more during his imprisonment.

"You're sure Paco was mixed up in the black market?" the bearded man said, ignoring Gonzalo's last statement. His voice was grim.

"It would help if I knew who Paco was," Gonzalo retorted.

"You don't know? Oh, shit." The man frowned. "Paco was the name of that dead guardia. The one who your Viviana was killed for. But what the hell was he doing with the black market? I thought you said he was a perfect choirboy?"

Gonzalo realized that the last question was not addressed to him but to the woman. She nodded. "I did. I thought he was." She sounded sad. "He was . . . oh, an ideal Fascist, I thought. Loud and blustery, and too shortsighted to know what he was fighting for. A stupid man, in many ways. But not a hypocrite."

"You knew him?" Gonzalo asked, with surprise and a touch of fear.

"Fairly well." The woman's voice might have been bitter, or amused, or simply rueful. It was hard to tell. "He was a very valuable source of information."

"You mean he was a spy?" Gonzalo blurted out the words before he could stop himself. He grieved briefly for a man who had died trying to serve the Republic, and then he realized that pinning the guardia's murder on Viviana might be tremendously convenient for . . . someone. He shuddered slightly. No wonder they were interested in finding out who had killed Viviana.

"Not precisely," the woman said, still rueful. The man frowned at her, gesturing her to silence, and she shook her head. "What difference does it make, Andrés? He's dead." She turned back to Gonzalo. "Paco thought he was in love with me. A real hearts and flowers affair. It wasn't hard to get him to talk about his work. He was the type who didn't think that women really troubled their heads over wars and politics." She sighed, and her voice shook slightly as she added, "As I said, a stupid man. But honest enough, in a clumsy sort of way. We assumed he'd died for that."

"You think someone found out about his connection to you?" Gonzalo asked, his mind working rapidly.

"Yes." The woman nodded. "It made sense. He is—he was—from a prominent family. It would have been embarrassing to them for him to be court-martialed. We thought they'd decided on a quiet assassination but we didn't know if he'd told them anything first. He could have identified me . . . and a few other people."

"How did they find out?" Gonzalo asked.

"The idiot sent money." Juan had apparently decided that it could not hurt to tell Gonzalo more. "To his 'fiancée.'" Juan snorted, either in contempt or amusement. "Not that we didn't appreciate Burgos currency. But someone was sure to notice it sooner or later. And try to trace this 'Isabel' who was receiving the payments."

"'Isabel' seems to be a name that turns up a lot," Gonzalo remarked dryly.

Juan smiled. "It's a common name, comrade."

Gonzalo nodded and suddenly remembered something. "The smuggler I talked to said that Paco didn't care about money. He said he 'sent it all to some girl.' Would that have been you, too?"

The woman—Isabel, for lack of a better name—looked thoughtful. "Yes, in fact . . . oh, yes, that makes sense. About six months ago he started sending money. He said . . ." She closed her eyes. "Let me get it right. Something like: 'I have a little extra pay now. I'm not proud of what I'm doing to earn it, but I don't have any choice. So if it's of help to you, I'm glad.'"

Juan laughed. "So he turned to a life of crime to help support Isabel?" he said. "That's pretty rich."

"Or else someone figured out who 'Isabel' really was," Gonzalo suggested. "And blackmailed him."

"If he was being blackmailed he wouldn't have had spare cash," Juan pointed out.

Isabel shook her head. "No, I see what he means. If Paco only got involved with the smugglers because he was coerced, he wouldn't care about the money." Her face softened for a moment. "It would be typical of him to try to give it away, if he felt it wasn't rightfully his. Naturally, all that he'd inherit from his father was 'rightful' but this wouldn't be. That was how he thought."

"Would he keep sending you information? If he knew you were on the other side?" Gonzalo said.

Juan swore softly. "For six months, he could have been feeding us false information!"

"No." Isabel was positive. "I told you. He could never have been an agent. He was too . . . open. Too poor a liar. I don't mean he couldn't keep his mouth shut because he was good at that. But you always *knew* he was hiding something. You might not know what, but you'd know it was *something*."

"But how else could he be blackmailed?" Juan objected.

This time it was Isabel's turn to snort softly. "Someone probably threatened to tell his mother he was still in contact with me. She didn't approve of me. Starched old bitch. He was the one who made a big thing about keeping our letters clandestine, 'until my mother is won over,' to use his own words. The entire system was so complicated that I knew for sure it would go wrong. That's what I mean about how he'd have made a poor agent."

Juan was tapping his glasses nervously against the table. "That doesn't change anything, then. They would have cared more about a security risk than about black marketeering."

"Probably," Isabel agreed. She smiled briefly at Gonzalo. "At least, thanks to your chocolate seller, we know the smugglers thought his death was a coincidence."

"I'm glad to be of help," Gonzalo said dryly. "I don't suppose there's any chance of finding this sergeant for me, in exchange for my information?"

Juan shook his head. "Absolutely not. We can't let personal grudges get in the way of the cause."

Gonzalo knew that Juan was right. But it was hard to care more about a cause than about Viviana. He brooded as Isabel said, "I still wish we knew more about Paco's involvement with the black market. If he told someone outside the Guardia Civil. . . ."

Juan nodded. "We'll find out. But first we have to get *him* out of here." He turned to Gonzalo. "You'll have to stay underground a little longer. It takes time to get papers. We'll get you out of the city when we can."

Gonzalo felt the stirring of rebellion. He was a man, not a suspicious parcel to be handed quickly from one person to the next. He supposed it was only natural for these people not to trust him fully but he wished that they would not treat him like an infant, fit only to be passed passively from hand to mysterious hand.

"Let me try to find out about your Paco's involvement with the black market," he volunteered. "No one knows me as part of your group, and I can spend my time in Madrid doing something useful then."

The man and woman exchanged considering glances. "It's not a bad idea," Isabel said slowly. "It doesn't risk any of us, but. . . ."

"But," the bearded man agreed. He studied Gonzalo through narrowed eyes. "Are you a Party member?"

Gonzalo hesitated. The truth might well be the wrong answer to this question. And the wrong answer could be dangerous. He had been a Socialist before the war, and simply a carbinero for the duration. None of his hosts (Rescuers? Captors? What was the right name for them?) had volunteered an affiliation. "Worried I'm a Fifth Columnist?" he asked, as lightly as possible.

"That," the bearded man agreed, "or simply a loose cannon. We can't let you hare off to shoot guardias for the sake of some private vengeance."

Gonzalo took a chance. "My word as a Party member," he said quietly. "I won't do anything that's not for the good of the cause."

Juan (or Andrés) looked at him for a long moment. Then he took out the revolver and handed it to the woman. "I'll see if my superiors agree," he said, without taking his eyes from Gonzalo's. "You won't mind waiting here."

"Here?" Gonzalo asked, with a feeble attempt at humor. "Or in the closet again?"

"Here," the man replied, smiling slightly. He turned to Isabel. "Watch him."

She nodded, and Gonzalo felt his stomach clench. They were being very polite, and even kind, to risk helping him. But he was still little better than a prisoner. Juan (or Andrés) departed, and Gonzalo was left sitting across from Isabel. Her face was friendly, but she was still holding the gun, and he had no doubt that she would use it if he made any attempt to escape.

Gonzalo could think of nothing to say that would not be construed as a suspicious request for information. The woman was equally silent. He invented a dialogue between them. "So, where are you from?" Her inky black hair and pale, Celtic features suggested an imagined answer. "Galicia, along the coast." "I've heard it's very pretty there." "Yes, beautiful. You're from Madrid?" "Yes." "When did you join the Party?" The imaginary conversation stopped here. Gonzalo wondered if the bearded man would try to verify his claim that he was a Communist. I gave my word to them as a Party member, Gonzalo thought. But if I get the chance to meet this sergeant it won't be breaking my word. Not if I was never a member in the first place. If only I get the chance. . . .

"Would you like something to eat?" Isabel's voice broke in on his reverie.

"Please," Gonzalo said.

She smiled. "There should be something in the icebox."

He was puzzled and then saw that the gun was trained on him. Isabel might be trying to be kind, but she was taking no chances. After a long pause, he rose and headed toward the icebox in the corner.

There was some stale cornbread. He ate and offered some to her as well. She refused, but with an apologetic smile. He munched in peaceable silence. The kitchen was dim now, shadowed as the sun dropped behind the building that backed onto it.

There was a sound of tramping feet, and it occurred to Gonzalo that the unsteady stairway leading down to the basement provided an excellent warning system. The gun had disappeared under the table and the woman's veil was slid over her face before he heard a knock at the door.

"Who's there?"

"Andrés, with news of Isabel."

The door opened, and Gonzalo's bearded guide reappeared. "All safe and sound here?" he asked.

Gonzalo nodded, too tense to say anything further.

"All right, then." The man came and sat beside him. "The others like your idea. Let's call it a way of paying for your documents."

"My pleasure." Gonzalo relaxed slightly.

"Good." The man looked at Isabel. "You want to meet at the usual place?"

She nodded and slid the revolver out from its hiding place, leaving it lying on the table. Then she stood and gathered her coat. At the doorway she turned. "Good-bye, Gonzalo. Good luck."

The man waited until the door had closed behind her and her footsteps on the stairs had died away. Then he leaned toward Gonzalo. "All right," he said in a low voice. "Here's the deal."

Chapter 19

Tejada was on his way to find food for Alejandra when Lieutenant Ramos intercepted him. "Tejada! Why are you still in that getup? Corporal Torres is waiting."

The sergeant began an explanation, but Ramos was in no mood to listen. "Look, you said you'd find the brat's mother and get rid of her. You can't spend the afternoon baby-sitting."

"But, sir," Tejada protested. "I think if I have just a little more time with Alejandra . . ."

"You're scheduled for patrol in five minutes," Ramos interrupted. "And you're out of uniform."

"But, sir," Tejada insisted. "If I can just give her lunch, she'll talk to me."

"Absolutely not!" the lieutenant said firmly. "The girl was one thing—and don't think I was fooled by that cousin nonsense for a minute, by the way—but you are not wasting our rations as a bribe for some Red brat."

Tejada breathed through his nostrils and suppressed the urge to take exception to his commander's tone when referring to Elena. "Sir," he began, hoping his voice was neutral. "If I—"

"Four minutes to be in uniform, Sergeant." Ramos's tone was final.

Tejada capitulated. At least, he thought, Ramos had not insisted that he drop off Alejandra at Cuatro Caminos that same afternoon. The child could wait. He met Corporal Torres within the designated four minutes, and the two of them set off.

Normally, Tejada rather liked foot patrol. The slow steady tramp gave him time to think. But today he dreaded being alone with his thoughts. How could Paco have gotten involved in the black market? The question was insistent, and painful. Paco could not have voluntarily allied himself with traitors and criminals. He would not have taken food from his own post to sell. Not willingly and cynically. Paco was never cynical, Tejada thought. I joined the movement because I saw what the Reds were capable of, and I knew they had to be stopped. But Paco joined because he believed. In a new, better world. I never believed like that. Somewhere at the back of the locked filing cabinet of his unconscious the sergeant knew that he was lying to himself. He *had* believed in the Movement. He had not merely wrapped himself in the glow of his friend's passionate conviction. But somehow his own certainties had gone. Perhaps they had been slowly flaking away like the edges of yellowing newsprint. Perhaps they had been shredded when Elena explained why Viviana had gone to fetch Alejandra's notebook and he had realized that he had killed a woman guilty of nothing more than trying to care for her niece. Perhaps they had disappeared the moment he had kissed Elena, terrified of what she might reveal and of his own awareness that he would take no action against her no matter what she said. But I haven't changed that much, Tejada told himself. And Paco wouldn't have changed that much. Paco *couldn't* have changed that much. He thought about the photograph of the smiling girl. How well did you ever know Paco? a voice in his head asked treacherously. As well as you knew Elena when you thought she was a spy because she wouldn't let you take her home? Or as well as Elena knew you when she said she assumed you weren't guilty of murder? Do you *know* that he believed in the Movement the same way you *knew* that damn miliciana had killed him?

Corporal Torres, who had been paired with Tejada before, was accustomed to the sergeant's taciturn ways. The two men were not friends, but they liked patrolling together. Their paces matched well, and they generally preserved a companionable silence while each pursued his own thoughts. In the normal course of things, Torres, who was himself an expert sharpshooter, scanned the upper windows with suspicion, while Tejada kept an eye on things at ground level. So Torres was surprised when the sergeant said suddenly, "Why did you join the Guardia, Corporal?"

"My father's a guardia, sir," Torres answered, wondering why the sergeant was interested.

"Was that all?" Tejada asked, disappointed. Surely other men joined the Guardia because they believed in . . . something. Something that they could explain to him, as a reminder.

"All?" Torres was somewhat offended. "It's a family tradition, sir."

"Of course." Tejada lapsed into silence again. He and Paco had been friends because they were not merely following a family tradition. Because each had understood that the other believed in something. So why did Paco get involved with the black market? Tejada could find no answer to the question, but he remained positive that it had not been Paco's own doing.

The two guardias civiles passed through the Plaza Mayor and headed southward. Near the Cathedral of San Isidro, a pair of priests nodded to them and saluted. Torres nodded back and gave a deferential greeting. Tejada nodded also, but said nothing. Confession tomorrow, he thought miserably. Elena . . . oh, God. Please let the priest be sympathetic.

The Plaza de la Cebada was crowded with people. Many of them seemed to be peasants who had come into the city for the holiday, perhaps to go to church. But Tejada noticed bitterly that they slipped away from the guardias civiles with the same furtiveness as the madrileños. At least they were not the only guardias in the square. Another pair of uniformed figures were orbiting the plaza in the opposite direction. And, Tejada realized with some surprise, a third guardia was crossing the plaza ahead of them, apparently unaccompanied. Off duty, the sergeant thought automatically, noting the absence of a three-cornered hat and the slouching posture with some disapproval all the same. And something about the slouch was familiar. He slowed down, watching the man, and Torres, who recognized the sudden change of pace as an alert, brought his attention back from the cornices of the roofs, and tried to follow his partner's gaze.

"Smugglers, sir?" Torres asked, without moving his lips.

"What?" Tejada spoke softly, without turning his head. "What makes you say that?"

"We're at the Plaza de la Cebada, you know, sir."

Tejada gave himself a mental kick. He did know. Everyone knew the rumors about the plaza. And here he was, watching a thin, stooping guardia who was behaving suspiciously. He imperceptibly changed course, crossing the square more directly to intercept the guardia, and Torres followed him. The man with the sloping shoulders was moving quickly though, and although the crowds cleared a path for the two of them, breaking into a run would have warned their prey.

"Torres," Tejada said quietly. "Alert the others."

"Yes, sir." Torres had already begun veering toward them.

The crowd shifted, and Tejada caught another brief glimpse of the rapidly moving lone guardia. He was closer now, and Tejada remembered where he had seen those sloping shoulders before. It was Sergeant de Rota, Paco's partner. The man who reported him missing, Tejada thought. And the one who tried to convince me that Paco was engaged in the black market. He picked up his pace. Paco must have been forced into it, Tejada thought grimly. And who'd be in a better position to do so than a superior officer? Bastard! But Paco wouldn't have gone along even if he was ordered. They must have had something to twist his arm with. And when I get my hands on Rota he's going to tell me *exactly* what it was.

Tejada glanced across the square. Corporal Torres had signaled the guardias from the other post. They were converging on a point a little ahead of Sergeant de Rota at a deceptively rapid pace. Rota had almost reached an archway leading off the square. Torres and the two other guardias disappeared into it just ahead of him. Tejada saw Rota pause and smiled in triumph. He reached for his pistol.

"Guardia Civil! Hands over your head!" To Tejada's chagrin, the cry came from within the archway. Two civilians, their hands raised high, came stumbling out followed by Torres and the two men he had enlisted.

Before Tejada could figure out what had happened, Rota stepped forward and saluted the three guardias civiles. "Good work, men. Do you need help with them?"

"No, sir." It was one of the strange guardias. "It's just these two."

"Excellent. Since I'm off duty, then. . . ."

"Very good, Sergeant."

Tejada opened his mouth to protest but Rota had already stepped past the guardias civiles and through the archway. By the time Tejada arrived, Rota had disappeared down one of the innumerable winding alleys that led from it.

"What are you doing?" Tejada demanded, as Corporal Torres and one of the strange guardias handcuffed the prisoners.

"The corporal told us you were looking for smugglers, sir." It was the other strange guardia.

"You have a good eye, sir," Torres added appreciatively. "I wouldn't have noticed the archway. But we've got them, dead to rights. Look in the suitcases."

The sergeant realized that berating the men would be both unfair and unwise, especially in front of the prisoners. There was no way for Torres to know that he had mistaken Tejada's target. Inwardly furious, Tejada bent to open the suitcases.

"My God!" One of the strange guardias leaned over his shoulder and inspected the contents. "Coffee! You think it's real? And look, canned milk, too! Is this stuff evidence, sir? I mean, do we take it, or . . . or what?" he finished, trying not to sound hopeful.

"It's yours if you want it, gentlemen," one of the prisoners broke in.

Tejada looked up at the man and raised his eyebrows. "Are you offering us a bribe?"

"No," said the more intelligent prisoner hastily, after glancing at the sergeant's face. "No, of course not, Officer."

"Chocolate," said one of the guardias dreamily, looking at the contents of the suitcase. He encountered Tejada's glare and added rapidly, "Evidence, sir, of course."

Tejada's one concern was to get back to the post as fast as possible. Sergeant de Rota had escaped for the time being. But the smugglers might be induced to name him if he was their contact. And even if he was not, it was worth reporting the man's suspicious behavior to Captain Morales. The captain had struck Tejada as a careful officer. Even without further evidence, he might set a watch on Rota. It occurred to Tejada that these prisoners provided an excellent reason to return to the post and question Alejandra as well. She must have received some impression of the man who killed Paco, Tejada thought optimistically. Thin, sloping shoulders, a slouch . . . I can ask. Biting back his irritation at Rota's escape, the sergeant gave orders to return to the post.

The two guardias from the Cuatro Caminos post readily agreed to accompany their colleagues and the evidence of smuggling. The walk back to the post was a quiet one. Guardias Díaz and Soriano were occupied in escorting the prisoners and speculating on what would become of the seized goods. Corporal Torres was wondering why Sergeant Tejada did not seem better pleased. Tejada was wishing that the party could travel faster.

Lieutenant Ramos was initially annoyed to see Tejada return early, but his irritation soon disappeared. He heard the formal report of the four guardias and then dismissed all of them but Tejada. "Well, Sergeant," he said, when the door had closed. "Do you think these are the men who have been receiving our supplies?"

Tejada paused before answering. "They might be, sir," he said. "But I'm not sure."

Ramos frowned. "Then why did you single them out? Do you think they have information?"

"It's possible." Tejada considered how best to admit that the men had in fact been arrested almost by accident. He could think of no way to do so without sounding incompetent. "But actually there was a slight miscommunication between Corporal Torres and me." He took a deep breath and then told his commander his version of their afternoon arrests.

Ramos shook his head when Tejada had finished. "Next time, make sure you make your target clear."

"Yes, sir."

"But I don't think there's any harm done," the lieutenant went on encouragingly. "You say that this Rota wasn't actually engaged in any criminal activity."

Tejada paused. He had been positive that there was something suspicious about Rota, but crossing a plaza while off duty wasn't a crime. "He *looked* suspicious, sir," he said, aware that it was a weak argument. "And he avoided assisting us with the smugglers."

"He did give a reason," the lieutenant pointed out.

"Well, yes," Tejada admitted. "But . . . well, he didn't acknowledge us at first."

"Weren't you trying to hide from him?" Ramos asked.

Tejada had to admit that the lieutenant had a point. "I suppose. But there was a *feeling* that something was wrong, sir. It's hard to quantify. But I was positive."

Ramos sighed. "I'm not saying there's no such thing as a hunch. But the man's an officer, Tejada. And it's a serious charge to level at someone of that rank with no proof."

"But there wouldn't need to be a formal charge, sir. If you could just alert Captain Morales informally, I'm sure that he'd take the necessary steps."

"How would you feel if someone informally alerted me about you?" Ramos demanded.

"No one would!" Tejada said, annoyed. "Because there's nothing to alert you about! I'm not making this up, sir. He disappeared too fast. No greeting. Nothing. It was suspicious."

"I'm not arguing," Ramos said. "But I can't call a superior officer and tell him that my sergeant thinks one of his men lacks social graces. If you just had something, Tejada . . . *any*thing more than just a feeling. Did he stop to speak to anyone in the square? Was he carrying any packages?"

For a moment, Tejada was tempted to invent a suspicious circumstance. Then he shook his head. "No, sir. I'm sorry, sir."

"Me, too," said the lieutenant. "But maybe it isn't a wasted effort. Talk to the prisoners. If they've got cans in their suitcases, they're not just running the small stuff. Try to find out about their supplier."

"Yes, sir." Tejada saluted. "Is there an unoccupied interrogation room, sir?"

The lieutenant snorted. "We're in a fucking dormitory, Tejada. What do you want, the Alcázar de Toledo?"

"Very good, sir," Tejada said, correctly interpreting this reply as a no. "Please inform me when a room becomes available."

"I will. Dismissed."

Tejada turned on his heel and left, wondering how he could persuade the prisoners to implicate Sergeant de Rota. After a moment's thought, he went to his room and checked the post duty roster. He was in luck. Guardia Eduardo Meléndez was on duty, but not scheduled for patrol. He found Meléndez on guard outside the makeshift prison. The guardia pulled himself to attention at the sight of Tejada.

"Sir!" Meléndez saluted.

Tejada looked measuringly at the salute. Meléndez's outstretched fingertips were barely within his reach. Guardia Meléndez was perhaps four inches taller than the sergeant and at least fifty pounds heavier. As a general rule, the sergeant preferred doing his own physical persuasion. But he was in a hurry, and Meléndez's presence during interrogations was known to be effective. "You know that a pair of smugglers were brought in this afternoon by Corporal Torres?" he asked.

"Yes, sir."

"I'm going to want to speak with them. I'd appreciate your assistance, Guardia."

"At your orders, Sergeant. Do you want me to warm them up a little first?"

Tejada considered. "Nothing too serious. I want them conscious and coherent. Start with one, maybe, and let the other stick around."

"Yes, sir. I know how it's done, sir."

"Excellent. I'll send for you when I'm ready for the first one."

"Yes, sir."

Unfortunately, the room Ramos provided had a window giving onto a courtyard, but Tejada drew the blinds and hoped for the best. He sent for the first smuggler within fifteen minutes of his meeting with Meléndez. When the man was shepherded into the room, he had a trickle of blood at one corner of his mouth, and appeared to be walking with some difficulty.

"Sit down," Tejada said. "I have a couple of questions."
Guardia Meléndez reinforced the command by leaning on the
prisoner's shoulders until he sat on the chair in front of the table.

Tejada picked up a notepad that had been lying on the table
and perched comfortably on the edge, looming over the prisoner. "Smuggling's a serious offense, you know," he said.

The man was silent. Meléndez cuffed the back of his head
lightly. "Answer the sergeant."

"Yes, sir, I know." The prisoner's voice was indistinct.

"I imagine this isn't a first offense, either," Tejada continued. "And I wonder what we'd find if we looked at your war
record."

"It's a first offense, sir," the prisoner said pleadingly.

"Of course," the sergeant said, "we could just put you up
against a wall and be done with it. And that might be simplest.
But I'd like to know who your suppliers are."

The prisoner looked slightly nauseous. "I—I don't know
who they are, sir."

"Such loyalty!" Tejada mused, shaking his head. "Honor
among thieves, would you say, Guardia?" He set down the pad,
leaned forward, and casually backhanded the prisoner, deliberately choosing the side that Meléndez had already hit. "Don't
lie to me."

"I-I'm not lying." There was a sob in the man's voice. "I've
never seen them. . . . Ow! . . . Oh, God . . . they'll kill me."

"So will I," Tejada said coolly. "And if you don't cooperate,
believe me, I'll take my time about it."

"I can't tell you." The sob was more pronounced now.
Tejada hit the other side of the man's mouth. "I *can't* tell you."

Half an hour later there was blood on the floor and the
sergeant's knuckles were starting to get sore. He knew that
patience was the key to successful interrogation but he was not
enjoying himself and he was more interested in confirmation
than information. He took a risk. "Why are you so frightened

of them?" he asked, switching questions. "Have they killed someone before?"

There were a few sobbing breaths, and then a defeated half-nod from the prisoner.

"Who?" Tejada took a firm grip on his excitement. Calm, he thought. Don't betray interest. Just keep calm.

The prisoner mumbled something. "Speak up," Tejada commanded sharply.

"An associate," the man repeated dully. "He tried to rat on them."

"A guardia civil?" The question slipped out before the sergeant could think better of it.

"No." The man shook his head. "No, just one of us." He looked up through puffy eyes and squinted at Tejada. "I . . . oh, God! Is this about that again?"

Tejada glanced over the prisoner's head at Meléndez, surprised. Meléndez shrugged in puzzlement. "Maybe," Tejada said, hoping that the answer hid his confusion. Again? he thought. Someone else has been asking questions? "It depends what 'that' is."

"Oh, shit." The man's voice was a groan. "About Paco. I told the truth before, you know."

"Told the truth to whom?" Tejada asked.

The prisoner said, "Look," in a voice that tried to be calculating but sounded pleading, "if I tell you what I know about Paco—about who was asking for him and everything—will you give me a chance? Please?"

"I'm listening," Tejada said, as neutrally as possible.

"I thought Paco was killed by a Red." The words were a mumble, partly because some of the prisoner's teeth were missing. "But then, this guy came—he pretended to be a customer—and he wanted to know all about Paco, and about the sniper who killed him, and about what had happened to the sniper."

"And you told him?" Tejada asked, scribbling notes furiously.

"He had a gun," the prisoner explained. "And I thought he might be a guardia. But what he was really interested in was who killed the sniper. Then he pulled a fast one and took off, and that's not like a guardia. And I thought maybe he was a Red too. But you're guardias, and now you want to know about Paco as well so . . ." He trailed off, sounding despairing.

Tejada had intended to work his way toward Sergeant de Rota, but the prisoner's information intrigued him. If someone else was asking questions about Paco's death, then perhaps Paco had in fact been killed by the Reds. Or perhaps someone was being clever, the way someone had been clever about the rations, and was trying to shift blame. "Tell me *exactly* how you met this man, and what he asked you, and what you told him," he commanded.

It was a long and tearful story, broken frequently by pleas and curses from the prisoner. But Tejada finally gathered that the unknown questioner had shown a surprising interest first in the sniper who had supposedly killed Paco, and then in the identity of the guardias who had been on the scene first. If someone's looking for me, he thought, it's because of the missing rations. . . . They know that I'm investigating that. But that's a funny way to identify me. Unless they really are interested in the sniper. . . . Alejandra's aunt, what was her name . . . Viviana. Who would be interested in her, unless she somehow was related to the black market? He needed time to think but he also knew that to relax his pressure on the prisoner would be fatal. "Tell me about your supplier," he ordered, returning to his original question, because he could think of no other one.

"I can't."

Thwack. "Give me a name." Tejada flexed his fingers surreptitiously. They felt bruised. He was severely tempted to turn the interrogation over to Meléndez and go somewhere quiet to let his hands recover and think over the information about Paco, but persistence was key. "A name," he repeated.

"Diego."

Tejada remembered the memo Lieutenant Ramos had shown him a few days earlier. ". . . *His partner, Sgt. Diego de Rota, reported him missing . . .*" He took a deep breath. "Surname."

"I don't know."

Thwack. "Surname."

"Báez. Diego Báez."

Tejada wished that he had had more experience with interrogation. He had come so close to getting information pointing to Sergeant de Rota. I'm an idiot, he thought. If I hadn't pushed, I could have gone to Ramos with just the given name. Of course, he could be lying. He tried to inspect the prisoner. The man's face was a bloody mess, so his expression was difficult to read. More experienced men presumably had a feel for when prisoners were telling the truth.

"Where can I find him?" Tejada asked, because that seemed like the next logical question.

The prisoner was silent. "In your own time, Guardia," Tejada said, nodding at Meléndez.

Watching Meléndez work was not pleasant but Tejada had to admit that he was effective. Within an hour, he had gathered that Diego Báez was an intermediary who received illegal merchandise from persons whom the prisoner insisted were unknown and passed it along. The prisoner maintained that he did not know where Báez was to be found but he admitted that he and his colleague were scheduled to meet with the mysterious Diego on Sunday afternoon at the grave of one Maria Dolores Torrecilla in the Eastern Cemetery. Tejada, judging that he had obtained all the information he was going to get, sent the exhausted man back to his cell.

When Meléndez and the prisoner had left, Tejada inspected his notes, meditatively sucking at one knuckle. He tasted blood and wondered absently if it was the prisoner's or if he had grazed his own hands. Lieutenant Ramos would probably be pleased to hear about Diego Báez. He would almost certainly be pleased if the guardia succeeded in capturing Báez on Sunday. It briefly occurred to Tejada that finding guardias willing to work over Easter would be something of a challenge. He decided that the ever-enthusiastic Jiménez would be a necessary addition to the party. But the information he had obtained was enigmatic. Is someone looking for me? he wondered. And why? Does it have to do with Alejandra's aunt? Idly, he doodled the dead miliciana's name on the pad. Viviana Llorente. The sister of Carmen Llorente, who was being held at Cuatro Caminos, in connection with the disappearance of her brother. Her brother Gonzalo, Tejada thought slowly, who is a Red. Who's been in hiding. Who might want to know who killed his sister. Gonzalo Llorente.

Tejada filed the name for future reference. Finding a former Republican soldier was a low priority, compared with locating the man stealing rations from the post. But Tejada reflected comfortably that if it ever became imperative to capture Gonzalo Llorente, he knew the perfect bait to use. After a moment's thought, he rose, and for the second time that day went in search of food for Llorente's niece.

A little knot of excited guardias drew Tejada's attention as he passed the cafeteria. They were clustered around one of the tables, apparently examining something. Snatches of conversation floated through the open doorway. "You shouldn't . . . not during Lent."

"Listen, Your Holiness, I haven't had a decent smoke in six months and these are the real thing."

"He's right. You could wait 'til after Easter."

"Screw you. You wouldn't be so holier-than-thou if it was a girl."

"What are '*bis-cu-its*'?"

"What are what? Oh, my God, *biscuits*. English butter cookies."

Tejada stepped into the room and raised his voice. "Has something exciting occurred?"

The conversations died, and a ring of sheepish guardias turned to face him. "Err . . . no, Sergeant. It's nothing," one of the younger men ventured.

"What's on the table?" Tejada asked mildly, noting that the guardias seemed to have bunched in front of one table as if to obscure his view. He recognized one of them. "Durán? Can you explain this?"

"Errr . . . we heard you'd captured a pair of smugglers, Sergeant," Durán gulped. "Guardia Soriano was just telling us about your your initiative, sir. About how sharp-eyed of you it was to spot them. And showing us the . . . the evidence, sir."

"Showing you?" Tejada raised his eyebrows. "It sounded as if there was a full-scale auction in progress."

Durán gulped again. "Surely, it's better than the Reds getting it, sir. And . . . and . . . well, I mean, there's Gauloises and everything."

"He'd sell his mother for a pack of Gauloises." The voice from the back of the crowd was indistinct.

Durán turned, indignant. "I didn't notice you offering to share any!"

The little group dissolved into recriminations. Tejada thought for a moment, wondering how literally true the statement "He'd sell his mother" might be. "I haven't spoken to Lieutenant Ramos about what to do with the seized goods," he said, raising his voice to make himself heard. "You understand that until it's been inventoried, no one has any claim to it."

There was a general sheepish mumble of "Yes, sir."

"However," Tejada went on, "two suitcases were seized. I imagine that one will be sufficient as evidence, provided that it is full and contains samples of every item found."

"Yes, sir!" The chorus was more enthusiastic this time.

Tejada stepped forward, and the group parted to let him see what was on the table. As he had expected, a suitcase was lying open, with its contents strewn about. The guardias quickly turned their attention back to the forbidden luxury goods, and negotiations resumed. Tejada picked up the brightly colored tin marked BISCUITS. There was stiff competition for the chocolate, and men would probably come to blows over the cigarettes and coffee before too long, but no one seemed to covet the little metal box particularly. He weighed it in his hand for a moment, considering. He had never been part of anything remotely illegal before. But he had loved English cookies as a child . . . *he'd sell his mother.* "Is anyone especially fond of these things?" he asked, holding up the tin.

The guardias briefly returned their attention to him, and then there was a general shaking of heads. "In that case . . ." The sergeant tucked the tin under his arm and made a discreet exit, leaving a favorable impression among the guardias.

"I thought we were in trouble there for a minute," Soriano commented.

"Nahh," one of the Manzanares post hastened to reassure him. "The sergeant's all right. He could have scooped everything, you know, or made us give up the cigarettes. But he's a gentleman."

"I wonder if he likes those cookie things? *Bis-cu-its*," said Durán thoughtfully.

Tejada headed for the infirmary. I won't ask, he told himself. I'll just offer them to her. And then maybe she'll *want* to tell me. To his surprise, he found Guardia Jiménez sitting by Alejandra's bedside, singing to her: "*Heaven, I'm in heaven/and the cares that hung around me through the week/seem to vanish, like a gambler's lucky streak . . .*" The young man stopped singing as Tejada approached. Alejandra, who had been sitting up in bed and smiling, slumped and regarded Tejada with wary eyes.

"Hello, sir," Jiménez said easily. "I've been trying to keep Aleja entertained."

"That's very kind of you, Guardia," Tejada said, bemused. "I didn't know you knew English," he added.

Jiménez smiled, flattered. "I don't really, sir. Just songs from the movies. And I saw *Top Hat* again, while I was on leave."

"Oh." Tejada nodded vaguely. He was aware of the existence of movies, but they were not a form of entertainment that had ever appealed to him.

"Listen, sir." Jiménez rose and dropped his voice, slightly. "I've found something out, I think. Aleja . . . her full name's Alejandra Palomino."

"Yes." Tejada nodded. "So?"

"So"—Jiménez cast another glance at the girl, who was sitting up and watching them closely—"I thought it sounded familiar, sir. And then I remembered. That was the name on that notebook we found last week. By the"—he glanced at Aleja again—"you know."

"I know," Tejada said dryly. "But it's an admirable deduction, Jiménez."

"I gave her her notebook back, sir." Jiménez seemed rather deflated. "I hope there wasn't anything wrong with that. But it was in Lieutenant Ramos's office, and he said to take it and . . . er . . . get it and the brat out of there, so . . . ."

"It's fine," Tejada said impatiently. "Was there anything else?"

"No." Jiménez was worried. Perhaps he had done something wrong and Tejada was too kind to say so. He justified himself by adding, a bit nervously, "That's how I found out that Aleja likes the movies, too. From that picture."

"What picture?" Tejada asked, startled.

"This one, sir. You must have stuck it in her notebook without thinking." Jiménez held out a little white square, anxious to please. "Aleja wanted to keep it but I said that it must be yours."

Tejada automatically took the photograph he was offered and looked down at the snapshot of Paco's Isabel. "What does this have to do with the movies?" he asked, feeling stupid.

"You don't recognize her, sir?" Jiménez said, a little disappointed at his idol's lapse from omniscience. "It's Ginger Rogers. The American actress."

Chapter 20

The long, cruel winter fought its last battle that weekend, and the bells that rang out on Easter morning clanged through air cold enough for madrileños to see their breath. Gonzalo, strolling toward the Eastern Cemetery, kept his hands buried in his pockets and wished that the weather had tempted more people outside. His cold fingers slipped around the slick-coated passport buried in one pocket: "José Hernández Ibañez. Date of birth: April 23, 1914. Place of birth: Illescas, province of Madrid." The passport slid away from his fingers, and a few pieces of paper crackled. He did not draw them out. He already knew their contents by heart. One was a handwritten note from María José Hernández, begging her dearest and best-beloved brother to make as much haste as possible to Navarra, where their poor mother, who had been taken ill, wanted desperately to see her son before she died. The other was an official permission to travel, which looked very impressive to Gonzalo, although the bearded Juan/Andrés had warned him not to let anyone examine it too closely.

José, Gonzalo thought to himself firmly. José. He and his mentors had spent Saturday practicing in the dimly lit kitchen. Long hours of casual conversation and always at an unexpected moment. "What do you think, José?" "Isn't that right, José?" Isabel and Juan had taken turns stepping out of the room and calling, at random moments, "José! Come quickly!" Perhaps because of his nervousness, and perhaps because the situation was in fact funny, Gonzalo had been unable to answer to the name "José" without grinning broadly the first few times. His coaches had been strict with him, though. He had gotten reasonably quick at responding to the new name.

Then they had rehearsed his story. Juan had put on his glasses and folded his arms across his chest. "May I see your papers, please? And where are you heading, Señor Hernández? No, no, José, don't offer to show your papers too quickly. They'll see you're nervous. Just answer the questions. Now, try it again. What business do you have in Navarra, Señor Hernández?"

It had been an entertaining way to pass the time. On Friday evening, Juan had returned with the news that Gonzalo's documents would not be ready until Easter. "That's fine, though," the bearded man had reassured Gonzalo. "Because it means you'll get to do some nosing around, to find out what Paco was doing in the black market."

"How?" Gonzalo had asked.

"Do you remember when . . . the other comrade asked if you'd ever heard of Diego Báez?" Juan had asked.

Gonzalo had nodded. All of his memories of the tense moments when Juan had stuck a gun in his back were very clear.

"Báez is a middleman," the bearded Communist had continued, satisfied at the wordless response. "The Fascists are too smart to deal directly." He spoke with a touch of regret. "We think this Báez knows who the guardias are who are involved and who the smugglers are. He takes a cut from both sides. They pay him for anonymity."

"Sounds like a dangerous job," Gonzalo had commented.

"Some people will do anything for money," the Communist sneered, with the fine scorn of someone who would do anything for a cause.

"How do I find him?" Gonzalo asked.

The bearded man (whom Gonzalo continued to think of as Juan) had tapped his glasses on the table, a nervous gesture the carbinero was beginning to recognize. "That part might be difficult. But we think that Báez is scheduled to meet with some of his distributors on Sunday."

"An Easter egg hunt?" Gonzalo asked dryly.

"Exactly," the other grinned. "At the Eastern Cemetery. But we don't know what time."

"I can't haunt a cemetery all day!" Gonzalo had protested. "I'll be spotted for sure."

"Why not? You're visiting your sainted mother's grave on Easter. Or you could just say you're checking to see if any of the dead have risen."

"For Christ's sake, Juan—"

"Exactly."

So Gonzalo, as José Hernández, was strolling toward the cemetery as the Easter bells tolled their joyful greeting that morning. His documents were in his coat pocket, for easy access. In the pocket of his shirt, hopefully secure from pickpockets, was a thick roll of bills—not the useless paper Carmen had given him, but a small fortune in Burgos currency.

"Let's call it Paco's last contribution to the cause," Juan had said the previous evening with a brief grin, as he handed it over to Gonzalo. "Use this to get whatever information you need. Oh, and José—"

Gonzalo blinked for a moment, and then managed to say, "Yes?"

"No funny business with guns this time. It won't work. According to our sources, Báez has close links to the Guardia Civil. He's tough."

So Gonzalo was unarmed. His hands clutched the passport again. He reached the main entrance to the cemetery, and strolled south, looking for the grave of María Dolores Torrecilla.

The newer section of the cemetery was crammed with identical, unadorned graves. The older part, up ahead, was full of smashed angels, and chipped headstones. He hurried past the new graves, with their grimly similar epitaphs: 1910–1936. 1915–1937. 1920–1938. FELL SERVING THE REPUBLIC. Gonzalo had rather liked cemeteries before the war. Now he had too many acquaintances in them. He winced each time a face attached itself to one of the names on the tombstones. Most of them had no flowers in remembrance, even today. It was dangerous to publicly mourn the soldiers of the Republic. He reached the elaborate pre-war tombs with relief. María Dolores Torrecilla's was deserted when he found it but directly opposite, a pair of proud families (perhaps rivals, in some distant past), had erected little family mausoleums, complete with doors to the niches within. One of the doors had been partially destroyed, either by accident, or through the zealous efforts of some anti-clerical madrileño. Gonzalo glanced around, and then stepped into the semidarkness and settled down below the statue of the Virgin to wait.

The cold of the marble seeped through his clothes, making his back ache, but gradually the spot where he was sitting warmed, and when he tried to shift his position some while later, he realized that the rest of the slab was icy in comparison. But the mausoleum was almost too good a hiding place. No one could see him, but he could not see anyone either. He would have to rely on his ears and hope that Báez or his compatriots made some sound to alert him. He strained to hear. Once in a great while he caught the clatter of wheels on cobblestones but few vehicles were out and about on Easter. The sounds of distant churchbells were clearer. They began muted and swelled to a climax as he waited. *Alleluia, alleluia.* The cacophonous clangs thundered through the cemetery with arrogant joy. God is risen again in Spain, now and forever. *Alleluia.* Gonzalo shivered in his hiding place and wondered if he would hear Báez's footsteps over the sound of the bells.

It was nearly noon, and the Easter mass was over when Gonzalo became aware that someone else was in the graveyard. It was not footsteps that alerted him but the sharp smell of pipe smoke. He risked a glance out of his hiding place. There was nothing to the left, but to the right, among the slabs near the entrance, a man in a gray-green trench coat was strolling along the path. He wore gloves and a scarf that partially covered his face.

Gonzalo took a deep breath and stepped out of the mausoleum. The man had paused in front of one of the graves and removed his hat. He seemed to be reading the inscription, lost in thought. Gonzalo walked toward him, trying to look like a mourner while surreptitiously observing the newcomer. "Dark," Juan had said. "Maybe five seven, five eight. And well fed, the bastard." The description could have fit many people. It fit the solitary mourner. It was the man's corpulence that decided Gonzalo. He cleared his throat. "Good morning, sir," he said as he raised his hat, hoping he sounded casual.

The man looked up. "Good morning." He sounded mildly surprised. "Happy Easter."

"And to you."

"Thank you." The man nodded and returned his attention to the unembellished grave.

Gonzalo wondered wildly how to continue the conversation without betraying himself or scaring off Báez—if it was Báez. "Fine day," he commented.

"Yes."

"But a bit cold."

The other nodded without replying.

"What brings you out here today then?" Gonzalo asked awkwardly, rapidly concocting a story about a promise to a dying grandfather to visit a grave every Easter, in the event that the unknown man asked him a similar question.

The man shrugged. "Personal reasons."

"Of course." Gonzalo hesitated. "Are you from around here?"

The man turned to face Gonzalo and raised his eyebrows. "Because," Gonzalo continued desperately, "if you are, I wonder if you might know a friend of mine. By the name of Báez."

The eyebrows contracted into a frown. "I might. What's your friend's first name?"

Gonzalo licked his lips. "Diego."

There was a long pause while the wind whistled loudly and Gonzalo grew acutely aware that he was defenseless. Then the man said, "What do you want with Diego Báez?"

"Information," Gonzalo said quietly. "He might know some things I want to find out."

The man was still frowning as he said, "I know Diego, a little. But he's pretty close mouthed. What makes you think he'll tell a stranger anything?"

The man emphasized the word *stranger* slightly, and Gonzalo noted that his claim of knowing Báez had been neatly discounted. He hesitated, and then took the plunge. "I might be able to make it worth his while."

"He stays in business by keeping his mouth shut," the man pointed out.

"This wouldn't hurt him," Gonzalo replied carefully. "And the pay is good."

The man glanced around, and then took a step closer to Gonzalo. "What are you interested in?"

Gonzalo felt a certain relief that the preliminary fencing was over. "A guardia civil named Paco López," he said softly. "He was killed a little over a week ago. How was he connected with the black market?"

"And who wants to know?"

It was Gonzalo's turn to keep silent and raise his eyebrows. The man shrugged and smiled slightly, tacitly admitting that this was an inappropriate question. "I have nothing to do with murder," he said flatly. It was not a completely convincing statement.

"I didn't say you did," Gonzalo replied evenly. "López's murder doesn't matter. I need to know who he was working with."

"And you're telling me this wouldn't shut my business down?" Báez shook his head, and half-turned away, as if to go. "Sorry."

"Two hundred pesetas," Gonzalo said quietly. He remembered the way Juan and Isabel had spoken mysteriously of "us." "We don't want to compete," he added. "We'd just like to know how he got involved, and when."

Báez turned back. "That's all?"

"Yes."

"No names?"

Gonzalo hesitated, and then nodded.

"For two hundred pesetas?"

Gonzalo nodded again.

"Make it three hundred."

Gonzalo, who had five hundred pesetas in his breast pocket, opened his mouth to agree, and then remembered that seeming too eager might be a bad idea. "Two fifty," he said.

For form's sake, Gonzalo allowed himself to be bargained up to two hundred and seventy-five. Báez seemed to be in a hurry, glancing at his watch frequently as they spoke.

"All right," he said quietly. "Paco got involved six months ago. He was brought in by someone else, as a messenger. I don't know details. Now give me the money and beat it. I've got another appointment."

"Who recruited him?"

"You said no names."

Gonzalo cursed mentally. "Three hundred pesetas," he said aloud.

One of Báez's gloved hands went to the pocket of his coat and for a moment Gonzalo wished fervently for a weapon. Then the hand emerged again, gripping a pencil and a scrap of paper. "Here." Báez bent over the marble slab, and leaned the paper against it to scribble something. "Call this number if you want more information." He smiled suddenly. "Just ask for Paco's boss. You'll get him."

"Thanks." Gonzalo took the scrap of paper and folded it with fingers made clumsy by the cold. He reached inside his coat and tucked the phone number into his breast pocket. Then he drew out the roll of bills. Báez watched avidly as Gonzalo counted out the twenty peseta notes.

"A pleasure doing business with you," Báez said. He smiled again, as if something amused him. "Now, if you'll allow me to say so, I don't think graveyards are very healthy places."

"I couldn't agree more." The voice came from behind the two men.

Gonzalo jumped, startled nearly out of his wits. Báez whirled around. A guardia civil was standing in back of the white marble slab behind them like a ghost newly risen from its grave. He was pointing a gun at the two men. "Don't move," he said, his voice conversational. "You're covered from behind as well."

Gonzalo stood, paralyzed. So close, he thought, with a familiar crushing sense of hopelessness. So close. Then Juan's last words came back to him with chilling clarity. If something does go wrong, try to hold out for twenty-four hours.

Báez had already recovered. "Good afternoon, Señor Guardia." To Gonzalo's amazement, he took a few steps toward the man with the gun. "I think perhaps we haven't met." Báez was at the edge of the pathway now, and he stepped onto the narrow strip of earth separating the headstones, as if to make his way toward the guardia. He extended his hand. "My name is . . ."

There was the brief report of a rifle, and then Báez fell between the graves. The guardia had not moved. "Good shot, Torres." He barely raised his voice. Then, to Gonzalo, he added, "I'd advise you not to move, Señor . . .?"

Gonzalo stood, mute. Would it be better, he wondered, to give his false name and passport, or would this only serve to implicate him further? Could he protect his mentors by giving his real name? But then, what about Carmen? He heard footsteps, and then felt someone grab him from behind. The guardias did have the graveyard surrounded, then. A trap, Gonzalo thought despairingly. But for me? Or for Juan and Isabel? Or maybe even Báez? But how did they *know*?

"Señor Llorente, perhaps?" the guardia asked courteously.

Gonzalo gasped. "How—" he began, and then swallowed his words, too late.

A smile flickered across the guardia's face. "A hypothesis. I overheard some of your conversation. I suspect you've been looking forward to our meeting for some time now. Though not, perhaps, under these circumstances. Search him," he added, addressing the man who had handcuffed Gonzalo.

The second guardia emptied Gonzalo's pockets. Several white sepulchres gave the impression of gaping wider as more guardias appeared from their hiding places. One of them took the papers and money and handed them to the man who had spoken.

"This is the money, sir. And there are some documents. Might be false. There are a couple of pieces of paper, too."

The officer passed hastily over the passport and bills and looked down at the scraps of paper. "Mike McCormick,

17 Plain View Terrace, Elizabeth, New Jersey, USA," he read. "You have American friends, Señor Llorente?"

Gonzalo choked back an urge to laugh. It was the address Carmen had given him, in the impossible hope that the American volunteer would provide some sort of asylum. Let them focus on that, he told himself. The less I tell them . . . try to hold out for twenty-four hours. . . . Oh, shit. The officer had moved on to the other paper. "That was the one in the breast pocket, sir," one of the guardias volunteered. "It's a phone number."

Gonzalo, watching the guardia civil intently, saw the paper crinkle in his hand as his fingers tightened on it and knew that Mike McCormick would not be a diversion for long. He saw Tejada staring at the paper, reading and rereading the scribbled phone number, and saw his lips move. But Gonzalo was too far away to hear the sergeant's astonished whisper. "Son of a *bitch!*"

Chapter 21

Tejada sat at his desk and stared at the phone number he had taken from Gonzalo Llorente an hour earlier. He felt as if he had spent most of the weekend staring stupidly at things and that he was not much the wiser for it.

A fair amount of Friday evening and almost all of Saturday had been devoted to staring at the photograph of Ginger Rogers that Jiménez had identified so easily and wondering if it was simply an innocent remembrance of a shared fondness for movies or if Paco had meant the actress to be mistaken for Isabel. And if the photo was a deliberate blind, why had it been so important to keep Isabel's identity a secret?

After a few dumbstruck moments while Jiménez looked at him anxiously, the sergeant had remembered his goal and presented Alejandra with the cookies. He had then questioned her gently about the guardia civil she had seen pass by Paco's body. "Was he a thin man?" he had asked. "With drooping shoulders, and a hunched back?"

Aleja had been wary and hesitant, but when Jiménez had finally coaxed her to speak, she had disappointed Tejada. She had only seen the man's legs. But they had looked like thick legs. Like a wrestler's. Not thin or droopy. And the man had been humming. Tejada kept a grip on his temper and reminded himself that to a starving child even someone as thin as Rota might look "thick." He had thanked Aleja, given her more cookies, and then taken her over to the Cuatro Caminos prison and returned her to her mother.

Carmen and Alejandra had both seemed overjoyed at the reunion. But Tejada, watching the gaunt woman cradle the child's bruised head, had felt a strange reluctance to abandon Aleja. The prison was clearly tremendously overcrowded. A number of the women in Carmen's cell were sobbing and wailing, and from other cells he could hear curses and subversive songs. It did not seem like an appropriate environment for a child, especially an injured one.

"Do you have family, Señora Llorente?" he had asked. And then, remembering that he had shot her sister, and that her brother was in hiding, had added, "I mean family who are alive and free?"

The woman had shaken her head wordlessly. Tejada felt awkward. "Is there anyone you'd like to send your daughter to?" he asked. "I mean, this isn't . . . a very pleasant place for her. I wouldn't mind dropping her off with them. . . ."

Carmen had shaken her head again, and Tejada had realized with a certain despair that she was probably afraid the question had an ulterior motive. "Well . . .," he said awkwardly. "I hope Llorente is found soon then. I mean, I hope you're released soon. I mean, I hope Alejandra recovers quickly. Good-bye, Aleja," he had added, to the back of the child's head. "Thank you for your help."

On his way back from the prison he had made one more effort to help Alejandra, somewhat against his better judgment. The streets looked very different in the daytime, but after some careful searching he had found what he thought was the building where he had dropped off Elena the evening before. He took a deep breath and knocked on the outer door, wondering if Elena would answer, what he would do if she did, and if it was even the right apartment building. No one responded to his knocking. He waited a few minutes and then knocked again, hesitantly. He was just turning to leave when a window on the second floor opened and a woman leaned out to look down at him.

"Are you looking for someone, Señor Guardia?"

Tejada turned back and hesitated, suddenly aware that Elena's neighbors might misinterpret his reasons for wishing to speak to her. But having come this far he had to say something. "Is there a young lady named Fernández living here?" he asked awkwardly.

A frown crossed the woman's face. "She's not in."

Had Tejada been less anxious to bring the encounter to a close, he would have noticed that the reply was too quick. He was too relieved by it to do anything more than say, "When she comes in, could you give her a message, please?"

"Yes, sir." The woman waited expectantly, and after a moment Tejada realized that there was no verbal message he could give that would not be impossibly complicated.

"Do you have a pen?" he asked.

The window closed with a rattle and a few moments later the woman reappeared at the door, with pen and paper. Tejada stepped into the shadow of the entry and leaned against the wall to write, uncomfortably aware of the last time he had stood there. He scribbled quickly, reflecting as he folded the note that it was stilted, but impossible to edit under the circumstances. After hasty thanks to the woman, he fled back to his office, to continue staring at the photograph again.

He knew the inscription by heart. "Dearest, Here is your 'souvenir of a happy time.' Love, Isabel." Who was Isabel? How had Paco met her? The preparations for the capture of Báez on Sunday had provided a brief diversion, but Tejada had no sooner taken his place behind the old grave than his mind went back to its favorite conundrum. Who was Isabel? Was she also involved somehow with the black market? Sergeant de Rota denied knowing her, Tejada thought. How does Rota fit

in? And how can I prove that he fits in? Maybe Báez will implicate him. Who's Isabel, if not the girl in the photo?

Tejada might have been gratified to know that his own
handwriting was haunting Elena much as Isabel's handwriting
was haunting him. After the door closed behind him, Señora
Rodríguez had hurried up the stairs to the fourth-floor room
that the young lady teacher rented, unfolding the sergeant's
note as she went. She would not normally have dreamed of
reading someone else's mail. Of course not. But teacher or no,
Señorita Fernández was still young, and Señora Rodríguez felt
a certain responsibility to keep her respectable. Besides, the
Guardia were trouble. Señora Rodríguez liked the teacher, but
if the note contained either proposals or threats, she would
have to be told to move. No one could afford that kind of trouble now.

The landlady was panting for breath and more than a little
puzzled by the time she reached Elena's room. She knocked
once, for formality's sake, and then pushed her way inside.
Elena was on her knees beside the dresser, packing a suitcase.
"A guardia civil was looking for you." Señora Rodríguez spoke
without preamble.

Elena's face, already grave, turned white. "Tell him I'm not
here."

"I did. He left a note."

Señora Rodríguez held out the sheet of paper, which she
had kindly refolded. Elena stretched out a hand for it automatically, without rising. The landlady made a discreet exit as
her lodger unfolded the letter and began to read. Señora
Rodríguez had already decided, to her relief, that nothing in
the letter indicated that Elena was in moral or political trouble, but it had made very little sense to her. So she lingered
on the landing. She was extremely surprised to hear what
sounded like muffled sniffling, and reviewed the contents of
the hastily read letter in her head.

I'm sorry to trouble you, but I couldn't think of anyone else. Alejandra Palomino is currently being held north of Cuatro Caminos, along with her mother. None of her family are able to care for her, and if you could take her until her mother is released it would be a kindness. The prison is over-crowded, and they won't mind if you pick her up. Hopefully, it won't be for a long time.—Carlos Tejada

Elena's first impulse on reading the letter had been to thor-oughly damn its author for reasons that were somewhat unclear. Her second, more rational, thought was to go and pick up Aleja as the letter suggested. But she had been pack-ing since the early morning, and her desire to flee the city and return to her parents' home was not lessened by the uncom-fortable reminder that Sergeant Tejada could easily find her if she stayed. Self-preservation warred with pity for Aleja and with an irrational desire to live up to the sergeant's good opin-ion of her. Caring for the little girl would not be difficult, now that she herself had no job, but feeding her would be. If it's just for a few days. . ., Elena thought. I could stay in the city that long. But he says 'hopefully' it won't be for a long time . . . and who knows how long 'long' is, anyway? It would be cruelly irre-sponsible to take Aleja home to Salamanca with her if Carmen expected to find her daughter waiting upon her release from prison. But if the days stretched into weeks, or months, and she was forced to find food for Aleja as well as herself in Madrid. . . . He would help with that probably, Elena thought. In exchange for what? responded her most cynical self.

Elena glared at the piece of paper, wishing that the innocuous-sounding phrases gave some clue to the sergeant's real intentions and almost sorry that she had not met him in person so that she could better judge him. Finally, after much deliberation and a few tears, she finished packing her bags and went to the post office to send a letter of her own: "Dear Mama,

I hope everything is fine in Salamanca. Things are a bit diffi-cult here. I want to come home. Please wire Burgos currency for a train ticket, as quickly as possible. I hope everyone is well. Love, Elena." Then she had returned to her room, to wait for money that could not come too quickly. Since most of her time was spent indoors, sleeping or fasting, she had little to do over Easter except think about how she had failed Alejandra and reread Tejada's note. Saturday morning it had seemed to mock her with its arrogant confidence. Saturday evening it reproached her with its mute dependence on her altruism.

On Easter morning, at around the time Tejada himself was wondering who Isabel was and why she had given Paco a pho-tograph of Ginger Rogers, Elena was wondering if it might not be a good idea to contact him about Alejandra after all. By the time Tejada had actually confronted Aleja's uncle, Elena had already given up the notion as useless and probably foolish. But while Elena's miserable preoccupation with the sergeant's note and her inability to respond as she would have liked lasted several more days, Tejada was given the advantage of more immediate distraction from his puzzlement over Isabel.

Báez had strolled into the graveyard around noon, just as the prisoner had said he would. Tejada had been about to give the signal to close in on him when the smuggler was accosted by another man. Curious and faintly uneasy, Tejada had delayed making an arrest and tried to listen to the conversation between the two men. It had been interesting but not enlight-ening. The sergeant felt a swift and well-controlled flash of fury when Corporal Torres shot down Báez. It was typical of Torres, Tejada thought, to show off his stupid skills as a marksman without thinking whether the man might have useful infor-mation. However, the other man might have information. The sergeant, narrowly inspecting the man, traced a resemblance to Carmen Llorente and made an inspired guess.

His satisfaction at guessing correctly evaporated when he saw the phone number Báez had given Llorente. This must be wrong, he thought, staring at the scrap of paper. There's a mistake. Or I haven't understood something. It must be Rota, trying to be clever again. . . . this can't be right. But he had no time to think where the error might lie. He gave orders to return to the post, bringing Llorente along.

"Do you want to question him, Sergeant?" Torres asked when they reached the post, gesturing toward the sullen Gonzalo.

Tejada nodded absently. "Stick him in solitary. I'll be right there."

"Should I send for Guardia Meléndez, sir?"

Tejada's mind, which had been stuck on puzzling out the meaning of the phone number on the scrap of paper, focused on the present again. If he's tough, he thought, Meléndez won't break him. And if he cracks easily, then he'll say anything. And I don't just want Rota's name now. I want to know what the hell this *really* means. He shook his head. "No," he said. "No one talks to him before I do." The phone number intruded on his thoughts again, and he added, "That's an order. Jiménez, you stand guard outside his cell. No one besides me goes in or out, got it?"

Jiménez noticed an odd tone in the sergeant's voice. "What about Lieutenant Ramos, sir?" he asked, not because he thought that the lieutenant would actually interfere, but because Tejada had stressed *no one* with surprising vehemence.

Tejada flashed him a brief, mirthless smile. "Guardia, if His Excellency Generalíssimo Franco comes to that cell door and asks to play dominoes with the prisoner you tell him that the sergeant's orders are that no one goes in or out. Do you understand me?"

"Yes, sir," Jiménez gulped. So did the prisoner, but probably for a different reason.

Jiménez must be wondering what was keeping him now, Tejada thought. With a sigh, he folded the scrap of paper, thrust it into the depths of one pocket, and went to meet Gonzalo Llorente.

The miliciano had the slightly rumpled appearance typical of all prisoners, but he did not seem to have been manhandled. Sitting with his hands bound, he closely resembled his sister Carmen, with her square shoulders and lank chestnut hair. Viviana, Tejada thought, had been slimmer and much darker than her siblings. Perhaps she had been a half-sister. Llorente said nothing as the sergeant sat opposite him, and the cell door swung shut.

"Suppose you tell me about it," Tejada suggested quietly.

The miliciano's face was grim. He said nothing. Tejada sighed. "Look, at the moment, we'll overlook why you weren't at Chamartín as you should have been. I want to know about Báez. And the black market." He paused a moment, and then added reluctantly, as if saying the name to a hostile stranger were a kind of violation, "And Paco López."

Gonzalo Llorente pinched his lips together. It was a gesture that Tejada recognized. It was one of Aleja's. "Stubbornness seems to be a family trait," he said dryly. And then, experimentally, "As I recall, your sister was stubborn as well."

The sergeant saw Llorente's eyes widen slightly at the use of the past tense. "What have you done to Carmen?"

"She's also stubborn," Tejada agreed. "But I meant your younger sister, Viviana."

The miliciano tensed, and for a moment Tejada was glad that the prisoner was unarmed and bound. "That was why you wanted to see Báez, wasn't it?" Tejada said, risking a hypothesis that seemed to make sense. "You were looking for the guardia civil who executed Viviana."

"Who murdered her," the prisoner spat, and for the first time Tejada saw a resemblance to the woman he had killed.

Tejada shrugged. "Semantics. Your sister Carmen is also in custody, by the way, and your niece. I don't suppose concern for them might make you more talkative?"

Llorente drew a long breath, and for a moment Tejada thought he would speak. Then he let it out again, noisily, saying nothing. The sergeant shook his head in exasperation. "I'll never understand the Reds," he said. "Who's worth protecting more than your own flesh and blood?"

Llorente was silent, and the sergeant wondered once more whether hitting him would help. Again, Tejada decided it probably would be useless. The man wasn't the type to start whimpering after being slapped around a little. In the hands of a professional interrogator, he might or might not decide to give information, but Tejada was incapable of conducting such an interrogation. He had neither training, nor materials, nor inclination. "We'll talk more," he said. "Maybe after I've spoken to some of your friends."

He left, knowing unhappily that the threat was an empty one. Jiménez met him at the doorway. "Lieutenant Ramos says that he's sending for a special investigator from Burgos, sir. He says in the meantime let Guardia Meléndez deal with him."

Tejada hesitated for an instant. Llorente's false documents were good ones. It was worth finding out where he had gotten them, and every hour wasted meant that whoever Llorente's contacts were had another hour to escape. It would be logical to question him about the documents, and, for that matter, about how he had known that Báez would be at the Eastern Cemetery. "Oh, and the lieutenant says get a photograph of him before you give him to Meléndez," Jiménez added.

"What?" the sergeant said, eyes narrowing.

Jiménez looked apologetic. "The lieutenant says it's useful for other prisoners, sir. So we can prove that we really have him."

"A photograph," the sergeant repeated.

"Yes, sir, a photograph."

"Stay here, Guardia. I'll be right back." Tejada was already in motion. "And the orders haven't changed."

"Should I call Meléndez, sir?" the young recruit called.

Tejada swung around. "The orders haven't changed," he repeated. "No one goes in or out besides me. I'll be right back."

The sergeant knew that every passing moment gave the Reds who had provided Llorente's passport time to regroup. But he was on the verge of discovering Paco's murderer. The Movement could wait. Paco had been his friend. He took the stairs to Lieutenant Ramos's office at a run.

The office was empty when he reached it. Tejada was first grateful and then worried. It was Easter Sunday after all. A lot of people would not be working. But he had to take the chance. "Alcalá-2136," he snapped and then counted the rings.

In the middle of the seventh ring he heard the click of a receiver being lifted from its cradle, and then the words: "Guardia Civil. Morales."

"I'd like to speak to Captain Morales, please." The sergeant held his voice steady with an effort.

"Speaking."

"Sergeant Carlos Tejada, Manzanares post, reporting, sir."

"Oh, good afternoon, Sergeant," Morales sounded slightly surprised. "Are you on duty today?"

"Yes, sir." Tejada took a deep breath. "I've found some information, sir. But are you sure this line is secure?"

"As much as it can be," the captain replied. "But if the information is delicate . . ."

"*Absolutely* secure," Tejada insisted. "You said it was a private line?"

"That's correct, Sergeant. Now, did you wish to meet?"

"There aren't other extensions," Tejada persisted. "There's only the one phone?"

"Yes."

"In your office?"

"Yes." Morales lost patience. "I assure you that I'm the only one who answers this phone. Now, Sergeant, was there something you wished to tell me?"

"Yes," Tejada said automatically. Then, very slowly, he added, "I think I've found the information you asked me about, sir. But I'd like to communicate it to you in private. As soon as possible."

"Monday morning?" the captain suggested, after a brief pause. "Ten o'clock?"

"If that is convenient, Captain. At your orders."

"Very good, Sergeant. I'll see you here on Monday morning then. Happy Easter."

"Thank you, sir."

"Arriba España."

"Arriba España." Tejada hung up the phone with his mouth slightly open.

Llorente, a distant corner of his mind prompted him. Go question Llorente about his false papers. Or give him to Meléndez. It doesn't matter about Paco now. You know, and you can deal with it later. Llorente has nothing to do with Paco . . . neither does Carmen or Alejandra . . . or Viviana. They're Reds. . . . The sergeant realized that he was rolling the piece of paper he had taken from Gonzalo Llorente into a tiny cylinder. Carefully, he unrolled it and stared again at the scribbled phone number. He had not misread it. There, lightly penciled, were the words Alcalá-2136. Diego Báez's mocking laugh sounded in his ears. "Just ask for Paco's boss. You'll get him."

Tejada was about to go talk to Llorente when he had another idea. Very slowly, he picked up the phone again. "Alcalá-2136," he repeated. This time the phone was answered more quickly.

"Yes, Sergeant Tejada, what is it?" Morales said with some impatience, when the sergeant had identified himself once again.

"I'm sorry to disturb you again, sir," Tejada apologized. "But I wondered if I could speak with your sergeant. Diego de Rota. I wanted to ask him a few questions."

"Sergeant de Rota?" Morales said, sounding surprised. "I'll see if he's at the post. Can he call you back?"

A private line, Tejada thought. "No," he said aloud. "There's no need. I'll try to see him in person."

He broke the connection and went to talk to Llorente again. Then he headed for the Alcalá post, to speak to Diego de Rota.

Chapter 22

Gonzalo lay on the floor of his cell and stared up into the dark. He had been a prisoner in so many small spaces recently that the experience was becoming familiar. Sooner or later the door opened and something unpleasant happened. He had been so close. . . . He had not realized how much he wanted to live until the moment when his hands were cuffed. He had been bent on vengeance for Viviana, because he had thought there was no hope. But then Juan and Isabel had offered him a chance, and for a few glorious moments it had seemed as if he might actually make it. "Try to hold out for twenty-four hours." They had given him hope. The least he could give them in return was time.

It seemed as if it might be possible. Twelve hours had passed since his arrest and he had not cracked yet. They had marched him toward the river and he had almost laughed as he recognized the Manzanares post and heard the commanding officer say to the guardia civil who had spoken to him: "Everything go according to plan, Sergeant?"

"Yes, sir." The sergeant saluted, and Gonzalo had stared at the tall, lean man and memorized every feature and every cadence of the calm voice, wondering if he was looking at Viviana's killer. There was a sickening hilarity to the thought.

The same man had come to talk to him a little later. To Gonzalo's surprise, the sergeant showed no tendency to use force.

He had been brusque and contemptuous even, but he had not raised his hands. When he reappeared, a few minutes afterwards, he had lost much of his brusqueness, and he seemed almost pleading. "Listen, Llorente," he said quietly, "I know that you were looking for the man who killed your Viviana. I . . . hell, if I were in your place I might have done the same thing. But look, she died because she was in the wrong place at the wrong time and someone thought she was guilty of murder. So whoever really committed that murder bears some responsibility, no?"

Gonzalo looked at the officer with disgust. Was the man actually going to have the gall to appeal to his moral sense? The sergeant continued, with considerable vehemence, "I'll tell you frankly, Llorente, the man who pulled the trigger was a cat's-paw, in more ways than one. But listen, I think I've found the man who's responsible . . . *really* responsible."

"So have I." Gonzalo's nausea got the better of his determination to stay silent.

"You stupid *shit!*" The sergeant lost patience. "Will you come down off your high horse before someone puts a noose around your neck! I've found the bastard who killed Paco, and indirectly caused that damn miliciana's death, and I can get him for it. All I need is confirmation from you! And if you *don't* talk to me now, you'll be damn sorry, because you'll have to talk to other people later, and believe me, they won't be as polite as I am. Or are you too dumb to understand that, you fucking peasant?"

"Maybe," Gonzalo said, managing to make the word almost nonchalant. He was a little puzzled as to why the guardias had not tortured him earlier. Perhaps they wanted the threat to hang over him. More fools they. He knew that waiting wasn't the worst part of combat.

The sergeant had left then, and for once the door to the cell slammed shut not to impress the prisoner with a sense of final doom but to relieve his guard of a fit of pique. Gonzalo had heard the guardia civil's voice, still sounding annoyed. "Fine, give him to Meléndez, and tell him to ask about the false documents. That's our first priority. Ignore anything else. It's just a red herring."

Gonzalo had smiled quietly to himself. Just want to know about Paco López, my ass, he thought, proud that he had seen through the trick. And then he was frightened, because he knew that the real interrogation was coming.

The beating had not been so bad until they discovered the scar of his wound and someone had the bright idea of hitting him in the stomach. After the first hour, Gonzalo abandoned his pride and wept. "Twenty-four hours." He clung to the words through a haze of pain. Only for twenty-four hours. He strained to hear clocks striking, to learn how much longer he would have to bear it, but someone had frozen time in the way that feet are frozen to the ground in a nightmare of an invisible pursuer. Surely twenty-four hours had passed? But they could not have. "No, I don't know. No, I don't know." Hold out for twenty-four hours. "Don't know, don't know, no, know, no." And then, just as he began to think that he would break, unconsciousness opened its kindly arms, and embraced him.

When he came to his senses he was lying on his back and it hurt to move. He lay still for a few moments, terrified that they would realize he was awake and begin questioning him again. Then he realized that he was alone in the darkness. Somewhere outside a clock began to strike. *Bong . . . bong . . . bong* . . . He counted eleven, and then the bells faded away. Twenty-four hours. Nearly twelve had already passed. He could lie still, pretending he had not regained consciousness. Surely they would wait until the morning then. And surely he could stand another few hours. Tears worked their way down his temples. Everything hurt.

They had taken his coat and the stone floor was cold, but moving was too much effort. A spasm of coughing shook him, and he tasted bile and blood. He lay still, grateful for each passing moment, afraid that somehow someone would freeze time again. It felt like a victory when he heard the clock strike midnight, but he was unsure he had counted the strokes correctly. Perhaps it was only eleven. Perhaps it was still eleven, and always would be, and twenty-four hours would never pass. He coughed again, and bloody phlegm dribbled down his chin. His head hurt, as it had when his wound had become infected, and the fever had set in. The bright, brief *bong* as the clock struck one seemed too good to be true. It was over so quickly that Gonzalo wondered if he had imagined it.

He was still trying to decide if his ears were playing tricks on him when the cell door opened again. It happened quickly this time, with no challenge from the guard outside, and no casually spoken words. A boot toe nudged him in the ribs. Against his will, he groaned.

"Good," said a voice quietly. "You're awake."

There was a click, and an electric flashlight cut through the darkness. The beam traveled along Gonzalo's recumbent body, inspecting him. He could not see who was holding it.

"Get up," Gonzalo recognized the voice. It was the man who had come to question him first.

"I can't."

"Nonsense." The flashlight beam danced crazily as the guardia leaned over Gonzalo and dragged him to his feet. He was not overly gentle, and Gonzalo moaned slightly.

"Shut up." The command was curt. "Or I'll gag you."

Gonzalo felt his arms twisted behind his back and then bound. Oh, God, he thought, suddenly remembering stories he had heard at the front. Not hung from the wrists. It's only twelve hours, or maybe thirteen. . . . Not dislocated shoulders, please God. . . . The guardia did not give any warning, so

Gonzalo's eyes were open (and uselessly focused on the bright dot where the flashlight hit the wall) when a blindfold was slipped over them and tightly tied.

"Come on."

Gonzalo felt his captor take him by the elbow and drag him along the corridor. He stumbled along blindly, tripping and blundering into the walls, as the guardia civil guided him through the prison. "Watch the stairs." If Tejeda had not been holding Gonzalo's elbow the warning would have come too late.

They passed through several doors. Gonzalo, blindfolded and bewildered, could make no sense of their progress until a door opened and he felt a cool breeze on his face. He could hear the wind and the ground under his feet was cobbled, unlike the smooth floors of the prison. A firing squad? he thought fuzzily. But it's not dawn yet, is it? I haven't cracked. Thank God, if it's a firing squad, I haven't cracked. The sergeant was pulling him forward again. He stumbled and struck his shins on something. He was almost grateful for the misstep. The minor pain distracted him from his greater ones.

"Get in." The guardia's voice was colorless.

"In?" Gonzalo repeated stupidly.

The man did not waste further words. Instead, Gonzalo heard a door opening and then felt himself being lifted under the armpits and placed on a seat. The guardia picked up Gonzalo's legs, swung them sideways, and then there was a slam. Gonzalo realized that he was sitting in some sort of truck. The noises were repeated, as the guardia climbed into the driver's seat.

Gonzalo was thrown backward as the guardia let out the clutch and the vehicle purred into life. He focused for a few moments on bracing himself with his feet. He was sorry to regain his balance. It meant that he had time to think about what might be happening. "Where are we going?" he asked, because he was more afraid of not asking.

"For a drive," the guardia said grimly.

In the midst of his pain and confusion an irony occurred to Gonzalo. "You're the sergeant, aren't you?" he said. "The one who killed Viviana."

There was a long pause. "Yes."

"And now you're going to kill me."

Another pause. "It's better than what's waiting for you back there."

Gonzalo was too proud to admit that the sergeant might be speaking the truth. "I can take beatings," he snapped.

The sergeant laughed softly. The sound was almost lost under the hum of the engine. "If it were just a beating, Llorente, I'd leave you to it, and welcome. You more than deserve it. But I've seen the way the professionals work. Believe me, you're better off this way."

Something penetrated Gonzalo's fog of fear and anguish. "You're not acting under orders," he said. He was thrown sideways as the truck made a sharp right turn. He had received no answer by the time he righted himself. "Why?" Gonzalo asked.

For a while, Gonzalo thought he would receive no reply. Then the driver said slowly, "Because I made a mistake, about Paco's murderer. And you helped me find it out."

"Viviana . . . was a *mistake?*" Gonzalo choked.

"I didn't mean your sister," the guardia said evenly.

"She wasn't my sister." Gonzalo spoke without thinking.

"Oh. Your lover, then." The word had a bad taste in the sergeant's mouth. "But that wasn't what I meant. You helped me find that phone number."

"I'm getting a nice reward for it," Gonzalo remarked as the jeep swung to the right again, and he braced himself.

The sergeant ignored the sarcasm. "Well, your . . . Viviana was a mistake, too. And I've met most of your family by now, I think. So this way seems best." He slowed slightly and added, "Balance yourself. We're turning."

Gonzalo said nothing more. He could think of nothing more to say. It was Tejada who interrupted the constant hum of the motor. "Your niece Alejandra told me Paco was killed by a 'thick' man, dressed like a guardia civil. I didn't understand what that meant, until I saw Morales's phone number."

"Whose phone number?" Gonzalo asked, momentarily distracted.

"Captain Morales, the head of the Alcalá post." Tejada's voice was very dry. "A very competent man and a highly respected officer." The sergeant drummed his thumbs on the steering wheel for a moment, and then continued speaking. "I talked to his sergeant this afternoon. Morales has been promoted fast. He got command of the Alcalá post after exposing a ring of thieves who were stealing rations at his last assignment. He punished them very publicly, too. And he was so modest about his own experience catching thieves that he asked Lieutenant Ramos to recommend a man to conduct an investigation when things started going missing there!"

Gonzalo wondered at the suppressed emotion in the sergeant's voice. "You're saying *he* was stealing them?" he asked.

"Oh, not just that." Tejada was bitter. "He has a system worked out. He pulls in the junior officers so he always has someone ready to take the fall. And he gets the credit for exposing corruption. But Paco wouldn't play. So he killed him and picked out a nice inexperienced sap to investigate the thefts of provisions. And if it was the sap who'd already executed someone for Paco's murder, so much the better!"

"What do you mean, 'Paco wouldn't play'?" Gonzalo demanded, interest getting the better of caution.

"I mean I think Paco was trying to pull out of it," Tejada snapped. "Morales threatened him with . . . well, it's none of your business, but Morales threatened him with something that wasn't true. So Paco went along. And I think as soon as the war ended he decided he was going to go to higher-ups. Paco was honorable, damn it! Whatever you say about him!" The sergeant's voice carried clearly above the humming engine now.

"I didn't say a thing," Gonzalo pointed out. His head hurt, and the temptation to needle his captor overrode his good judgment. "Morales threatened to expose Paco as a Communist, didn't he?"

"Paco wasn't a Red!" The sergeant rapped out the words. "He was trying to hide a girlfriend's identity, so he did something stupid and pretended that a photograph was a picture of her when it wasn't. But that's all!"

"Who told you that?" Gonzalo asked, wondering how Morales had seen through the deception. Probably it had been Paco's great inspiration. One of the over-elaborate lies that Isabel had said would have made him a poor agent.

"Morales's sergeant again," Tejada replied absently. "He's in it too, of course, but I suspect under some sort of compulsion. He wouldn't tell me what he's being blackmailed with. He's scared stiff that Morales will bump him off or set him up as the fall guy. He tried to warn me that the girl wasn't the important thing in the photo but he's such a fucking incompetent that all he did was make me suspicious of him."

Gonzalo reflected sadly that he had just gathered all the information Juan and Isabel had asked him for. It seemed that Isabel's identity had been guessed at by Captain Morales, but the information had been used for other purposes. It was a shame that he would not have a chance to report back to them. "I suppose this sergeant's not a Communist either," he ventured.

"I told you, Paco wasn't a Red!" Tejada snapped. He thought about his conversation with Rota, and about the photograph again, and then added reluctantly, "Was he?" His voice pleaded for a negative reply.

"No," Gonzalo answered, glad that he was telling the truth, for reasons that he could not analyze. "No, he was one of you."

"I knew it," Tejada sighed. He was speaking to himself now. "He might have made a mistake. But Paco loved Spain. He would never have willingly done anything to hurt his country."

"Why are you telling me this?" Gonzalo asked, wishing that he could see the other man's face.

"Because . . ." Tejada paused and thought. He understood suddenly why prisoners sometimes confessed even without threats. He wanted to talk. "Because you're a safe audience," he admitted.

Gonzalo coughed violently, almost retching, and wondered if his ribs were broken. "Silent as the grave?" he gasped, when he could speak again.

The guardia civil snorted. "Something like that. Besides, you knew Paco was involved with the black market. It's fair you know why."

It was odd, Gonzalo thought, that he was still able to be interested in trifles even though he knew that he would be dead in a few minutes. "How did you know I knew?" he asked, since there was nothing to lose by the question.

"I picked up that smuggler you questioned last week," Tejada said frankly. "That's how I found out about Báez too."

"Nice work."

"Sheer luck," the sergeant corrected. "I was hot on the wrong trail and happened to stumble over him." He paused and braked for a sign that Gonzalo could not see. "I've screwed up nearly everything in this investigation," he added ruefully.

Gonzalo's silence did not contradict him. The vehicle rattled along for a while. Gonzalo wondered again where they were going. Out into the countryside probably. It was the logical place to dump a body. "What will you tell them about me?" he asked.

Gonzalo heard a smile in the sergeant's voice. "Paco's murder is officially a closed case. But the lieutenant knows he was a friend of mine. If I tell him I found out you were responsible and took you out because I wanted to question you personally, he'll understand. He'll be annoyed, of course, because we do want to know where you obtained your forged papers, but I'll tell him I hit a little harder than I meant to or that you were weaker than I thought. These things happen."

"Jesus!" Gonzalo commented. "You could be court-martialed."

Tejada shook his head, forgetting that his prisoner was blindfolded. "I'd be court-martialed if I let you escape. I did think of that, but there's no way in hell you'd reach the border, and I'm not interested in staring down a firing squad."

"Why is this so important to you?" Gonzalo asked as the truck turned and then accelerated.

For a while, Gonzalo thought he would receive no reply. Then he heard the driver say shortly, "You're a Red. You wouldn't understand."

"Try me."

"I told you . . . I owe you. And I don't like being in people's debt."

"It's only the repayment part that I'm having trouble understanding." To the surprise of both men, Gonzalo's voice was almost jocular.

Tejada actually laughed. "I told you. It's the best I can do under the circumstances. I'll try to see that your sister's released soon, too. She was arrested for hiding you, so we really have nothing to hold her for now."

"Thanks a lot," Gonzalo meant the words ironically. They came out sounding sincere.

"It's really Aleja I feel sorry for," the sergeant explained. "This whole business has been hard on her. And it's not her fault her people are Reds."

"Or that you shot her aunt," Gonzalo pointed out.

"Fuck you, Llorente." The words were muffled by the grinding of gears.

"And uncle," Gonzalo murmured experimentally, trying out the concept. It was difficult to imagine being dead. Presumably it meant that various parts of his body would stop hurting.

Tejada deliberately ignored the miliciano. "Yes, Carmen should be released soon," he said. "But sometimes the process takes time and we're overworked at the moment. I was thinking . . . I was thinking, the wait won't be good for Aleja."

"Probably not," Gonzalo agreed. Knowing that he would not be there to see to Aleja gave death a context, made it seem more real, and permanent.

"I thought . . ." Tejada tapped his thumbs on the steering wheel again. "I thought maybe I'd send her to Granada. My brother's oldest daughter is in school there at the Convent of the Sacred Heart. I'm sure the nuns would take Aleja too, and my brother's family could take her on weekends, and during holidays."

"You wouldn't dare!"

The loathing in Gonzalo's voice startled the sergeant. "Her father's dead," he pointed out. "And *you* won't be around to take care of her. She'd get a good education, and she wouldn't be tagged as the daughter of a Red."

"You scum!" Gonzalo retched again and twisted in his seat, hating his body's helplessness and his tongue's inability to express his rage. "How could you, knowing what she means to Carmen?"

"You'd rather she starved in the street?" Tejada asked. "I assure you, it won't be easy for an ex-convict with a brother who's been executed to find work. And—" His face twisted for an instant. "I thought Aleja's education was important to you."

"I'd rather she starved in the street than learned what you would teach her!" Gonzalo hissed.

Tejada shook his head again. "I'll never understand the Reds."

The man was sincere, Gonzalo thought. He genuinely couldn't see what was wrong with taking Aleja away from every-thing she held dear. He had a niece of his own, and he would have screamed that the minions of Satan were kidnapping her if she had been so much as enrolled in a secular school, and yet he would take Aleja away and call it kindness. "I'll never understand you either," he said, and suddenly his anger was washed away by sadness.

"It was just an idea." The sergeant's voice was a little stiff. "I thought you might be relieved by it."

"I'm surprised you didn't bring a priest along," Gonzalo remarked sarcastically.

The sergeant laughed again. "I didn't think one would be necessary or appreciated. Should I have found one?"

"No, thanks." Gonzalo found himself smiling in the dark-ness and was appalled. How could he be sitting here in the darkness chatting with Viviana's murderer, and his own? "This is a very odd conversation," he said aloud.

"Very," Tejada agreed. For a moment, his mind flitted back to Elena, and he said reflectively, "Maybe it's easier to say things in the dark."

"When you can't see someone's face," Gonzalo agreed, star-ing at the inside of the blindfold, and wondering how far the sergeant was planning to drive him.

"That's why confessionals are dim, I suppose," Tejada said. "Brace your feet. We're turning."

The truck swung to the right, and Gonzalo, swaying to keep his balance, brushed against the sergeant's shoulder. Tejada righted his prisoner with one hand. "*The night became intimate, like a little plaza,*" Gonzalo quoted.

"Yes." The sergeant threw a quick, surprised glance at his prisoner's profile, wondering where Llorente had picked up the bit of poetry. "Yes, that describes it exactly. Except that I'm not drunk," he added, and then realized that Llorente probably did not know the entire poem, and would therefore miss the reference.

Gonzalo turned his head rapidly toward the guardia civil's voice, a gesture made useless by the blindfold. "You mean *you've* read Lorca!" he exclaimed.

"You mean *you* have?" Tejada said, disbelieving.

"Of course. All of Federico's work was in the union library." Gonzalo raised his chin, laying claim to the poet.

"My cousins lived up the street from his parents," Tejada explained. "I met him a few times, as a kid."

Gonzalo's jaw dropped. "But you've *read* him?" he asked, incredulous.

"Yes, of course. Well, all his early work. Some of the *Cante jondo* is beautiful. A shame he got off into all that surrealist crap." Tejada had few, but decided, opinions about poetry.

"So, you like the '*Romance de la Guardia Civil Española*'?" Gonzalo suggested mischievously.

Tejada snorted. "Communist crap. But I've always liked '*Preciosa y el Aire.*'"

"I wouldn't have figured you were so sentimental."

"I've always liked '*Preciosa y el Aire.*'" Tejada repeated, with a certain emphasis. He braked sharply and Gonzalo slid forward, wondering unhappily if they were reaching the journey's end.

"He was the greatest poet of his generation," the miliciano said, a little defiantly.

"Agreed."

"And your side killed him."

"A regrettable mistake. Accidents happen in wartime." Tejada was busy with the clutch.

"The way Viviana was a mistake?" Gonzalo asked. "How many mistakes do you allow yourself, Sergeant?"

"Fuck off." The gears ground, partly because Tejada's hands were shaking. The vehicle lurched to a stop. "Sorry I don't have more time to analyze poetry with you, Llorente. But we're here."

"Where?"

"Where you get off."

The engine died, and then there was the sound of the door opening and slamming. Gonzalo sat rigid, trying to accustom himself to the imminence of death. He heard the door on his side of the truck open, and then the guardia civil was pulling him down and setting him on his feet.

"Back up," the sergeant said quietly, and Gonzalo felt something that could have been a rifle barrel nudge him in the chest. He backed up, stumbling slightly, and found himself still on paving stones. There was still a paved road here then. Odd, considering how long they had driven.

"You fucking Red," Tejada said. "Paco was worth ten of you. Ten! And he died, and you're still here! And you damn well don't deserve to be! Communist traitor!" The sergeant's voice was rising steadily.

Gonzalo felt the rifle strike him lightly on the chest again. He stumbled a few steps backward and found his shoulders in contact with a wall. This is it, he thought. But I didn't crack. *Viva la República, I didn't crack.*

"Communist!" Tejada shouted again. "Spain should be purged of all of you! You don't deserve to breathe Spanish air! Red! Communist!" There was a hysterical note in the sergeant's voice, and Gonzalo wondered what had become of their fleeting camaraderie. "Filthy Communist!"

It all happened very suddenly. One moment, Gonzalo was backed up against a wall, as the guardia civil screamed insults, and the next moment the pressure on his shoulder blades had disappeared, and a hand behind him drew him inside. Then he heard the gentle thud of a door swinging shut, and Tejada's cries were muffled. Then someone pulled off his blindfold.

"You are a member of the Party?" a man whispered.

Gonzalo blinked stupidly. After so many hours in total blackness, the lamp shining in his eyes seemed as brilliant as the sun. He stared at the shadows on the floor and realized that he was in some sort of foyer. From the echoes of the whisper, it was a large space. "A Party member?" the man asked again, with a certain urgency. He had a thick accent, which flattened and squared off the vowels. German? Gonzalo thought, with a flash of fear. Outside, the guardia civil was still shouting. Then there was a burst of gunfire outside the door.

Gonzalo turned to his rescuer. "I . . . yes, I suppose, but you must let me out, sir. He's a guardia civil. He'll shoot open the door if he has to."

"No, he cannot." The foreigner spoke with absolute confidence. "Please turn around." He gently spun Gonzalo and began to work at the knots holding the miliciano's hands.

There was another burst of gunfire. "Comrade, thank you," Gonzalo said urgently. "I can tell you're a foreigner, but in Spain now, even foreigners—"

"We are not in Spain!" The foreigner's flat vowels took on a haughty tone. "This is the British Embassy."

Gonzalo twisted around and stared at the man. "But . . . who . . . how?" he gasped.

The man smiled and tapped his nose, a gesture made grotesque by the shadows thrown by the lamp. "It is a little irregular, comrade. But I think we can grant you asylum. If we twist . . . no, that's not right . . . if we *bend* the rules."

As Gonzalo stared, speculations whirling wildly in his brain, he heard the sound of a truck gunning its engine and then driving off into the night.

"There," said the man with satisfaction. "The guardia civil is gone, you see."

"How did you know I would be here now?" Gonzalo asked slowly.

The man tapped his nose again. "A tip. You understand, the embassy is neutral. But some of us who work here are sympathizers."

"A tip," Gonzalo repeated. "But who . . . ?"

"I understand he gave the name Paco López," the Englishman said.

Gonzalo's hands were free. He brought them slowly to his mouth, as pieces of his conversation with the sergeant whirled through his brain like confetti at a parade: *Sorry I don't have more time to analyze poetry with you, Llorente . . . I've always liked 'Preciosa y el Aire.'*

"Paco López," he breathed, as the last sounds of the truck died away in the distance. And then, under the concerned gaze of the Englishman, he leaned against the door of the embassy and laughed until he cried.

Chapter 23

"Citizens to the right, please. Citizens to the right. All passengers with foreign visas to the left. The *left*, sir, if you please. *A gauche.*"

Gonzalo did not understand the words but the guard's gesture was clear enough, and he guessed the meaning of the two lines. The line on the right was moving slowly but steadily down the gangplank, filled with people waving to friends and shouting incomprehensible greetings in English. The mass of people herded to the left were milling around the deck or sitting on their luggage, looking purposeless, annoyed, or distressed. Gonzalo, whose luggage consisted of a single duffel bag filled with gifts from members of the Association of Friends of the Spanish Republic, leaned against the railing and watched the fortunate holders of blue passports disembark. They were quickly swallowed by the crowd on the pier.

Gonzalo stared downward, past the greenish water where the boat gently rocked to the unmistakably dry and solid ground a few yards away. It was difficult to believe that in a few hours he might actually be stepping onto land again. He turned his gaze downstream before the hope became too strong. A bend in the river hid the harbor from view. Gonzalo had gone up on deck at dawn, along with most of the boat's passengers, to see the Statue of Liberty as they passed it. The statue's torch glowed in the rising sun, clenched in an eternally upraised fist, and Gonzalo had blinked, and yawned, and pinched himself to make sure that he was awake. The skyline of New York rose out of the water with shocking suddenness, too strange to seem beautiful, or even real. Gonzalo had wondered if some trick of the light made the buildings seem grayer than they really were. Now, looking at them in the full light of the golden September sun, he saw that the buildings were a perfectly normal color. He had thought that they should look green, because the sight had reminded him of the Emerald City of Oz in a book that Aleja had loved.

The air around Gonzalo hummed with tension. He watched, detached, as lines formed and uniformed men began to move from passenger to passenger, inspecting papers and luggage. A number of the English passengers were arguing loudly in their mother tongue with the inspectors. The Americans were courteous to the British, and more impatient with the French, who saw no need to translate their displeasure. No one enjoyed going through customs, but Gonzalo noticed that the inspectors did seem to be allowing people to leave the boat.

He had become a keen observer in the last few months because he was forced to gain all of his information through observation. No one on the London–New York steamer spoke Spanish. Gonzalo, who had been severely seasick for much of the voyage, had spoken to no one since waving farewell to his well-wishers in London. He was still being treated like a brown paper parcel. Well wrapped up, and mailed from city to city, COD, he thought sadly, and then reproached himself for being ungrateful. He owed his life to the people who had treated him like a package. After a tense week hiding in the English embassy, he had been smuggled to France along with a packet of diplomatic mail. From there, he had taken a boat for London, where he had been met by a delegation of the Association of Friends of the Spanish Republic. They were the ones who had raised the money for his passage to New York. They had done it for the best. They could not have known how terrible it was to be seasick and alone, with no one even to understand your misery.

"Your papers, sir. *Vos papiers, s'il vous plait.*" The voice jerked Gonzalo back to the present. A man in a dark blue uniform was holding out his hand, looking impatient.

Gonzalo hastily handed over his visa. The man glanced at it and then frowned, looking more closely. "May I see your passport, sir?"

Gonzalo gathered that he was being asked for more information, but was unclear of what kind. "I . . . I'm sorry. I don't understand." He had learned the English words during his brief stay in London, and had found them extremely useful.

"Your passport. *Passeport.* Look, do you speak French? *Parlez-vous français?*"

"No." Gonzalo shook his head. "I'm sorry." He had in fact understood the guard's request but had no idea how he could explain that he did not actually have a passport, and why.

The American gave an incomprehensible exclamation of annoyance, and then gestured to Gonzalo, speaking loudly and slowly. "Look, wait here, please. *Wait. Here.*" He turned, still holding Gonzalo's visa, and hurried across the deck to another uniformed man. The inspectors spoke rapidly together for a few moments. Then one of them called over a third. Gonzalo watched them, and felt himself starting to sweat.

The three men approached Gonzalo. "I don't speak Spanish." It was the third man, sounding annoyed.

"Come on, Tony, it's the best we can do," It was the more senior inspector.

"Ok, ok. Ummm . . . *Voi siete di Ispagna?*" To Gonzalo's surprise the question was in Italian.

He nodded. "Yes."

"*Ispagnole di repúbblica?*"

Gonzalo sensed a crevasse opening before his feet. This was not a good question to answer in Italian. As he hesitated, he heard a commotion in English. A red-headed man in a rumpled brown suit was pushing his way up the gangplank, arguing loudly with customs officials. "Look, he doesn't speak English. He'll need me to . . . There he is! Hey, Gonzalo! Gonzalo! *Viva la República*!" As Gonzalo watched, horrified, the young man thrust his fist into the air, practically under the nose of the hostile customs inspector. Helplessly, Gonzalo nodded, and raised one hand in reply, reflecting that the Italian guard's question had just been answered.

Gonzalo's interrogators turned to greet the newcomer. "And you are?" It was the French-speaking guard who had originally approached Gonzalo.

"Michael McCormick, sir." The redhead held out his hand. "I'm sponsoring this gentleman for citizenship."

The uniformed heads bent over Gonzalo's visa again and conferred. Michael grinned over them and winked at Gonzalo. "Do you speak Spanish?" the senior guard asked.

"Yes, of course. *¿Oyes, Gonzalo? ¡Quieren saber si hablo español!*" Mike McCormick was still grinning like a bride. Gonzalo smiled back, more relieved than he could say to hear his native tongue, and grateful to Miguel for being kind enough to translate.

"Could you ask Mr. Lo-ren-te"—the official struggled valiantly with the foreign name—"who paid his passage?"

"Sure." Mike rapidly translated the question, and Gonzalo's slightly bewildered reply.

"And what he plans to do after entering the U.S.?"

Gonzalo blinked when Mike translated. The American, with his imperfect grip on Spanish idiom, had inadvertently used the future tense for the question, instead of the more common "going to do." The phrase implied a long-term future that Gonzalo had barely been able to imagine. "Look for work, I guess," he said. "I don't want to be a burden to you."

"*Buena respuesta.*" Mike nodded approvingly and translated.

The customs officials nodded approvingly also. The next few questions were rapid and uninterested. Then Mike was hoisting Gonzalo's duffel onto one shoulder and guiding him toward the gangplank, speaking in rapid-fire, oddly accented bursts of Spanish. "Damn, I'm glad to see you, Gonzalo. I almost died with surprise when I got your letter from London. Watch your step." Gonzalo had stumbled slightly when he reached the pier, unable to reaccustom himself to solid ground after so many days at sea.

"I'm so sorry about Pedro," Mike continued. "He wrote me when I was in Barcelona, you know. I still have the letter. I can show it to you. No, we don't want a cab. We can walk to the station, your bag's light. Come on."

Gonzalo followed the American out of the echoing hangar that enclosed the pier, and into a chaos of automobiles. "Are there always this many cars?" he asked.

"Yeah, pretty much. This is Twelfth Avenue and Twenty-third Street, by the way. We're going to Eighth and Thirty-fourth."

"Streets don't have names?"

"No, not in Manhattan. Well, not—shit, I don't know the word—not *uptown*. Not in the north."

Mike saw Gonzalo's look of distress, and clapped him on the back with his free hand. "I know, comrade. It's not the Calle Tres Peces. But it's not so bad, really. And pretty soon it won't even be confusing."

Gonzalo nodded, and fell into step. As they walked eastward, Mike lowered his voice and said, "Listen, after I got your letter I tried to find out about Carmen."

"Oh?" Gonzalo tried not to be hopeful.

"It's kind of a long shot," Mike said apologetically. "But the State Department says there's a Maria Carmen Llorente de Palomino in Granada."

"In Granada?" Gonzalo repeated, and shook his head. "It must be a different woman then."

"That's what I thought," the American agreed. "But I have a friend who works for the Red Cross, and *he* knows people in Switzerland who know people in Spain, and . . . well, it's a long story, but it looks like there's an Aleja Palomino in Granada, too. And I'd call *that* a long shot, because my friend says that this kid is in a convent school, and that doesn't seem too likely, but if Carmen's there . . ." He trailed off.

"Jesus Christ," Gonzalo said softly.

"It was the best I could do," Mike explained anxiously. "This Carmen Llorente in Granada, the profession given was domestic. She's working for a rich family, it seems. I don't know the name. Can you think of anyone, Gonzalo? Who were the people she worked for in Madrid?"

"Del Valle," Gonzalo said automatically. "But this is someone different."

"You think you know who, then?"

Gonzalo took a deep breath. "I have an idea," he said slowly. "But I don't even know the name. It's a long story."

They had reached the corner of Eighth Avenue and Twenty-third Street. Mike, peering at his guest, saw that Gonzalo looked gray. "Why don't we stop and grab a coffee," he said. "We can take the subway uptown and still catch our train."

Gonzalo nodded, still looking abstracted, and allowed Mike to shepherd him into the deli on the corner. "See, the Metro—the subway—is right there," Mike explained, pointing to a staircase surmounted by a greenish globule, which looked singularly ugly to Gonzalo. "It takes us right to the train station. A beautiful station, Gonzalo. As beautiful as Atocha. You'll like it."

Mike realized that he was talking too much, but the faraway expression in Gonzalo's eyes unnerved him. Exchanging a few words in English with the man behind the counter was a relief. Remembering the Spanish habit of large midday meals, the

American ordered coffee and gargantuan sandwiches for both himself and his guest. Seated comfortably in a booth, surrounded by shining blue and white linoleum, Mike inspected Gonzalo. To his relief, the Spanish veteran was looking more lively. "It must have been a tough trip," he commented.

"Yes." Gonzalo appreciated Mike's kindness. But he felt too overwhelmed to respond at the moment. "I'll tell you all about it later, in private, if you like."

"Sure," Mike agreed. He smiled, prepared to joke with Gonzalo. "I've been scared stiff the last few days that your ship would go down."

Gonzalo smiled back. "Now that was one part I *didn't* worry about!"

"Ahh, you're too used to wartime. I bet everyone else on the boat was worried."

Gonzalo saw that Mike was only half-joking. "Why?" he said simply. "Who would sink the ship?"

The American's jaw dropped, revealing a considerable amount of BLT. "You don't *know?* Jesus, Gonzalo, you might as well have been at the bottom of the sea! Didn't you get *any* news on board?"

"It was a London–New York passage," Gonzalo explained apologetically. "All of the news was in English. And I didn't know anyone."

"Jesus, Gonzalo, I thought . . . I . . . Jesus! Hitler invaded Poland four days ago. Germany and England are at war. And France and Italy, too, because of their alliances."

The clatter of crockery suddenly faded into background noise for Gonzalo. "Spain?" he asked urgently.

"Neutral." Mike shook his head. "So far. But this is it, Gonzalo. If Germany and Italy are at war, then it's only a matter of time before Franco's pulled in. And then, once the English and French *have* to fight him. . . ." He grinned and clenched one fist in front of his plate. "*Viva la República.*"

"You're an optimist." The words were dampening, but a smile was pulling at the corners of Gonzalo's mouth.

"It's a funny kind of optimist who hopes for war." For a moment Michael McCormick spoke seriously, as a veteran. Then his puppylike eagerness reappeared, and he grinned. "But you have to admit it's a wonderful opportunity!"

"It's a bit sudden," Ramos said self-consciously. "But it's a wonderful opportunity."

"You deserve it, sir," Tejada replied, with every appearance of sincerity.

Ramos fidgeted with the cuffs of his new uniform. "I feel a bit guilty about it," he confessed. "As if it were taking advantage of someone else's misfortune."

"Not at all, sir," Tejada said reassuringly. "You weren't responsible for the accident."

"No," his commander admitted. "I suppose if anyone is, it's the damn fool who was the buildings inspector when the Reds were in power."

"It's no one's fault, really," Tejada said soothingly, and with complete disregard for the truth. In fact, it had taken him nearly three months to figure out a way to engineer the late Captain Morales's fatal accident.

The idea had come to him during a stretch patrolling with Corporal Torres. The corporal's unremitting interest in the rooftops had finally led Tejada to wonder how stable the chunks of crumbling stone that adorned the tops of Madrid's houses really were. Surely, after years of bombardment, one or two sizable pieces must have been shaken loose, ready to fall onto unwary pedestrians. Another month of careful observation of the captain's patterns of movement and the buildings under which he passed had given the sergeant the further information he needed. One sweltering August afternoon, the inhabitants of an old apartment building in one of the less salu-brious neighborhoods had been pulled from their siestas by the crash of falling masonry and had discovered a guardia civil lying dead beneath it. The brothel up the street had discreetly closed during the investigation. And the neighbors had all been unable to recollect seeing Captain Morales before. The civil authorities had condemned the building as unsafe, and Madrid's Guardia Civil posts had lowered their flags to half-mast and held a memorial service for an exemplary officer.

A few weeks later, Lieutenant Ramos received notification that he had been promoted to captain and was going to be transferred to command of the Alcalá post. Now, standing in his office at Manzanares, surrounded by piles of boxes, and with his desk unnaturally bare, he looked slightly sheepish. "I guess you're right," he said. "But thank you."

"It's nothing, Captain." Tejada enjoyed watching the way Ramos's lips tugged upward at their corners whenever he heard his new title.

"Oh, and Tejada." Ramos leaned absentmindedly on the desk, and it rocked.

"Captain?"

"When this came through I recommended you for a pro-motion, too. It won't go through this time, I'm afraid. But I wanted you to know."

"Thank you, Captain," Tejada said, touched. "That's very kind of you."

"Not at all," Ramos said, coming around the desk and hold-ing out his hand. "It's been a pleasure to work with you. And honestly, I think the only reason the higher-ups didn't go for it was because of that business with Llorente."

"Yes, sir." Tejada kept his face carefully blank.

"I understand perfectly, you know," Ramos went on, confi-dentially. "And I told them that there were mitigating circumstances. Off the record, of course. So I don't think it should hurt your prospects permanently."

"Thank you, sir."

"Well." Ramos smiled. "We're all human. We make mistakes. They shouldn't have to be fatal."

"No, sir," Tejada agreed sadly, following the captain out of the room. "They shouldn't have to be fatal."

Acknowledgments

This book would never have been written without many people, but a few outstanding contributions should be mentioned.

First and foremost, my eternal gratitude to Persephone Braham, for giving me the idea, and encouraging me to actually write the book, and to Chalcey Wilding for giving me chapter-by-chapter critique and encouragement.

Then to my parents, for putting up with my obsession with postwar Madrid, and to everyone at Columbia's Administrative Information Services for giving me time to indulge it.

Finally, my thanks to Aurelio Mena, and the other creators of the magnificent Web site, "*La guerra de nuestros abuelos*" (http://platea.pntic.mec.es/~anilo/abuelos/primera.htm) for making available so many oral histories of the Spanish Civil War and the postwar period, and to the Madrid Metro's official site (http://www.metromadrid.es) for the history of the Metro during the war.

Other Titles in the Soho Crime Series

Janwillem van de Wetering

Outsider in Amsterdam
Tumbleweed
The Corpse on the Dike
Death of a Hawker
The Japanese Corpse
The Blond Baboon
The Maine Massacre
Just a Corpse at Twilight
The Streetbird
The Hollow-Eyed Angel
The Mind-Murders
The Rattle-Rat
Hard Rain
The Perfidious Parrot
The Amsterdam Cops: Collected Stories

Seichō Matsumoto
Inspector Imanishi Investigates

Qiu Xiaolong
Death of a Red Heroine
A Loyal Character Dancer

Jim Cirni
The Kiss Off
The Come On
The Big Squeeze

J. Robert Janes
Stonekiller
Sandman
Mayhem
Salamander
Mannequin
Carousel
Kaleidoscope
Dollmaker

Patricia Carlon
The Souvenir
The Whispering Wall
The Running Woman
Crime of Silence
The Price of an Orphan
The Unquiet Night
Hush, It's a Game
Death by Demonstration
Who Are You, Linda Condrick?

Akimitsu Takagi
Honeymoon to Nowhere
The Informer
The Tattoo Murder Case

Peter Lovesey
The Vault
The Last Detective
On the Edge
The Reaper
Rough Cider
The False Inspector Dew
Diamond Dust
Diamond Solitaire
The House Sitter

Stan Jones
White Sky, Black Ice
Shaman Pass

Timothy Watts
Cons
Money Lovers

Penelope Evans
Freezing
First Fruits

John Westermann
Exit Wounds
High Crimes
Sweet Deal

Charlotte Jay
Beat Not the Bones

Martin Limón
Jade Lady Burning

Magdalen Nabb
Property of Blood
Death of an Englishman
Some Bitter Taste
The Marshal and the Madwoman
The Marshal and the Murderer
Death in Autumn

Cara Black
Murder in the Marais
Murder in Belleville
Murder in the Sentier
Murder in the Bastille

Cheryl Benard
Moghul Buffet

Tod Goldberg
Living Dead Girl